# Moody
## Forever

**Also by Steve Oliver**

*Moody Gets the Blues*

# Moody Forever

## Steve Oliver

St. Martin's Press ⋈ New York

Library of Congress Cataloging-in-Publication Data

Oliver, Steve.
    Moody forever / by Steve Oliver.
        p.    cm.
    ISBN 0-312-19301-7
    I. Title.
PS3565.L519M65    1998
813'.54—dc21                                    98-21446
                                                   CIP

First Edition: November 1998

10   9   8   7   6   5   4   3   2   1

To all those who have lost their lives, and
therefore all their dreams, possessions, and loved
ones. For you, I grieve.

My thanks to the following people for their help and support:

Michael Connelly

Rod Thorp

Dick Quirk

Abigail Padgett

Sandra Dijkstra

Vida Rossi

Douglas Kazdoy

Debra Schade

Renea Huber

Pete Delaney

Brook Blumenstein

Barbara Blumenstein

# Moody
## Forever

# One

Outside the café a cordon of officers kept unwanted civilians from corrupting the crime scene. I flashed my badge as I entered the building. The sun was shining, but it seemed dark somehow, as though it were bright moonlight. My vision wasn't quite right either. It was afflicted by a kind of tunnel vision, dark at the edges.

Inside, officers were milling around, collecting statements from the patrons of the café and from the cook, a sweaty fat man who looked a lot like Sidney Greenstreet in *The Maltese Falcon*, except that he was not so nattily dressed—he was in a sleeveless T-shirt, threadbare and wet from perspiration. He was waving a spatula at the questioning officer.

I looked around for my partner, who had arrived earlier. It was funny that I couldn't remember his name, but when I saw him across the room it was obvious that he had remembered mine.

"Moody," he said, "it's back here." He was standing in an open doorway to one of the banquet rooms. I don't know how I knew it was a banquet room, but somehow I did. I walked toward him, feeling like I was floating on air.

I still couldn't remember my partner's name, so as I came near him I merely nodded in greeting. I didn't feel like I knew the right thing to say, so I didn't say anything. I waited for him to say something. He looked so familiar. He was short and dark, Mexican or Italian, and was wearing a trench coat, just what I would have expected a detective to wear in the dead of winter; but it seemed to me, vaguely, that it was the dead of summer.

"Looks like someone came up behind him," my partner said. Apparently he wasn't having problems remembering things, or seeing things, so I listened like everything was okay. He led me farther into the room.

"He was sitting right there, in the egg cup," he said, "when somebody apparently came up behind him and decapitated him—perhaps with a butter knife."

I looked at the crime scene and saw the victim, a six-foot soft-boiled egg, lying on the floor on its side. The top of its head was nearby, the tan shells' ragged edges still holding soft-cooked egg white. Yolk oozed from the opening at the top of the corpse. We were near the body now, me and my partner, both in trench coats and fedoras.

I looked at the egg. It was obvious that the murderer had taken his time. There were toast crumbs everywhere and a good part of the victim was missing.

Then I did something that wasn't very professional—I absentmindedly leaned over, put my finger in the yolk, then licked it off as I surveyed the scene.

"Hey," said one of the other officers, "you should eat before you turn up at a crime scene."

Even though the egg tasted pretty good, it was beginning to become obvious that there was something wrong with this scenario. This scene didn't seem likely to be taking place in the real world. I probably wasn't really a detective investigating the murder of a giant egg. But who was I?

One thing I was sure of was that I didn't belong at any murder scene. I had been to one only once and had ended up as a suspect—not the investigating officer.

*Where* was I? I was somewhere having a dream. Not an unpleasant dream. It was a silly dream. Yet it horrified me. Which was okay. Everything horrified me. Especially at night, when I slept. And while I was waking up. That's what was happening. I was waking up. When I woke up, I always went through several minutes of horror. It was part of my routine.

I began to become aware of my surroundings and the horrible clanging of a cheap alarm clock. I slapped the clock silent with a panicky motion of my hand, as I would have dispatched a spider that turned up in my bed. Naturally, I was in some kind of sloppy bedroom. My sheets were balled up around me. I felt like a claustrophobic mummy. And I was the captive of a sense of absolute dread. I felt that everyone I had ever known was going to die, and that I would die also.

I gradually sat up in bed. As the feelings of horror and dread subsided, I lit a cigarette. I was having to make a specific effort to put together the pieces of my identity and my life.

I smoked as I waited for my memory to kick in. Who was I? Where was I? I was still in that nightmarish state so common to my waking up. I had no recollection of my identity, only fragments combined with imagination. Something had put an almost muscular hold on my mind, keeping my memory from me. It would be released in a minute or two, but for now it was painful and frightening. I was Scott Moody, of that I was vaguely aware, especially since I had been named in my dream. But *what* was I? *Was* I a detective? No. I had been a private detective in Spokane until a murder case had spoiled that pastime. Was I driving cab? Yeah, that was it. I was driving nights in the Spokane Valley. But there was more to remember and somehow I got the feeling I wouldn't like the news. There was a reason the alarm was going off at this ungodly time of the day. I had only been sleeping for a couple of hours. I had driven cab until six in the morning.

I looked around the room, seeking clues. I took a drag on

the cigarette. Then I saw the notebook and remembered. It was worse than I thought. I wasn't just a cab driver; I was a reporter, too. And I was late for work.

I scrambled as I donned the white cotton trousers and yellow-striped shirt I had worn the day before. I pulled on my blue and red sneakers and stumbled down the stairs from my second-story apartment—the top floor of an old house.

For just a moment or two I cursed my ex-wife for getting me this job. Of course, she had intended well; she didn't want to see me driving cab as a career. She wanted me to aspire to better things, and when an opening came up on her suburban semi-weekly, the *Daily Sun,* she recommended me. I took the job partly because I *did* have higher aspirations and because for some reason I still wanted my ex-wife to think well of me. I had moved to this small town near Spokane and asked the cab company to put me driving nights out in the valley so I would be near the new job. Of course, I didn't tell the newspaper I was moonlighting, and I didn't tell the cab company I was *Sun*-lighting, so I had to keep each of them in the dark about the other.

The one thing that had not changed in the six months since I took the job were my nightmares—they were still about murder. An amateur psychiatrist would have made much of this particular dream because it was common for a schizophrenic to live out fantasies from *Mother Goose* and *Alice in Wonderland.* But my dream was not based on Humpty Dumpty. There was a more ordinary reason: among my other duties, I had recently become the food editor.

I climbed into my Pinto, coaxed it to life, and schlepped away. The sun might have been shining; I wasn't sure.

Though I was late, I took the long way around, through the back streets of the small town to the day-care center. I slowed as I drove by and, sure enough, caught a glimpse of my daughter, blonde, blue-eyed Allison, on the playground with the other kids. My ex was an early riser and had already dropped her off on the way to work. I waved and said, "I love you," though I knew Allison could neither see nor hear me.

It was for Allison's sake that I kept going. And for the satisfaction of defeating the internal forces that seemed to be trying to kill me.

On the surface, things were fine. I was not known in this small town as a cab driver and mental patient, but as a reporter, respected for that professional skill. I looked healthier now, up to a hundred and eighty-five pounds on a six-foot frame. I was still what a kind person might have called ruggedly handsome, the "rugged" being a nose that had been broken half a dozen times. My black hair was longish and my mustache unkempt, so for 1979 I was right in style.

Beneath the surface, of course, things were not quite so swell. My ex-wife knew I had an obsession with death—I thought about it every ten seconds. But she didn't know how often I had panic attacks while doing interviews, while trying to remember the topic of the interview, or the next question, or the answer to the last question. She didn't know that I still listened for voices in my head, afraid I couldn't prevent them from speaking to me. People seeing me walk down the street couldn't know that my mind was still divided between the light and the darkness: the light of the present, the here and now, the tangible; the darkness of my terrible fantasies, my dark memories, my time living with dead people.

It was funny how different things were at the end of this decade than they had been in the beginning.

In 1970 I had still believed in the sixties. I had believed in drugs. I had believed in the afterlife. Now, in July of 1979, I had a much smaller set of beliefs. I believed in certain kinds of love. I believed in the most obvious forms of physical reality. I believed in watching out behind you—especially on a nice morning like this, driving a Pinto to a job at the *Sun*.

The *Sun* was a small twice-weekly newspaper, inadequately serving the needs of about five thousand people in the small town of Mill City, Washington, out in the Spokane Valley, about fifteen miles from the city. My ex-wife, Andrea, had landed a job as the governmental reporter, which was a pretty good deal for her since she had been a typesetter up until then. When she got me a job, she didn't give many details, but, as it turned out, I was to be the reporter for what used to be called the women's page. The first of the two editions came out on Tuesday, and my page focused on home, garden, and business. The second page, on Thursday, combined church and food in an uneasy alliance. To complete my page all I had to do was keep filling a file folder until it would cover the empty space between the ads and eternity.

What was it today? Thursday? That meant it was church and . . . food? Naturally. No wonder I'd had that dream. I looked in my mental file. Church announcements would be easy. As for food, I had saved recipes and articles from last week's torrent of filler material from agribusiness. All I had to do was edit and dummy out the pages with a nice publicity photo of Swedish tortillas or whatever the foodies had come up with this time. At least I didn't have to pay attention to what was going on in the "real" news. After all, Jimmy Carter was still president, so that news wasn't good.

I pulled up near the office, holding up a hand to block the glare of a yellow light that was murdering my eyes. That's right, it was July. So the sun *was* shining.

I eased through the front door of the office, walked through the reception area and through the saloon-type swinging doors into the back.

The reporters were crowded into a small cubicle with old oak newspaper desks lined in a row. The cubicle was separated from the printing and layout functions by an eight-foot divider, which allowed for all the noise and chemical smells to reach the reporting staff with a vengeance. A dozen fluorescent lamps radiated us from above.

And there were only four seats for five reporters. One of us had to float around the *Sun* office without a typewriter or a place to sit. This morning all the chairs were taken. As I entered, Andrea looked up from her desk where she was editing some UPI copy. She was a senior reporter at the *Sun* and had a permanent place—her own desk. She had been a reporter for nearly a year, the average tenure before reporters quit. I had been at the job half that time and was hanging on by a thread. I only rated a permanent file drawer for my copy and the chance to occupy one of the desks when someone else was out.

"Good morning, Scott," she said cheerily. She was a handsome woman I should have remained married to. She had a firm chin, strong cheekbones and forehead, a prominent nose, and beautiful green eyes. Her reddish brown hair was combed up this morning, and she was dressed in a dark suit—too good for Mill City.

"Hi, Shamus," chimed in Billy Hart, the neophyte police and sports reporter from Yakima. He was twenty-two, blond, and soft-faced as a puppy's belly. He had started calling me "Shamus" the moment he learned of my PI past.

"Hi there, ya twerp," I responded as Andrea ignored us and edited copy. Billy was studying her, with a leer, I thought. I considered stapling his ears to his head.

Instead I said, "Anyone planning to be out of the office awhile? I have some copy to edit." No one moved or replied. The editor, Albert Swallow, sat quietly, smoking his pipe and reading *Editor and Publisher*. Swallow belonged on the eighteenth-century staff of *The Tatler* or *The Observer*. Under careful tutelage he might have eventually become a mediocre reporter perennially late with trifling stories. He was a frail-looking man whose out-of-date sports jackets seemed to engulf him and whose thoughtful, pipe-smoking countenance was spoiled by the swimmy, bloodhound eyes that seemed always on the verge of tears. I decided not to insult him by suggesting that his chair could be more usefully occupied.

And I certainly wasn't going to bother the fifth member of the staff. She was the most recent addition, a lady one of us called Jan the Barracuda. She was at the bottom rung of a very short ladder in which seniority was measured by a very few months. She was stuck with all the shit work: the unwanted editing, most of the obits, though I usually got a few of them each day, and the odd story assigned by the editor. She did all her work with ambitious intensity and consistently suggested ways to improve the other reporters' beats, usually within hearing of Albert Swallow or the publisher. She was the congenital news hawk, doing her level best to be noticed and going out of her way to be inconvenient to the established staff. She was in her midtwenties, thin, fish-eyed, sharp featured, and wore her hair in a long, sandy-blonde ponytail, which emphasized her eyes and the thick glasses she wore over them. I considered Jan especially dangerous because they had hired her about four months after I started work. Since we were both part-time that meant they had declined to offer me full-time work in favor of giving her a part-time position. This implied that she might be my replacement, or someone to spur me on to harder work. I did my best to stay out of her way.

Surprisingly, she volunteered the seat. "I'll be leaving in a few minutes, Scott. I've got a million things to do. I've got to catch the police beat this morning in addition to my story about the new health food store."

I looked at Billy. He shrugged as if to say, "I couldn't help it." She had evidently bullied the police beat from him this morning, and the business story would usually have been mine. I didn't mind. If she wanted some of my work, she was welcome to it. Jan would eventually rise to the top as one of us got tired of the pace or the low pay and quit. Unfortunately, the best candidate for that fate was me. This was one of the prices for being on your way up from the bottom. When I drove cab it didn't matter. Nobody was going to fire me because nobody wanted the job. Here, in a small way, I was somebody. I could lose this position and become nobody again. I had to worry again. Still, I tried not to overdo it. "Thanks, Jan," I said as she collected her files and purse and left the office in a rush of importance.

I edited my religion copy—God was still winning, had the devil on the run, and still seemed very fond of rummage sales as a funding device. Then I went on to the food copy—a story on how hot dogs were summer food and a piece on lemon meringue pie—threw them into the typesetters' bin, and checked my basket. There was a small mound of minor editorial filler and a few obits, no doubt deposited there by Jan. Underneath I found a letter from the Triple-A Collection Agency. They had traced me to the newspaper. They were threatening to sue me over a car I had purchased a few years back, which I had abandoned when I went crazy. I tossed the notice into the wastebasket.

When I looked up, Andrea was smiling at me. I smiled back. Working in the same office with ex-wives can be an amazing thing. I tried to keep eye contact with her and make it significant, but she just winked and went back to her copy. I had been trying to get something going with Andrea again for months, but no such luck. I wasn't sure I wanted the relationship for the right reasons—I wanted the safety of being with her because she had custody of Allison.

Andrea was currently going out with a Mill City logger. I had retaliated by dating a local girl, Xanthia Welch. My relationship with my former girlfriend, Sheila, had lapsed almost entirely since I had moved to Mill City. I had met Xanthia when I did a story on her new business, a shop selling various New Age remedies and massage products. She was very pretty, and I discounted her intelligence and assumed that I would have a brief and casual relationship. My effort had backfired a bit because I now felt myself falling in love with her. Of course, that didn't stop me from thinking about death all the time, but it made the thoughts a little more cheery—I now saw myself having a well-attended funeral.

"So, tonight's the big dinner," said Andrea.

"Don't remind me," I said. I had forgotten that I had told Andrea about it.

"You're going to her dad's restaurant."

"Yeah, the Atrium."

"Pretty fancy. You having dinner with her father?"

"No. He's treating. He has guests from out of town he needs to visit with privately, so we're just doing a brief stop-by at his table to visit." There was a sense of unreality to this. If I were going to date someone after being crazy and considering myself scum, perhaps I should have started at the bottom of the social ladder—sort of crawling before you walk. But there was no getting out of it; I was going to a fancy dinner with my beautiful socialite girlfriend.

"You don't have to drive cab afterward, do you?" she asked.

"No. Tonight's a night off. I drive tomorrow night."

"I hope you have a wonderful time," said Andrea.

"Thanks," I answered, but I wasn't really listening. I was thinking about death again.

# Two

I arrived at Xanthia's house at a little before seven. I wore a corduroy sports jacket, jeans, and tennis shoes. I hoped this would suffice. I walked from my Pinto toward the Welch house, a large and lovely A-frame that was a clear symbol of the wealth I did not have. The 1954 MG TF that Welch drove only on weekends was parked in the driveway. I rang the bell by the glass sliding door.

Xanthia came to the door dressed in a cotton peasant blouse, jeans, and moccasins. It didn't matter what Xanthia wore since her good looks and social ease made it possible for her to fit in anywhere. She was of average height, five-five or so, but there was nothing else that was average about her. She seemed to be royalty from some other time and place, from some ancient world. With her long, dark hair and brown eyes, she could have been Italian or Middle Eastern. Her almond-shaped eyes were a little too narrow, and her nose a little too large, and yet this combination didn't produce someone who was less attractive, but someone so striking that people stopped what they were doing and stared at her as she went by. Men fell down in her path to get her to notice them. I was still trying to figure out what the hell she was doing with me.

"Scott," she said, when she came to the door, "you look very nice."

"Thanks," I grunted, sure that she was more polite than accurate.

She locked the door, then turned toward me, lifting her face for a kiss. I touched her lips lightly and wondered again what the hell I was doing in this particular fairy tale. For just a moment I thought about death.

We drove in my little Pinto the few blocks from the fine house to the fine restaurant owned by Andrew Welch.

The restaurant, the Atrium, was one of two or three really classy establishments in Mill City—symptoms of a recent change from logging community to burgeoning tourist center. A large building composed mostly of glass, its supporting structure looked like Roman columns. Inside, the marble, Roman statuary, fountains, and plants gave an impression of Rome in ancient times.

Xanthia breezed by the maître d' with a wave of her hand as we entered. Fortunately, I was close enough behind her that he allowed me to pass as well.

Andrew Welch and his party were at a table on the far side of the dining room. It was an intimate table, like most at the Atrium, separated by plants and short dividing walls and individually lit. He and his friends were having a good time—we could hear them laughing from a distance as we made our way across the room.

We approached, Xanthia confident and beaming with smiles, me tagging along behind like a poor relation.

"My sweet Xanthia," said Welch, as we approached. He rose from his place in the circular booth and kissed her on the cheek. He looked past her to me, shook my hand, and said, "Scott," in acknowledgment, perhaps a little coolly. He was a very handsome man of forty-nine. His blond, graying hair was cut unfashionably short and neat for 1979, which gave him an elegance that dated from earlier, more stylish years. Xanthia must have favored her mother, for Welch was WASPish, with small, regular features and blue eyes. He was shorter than me, but not much, and very fit. He wore a white shirt this evening with khaki pants and penny loafers. He sported a gold Rolex. And he was tan. It was midsummer, but I was still fish-belly white.

"I'd like you to meet my friends, Jack and Diane," Welch said, gesturing toward the couple sitting with him at the table. Jack was wearing a powder blue leisure suit, a gold jeweled watch, and an enormous gold ring with a large red stone. His hair was so red that it looked like he dyed it. He combed it in the style of teenagers in the fifties, kind of early-Elvis. A handsome, hawk-faced man, his clothes and hairstyle made him look like a movie star in some satire of the styles of our time.

Diane was classier. Her silk blouse was cream colored; her earrings and necklace were pearls. Her graying hair was beautifully styled and she was handsome, a Lauren Bacall type.

"What do you do for a living, Scott?" asked Diane.

"Scott here is a scrivener," volunteered Welch.

"A scrivener? What's that?" she asked.

"A journalist," I told her. "I work for the local paper." I thought how nice it was that no one knew that I had a secret life as an ex-mental-patient cab driver, but I was always nervous that someone might find out. It was the opposite of the problem faced by Clark Kent.

"But destined for greater things," said Welch, smiling at me, more ebullient than usual, but something else also—ironic? He was usually a reserved, careful, tasteful man. Tonight he seemed more outgoing and carefree. I glanced at his place at the table and saw that he was still drinking the usual sparkling water, not alcohol.

"A writer. That's wonderful," said Diane. "I've always wished I could write." She looked at Welch. "I'd certainly have enough to write about."

He laughed at some shared knowledge. "Perhaps later in your life you'll be able to tell the story. After the statute of limitations."

"He sort of reminds me of Grant Wilson," said the woman. "Do you remember him?"

Jack laughed his braying laugh. "Remember him? He screwed up the whole affair with Gladys Spofford." He laughed again. Diane chuckled politely, then sipped on her gin and tonic.

Welch turned toward us and smiled. "We're recalling old times," he said. "We haven't seen each other in a while."

I thought the scene silly and intimidating, but standing beside the lovely Xanthia I would have endured it for hours. Fortunately, Welch turned toward us, smiled with his patrician good looks, and said, "Perhaps you and Scott will be better served by sitting at the table I've arranged for you on the terrace. We're doing a little too much reminiscing for young people to enjoy." He kissed Xanthia on the cheek. "I'll see you soon, sweetie."

She started toward the maître d'. I began to follow, but Welch grabbed my elbow, quite firmly. "We have to have a talk sometime," he said. "I know all about you."

"Huh?" I answered, too eloquent for words.

"We'll talk," he said, pointing a finger at me as I began walking away.

I wished to get as far away as I could, so I just nodded and followed Xanthia.

"Are they going?" asked Jack, just getting the drift.

"Yes. They have their own table." Welch winked at me.

"That's too bad." Jack said.

"Now what about Grant Wilson?" asked Welch, rejoining the conversation.

We took our table on the terrace and spent the next hour or so having a wonderful dinner and staring into each other's eyes.

I had not been so happy for a long time, and I was quite worried about it.

We could see Welch and his companions through the large windows that bordered the terrace. They lingered there the whole time we were having dinner and were there when we left. Their dinner reminded me of the ones I used to attend in an earlier life as a salesman. At the end of the day we would get together for an expensive meal and drinks and talk about our victories and defeats. That's the kind of dinner Welch was having—hunters around the campfire after a day spent stalking prey.

And speaking of prey, what the hell did Welch mean, "We'll talk"? Did he want me out of Xanthia's life? Did he want to expose me? And expose what? My mental illness? I doubted that it would make a difference to Xanthia. But Welch had my attention. He was smart and, from my perspective, powerful. If he didn't like me, I was going to worry about it. But I tried not to let it affect me this evening.

When we finished dinner, we returned to the Welch house and repaired to the upstairs, which was Xanthia's domain. Xanthia ran a shop downtown called the Perfect Touch, an outlet for expensive and sensual products like body oils and natural scents. She used some of the products on me as she gave me a massage on her bed by a window overlooking the lake. It was a sensual massage that began with my excitement at the mere sensation of her fingers touching the nape of my neck and did not end even after she had gently performed fellatio. I felt a hunger to touch every part of her body with my mouth. I felt such gratitude for the level of sexual joy between us, a level I had not felt since before my illness, even with Sheila, my girlfriend from Spokane. Xanthia's presence had made me forget all other women but Andrea, the mother of my daughter.

When finally we were finished, we slept, arms and legs entwined with the sheets in the summer warmth.

As usual, I dreamt. That they were bad dreams goes without saying. But this night was the first in a while of the pyramid dream. This was a dream I had experienced since I was a boy, upon reading about ancient Egypt. In these dreams I was a prince who had returned to his people only to be marked for death in the tomb. And, in one of the pyramids at Giza, I was trapped, pursued through the claustrophobic tunnels, squeezed ever more tightly by the earth and stone closing in on me. The men pursuing me wore the clothes of ancient Egyptians, but I could never quite tell whether they were workers or priests or why it was that they wanted me dead and buried.

When I woke in the morning I was not so sure of my reality—to be lying nude with this gorgeous, bronze Middle-Eastern beauty, feeling the warmth and elasticity of her. It was a considerably more positive outcome than my previous pyramid dreams.

In time, of course, my mind told me the tale that I was Scott Moody, not an Egyptian prince, and that I was late for work. I kissed Xanthia good-bye, as she drowsily acknowledged me. Then I exited down the stairs and out of the house, hoping against hope that I would not have to encounter Andrew Welch, who wanted to talk to me.

# Three

When I got to the office I was accompanied by a sense of foreboding. I couldn't come up with a good reason for it other than that things had been going too well for me and that a sense of foreboding was a fairly regular companion. Albert Swallow didn't improve things. He had come up with another story.

"This chap's led an immensely interesting life," Albert explained through the smoke from his pipe. Albert was ensconced in 18th-century England in his corner of the room, while everyone else scrambled to get stories edited and dummied by deadline. The ad people had, only a few minutes earlier, given the ad sizes and locations so the other reporters were hurriedly measuring and fitting stories. Albert had asked Billy to lay out my page while he explained his idea to me. This pissed both of us off, but little could be done about it; until Albert got fired, he was the editor. From the other side of the partition the typesetters clattered and beeped, while layout people screamed at one another and at the reporters.

"He'd be a marvelous story," Albert continued. "He's a real character who knows about the old days around here. But it's also a kind of summing up of a life because he's dying of leukemia—and he's willing to talk about it."

I fixed Albert with a stare that normally sent him looking for a place to hide. He knew that I hated stories about death; I had made that clear enough by my bitching about doing obits.

"I thought it might make a good series," he concluded weakly. He looked down at the front page he was laying out badly and puffed on his pipe. He had probably been working on that page for over an hour, and it irritated the hell out of me. So did his story idea. Of course I thought it a reasonable human interest story for a small town, but it would make me confront another death.

Albert gave me the man's name and a phone number. The man had some months yet to live and was staying at home between transfusions and other treatments. His name was Frosty Shields and he was eighty years old.

We were late getting the paper out that afternoon, and when it was finally put to bed, I hung around to edit some copy for the following day. Jan and Billy were gone. Albert was in conference with the publisher. Andrea was working on a planning department story about the upcoming widening of Pine Street and the local opposition.

As I was staring at an article on kitchen remodeling, not really reading it, more depressed by the concept, she said, "I'm going to pick up Ally soon. I wondered if I could ask you a favor."

I tossed my pencil down, lit a cigarette, and leaned back. "Shoot."

"I've got to go to that city council meeting tonight and it's going to be a whopper—till nine-thirty or ten at least. I was hoping you could watch Allison—maybe do a little visiting. Babysitters are ruining my budget."

"Only if you get in no later than, say, nine forty-five. I have to drive cab tonight. I can put them off until ten, then things start getting busy."

"I think I can do that," she said.

I exhaled smoke through my nose, watching with disgust as it rolled out like some vapor from a dragon's nostrils. What a repulsive habit. My eyes fixed on a slip of paper: Frosty Shields's name and address. I sighed.

"Scott," Andrea mouthed with an exasperation only she could express in a single syllable, "how old are you?"

"Thirty-six. You know that."

"That old man is *eighty*. You won't be eighty for *forty-five* years. That's longer than you've even been alive. God, you've got to give up this obsession with death. Everyone dies."

"That's what worries me."

"Do you still carry your will around with you?"

"Sure," I said, pulling a single sheet of paper out of my shirt pocket. I didn't have that much to give away.

"You are a *nut,*" she told me, then, looking sheepish, added, "Sorry, Scott."

"Did you know that the average life span for an aardvark is ten years?" I asked, deciding to change the subject.

"No, I didn't. Where'd you dig up that fascinating tidbit?"

"A book." I pulled it out of my drawer. "It's called *Life Spans.* It tells how long everything lasts—including people and animals. One tortoise lived over 150 years—from 1766 to 1918. Can you imagine that?"

"Scott, you're impossible," she said, showing the anger of frustration that was central to our relationship. She turned to go as I spoke.

"They say in the book that you add four years to your own life span by living with someone."

Andrea's eyelids narrowed. "I won't be ready to think about that for a long time, maybe as long as several mosquito lives." She stalked out as I searched through the book looking for information on the mosquito life span.

By the time I arrived at her house that evening Andrea had cooled down. She bustled around for a few minutes, showing me where everything was in the old run-down house, then left for the meeting. As the door shut, Allison and I looked at one another and burst out in a fit of giggles. We were always tickled to be together. She was wearing a little flowered dress and white sandals I had bought her a couple of weeks earlier. Her blonde hair was braided into pigtails, which made her even cuter than usual.

"Daddy, swing me," she said.

"Okay, kiddo. C'mon."

We went out into the yard and I took her hands in mine and swung her around in a circle so her legs were almost parallel to the ground. We did that until Dad was worn out, then she got up on my shoulders and we took a walk. Then, after a little wrestling on the lawn, Allison decided she was hungry, so we went inside for a peanut butter and jelly sandwich and a banana. I poured her a glass of milk, but she said she didn't want it.

"Don't you like milk anymore?"

"No."

"You used to drink it all the time. Do you know that when you were a little baby that's all you could eat?"

"I ate hot dogs and ice cream, too."

"No, just milk. You wouldn't go to sleep without your bottle."

"That was when I was a baby. I'm bigger now."

"I have a picture of you when you were a little baby—right after you were born. Do you want to see it?"

"Yes." She moved nearer, munching on her sandwich. Her cheeks were all puffed out from the mass of food in her mouth.

I pulled out my wallet and thumbed through the ID, notes, and business cards until I found the picture of her that was taken at the hospital. "See how tiny you were," I said, pointing at the little picture.

"Is that me?" she asked, somewhat shocked. "That's not me."

"Yes, it is. It's what you looked like when you were really little."

"Who's that?" she asked, putting a sticky finger up beside

the photo opposite her baby picture. It was a picture of my father and mother some thirty years ago.

"That's my daddy and mommy. Your grandpa and grandma."

"That's not Grampa. He has gray hair."

"He didn't have gray hair then, and neither did Grandma."

"I don't know her."

"Well, honey, Grandma died a long time ago. She's not here anymore."

"Where is she?"

"She's dead, honey. People die sometimes, just like animals do. Do you remember Otis?" Otis was a big old gray cat we'd had when she was about two.

"My kitty cat?"

"Uh huh. Well, Grandma died just like Otis did."

"Who's your mommy now?"

"I don't have a mommy anymore."

"Well, you better buy yourself a new mommy," she said with emphasis.

"You can't buy a mommy, Allison. When people die you can't replace them like that. I just don't have a mommy anymore."

"Daddy."

"Yes, honey."

"Can I have a glass of milk?"


Andrea was true to her word—arrived home at a quarter to ten, allowing me just enough time to get to the cab lot in the valley and check out a car. The lot was a satellite of the one in town, and looked it. It was a rough fenced-in area where the crummy yellow cabs were scattered around, waiting for drivers and for someone to fix them. The cab I got was an older Chevy, dented on all four fenders and had lots of holes in the blue seats. I gassed it up and signed out.

The next three days were devoted exclusively to the cabby life. Weekends were the staple of the cab driver income and I devoted twelve or fourteen hours each night, then spent the days sleeping, trying to make up for the divided life of the work week when I split my time between driving and reporting. On Monday I worked on a couple of stories I was preparing for Tuesday's edition of the *Sun*, then I reported for work at the cab lot in the evening. This was one of the two nights I really hated because I would work all night, then have to report to the newspaper for my day job.

My first few fares were pretty good and put me into a good mood. Cabbing was not the same as it had been when I'd started driving the previous year in Spokane. My optimism about life had improved. I tended to be polite to other drivers now. When someone signaled to change lanes, I let them in without a struggle. I didn't cut people off, and I didn't brake suddenly just to piss them off. All in all I had become a pretty boring cab driver.

The valley made a difference, too. In the city I got more drunks and welfare cases. In the valley, the fares were relatively normal. My fares this evening had been so decent and polite that I was maudlin with satisfaction over my new life by the time I picked up my fourth fare, an elderly lady in a walker, and proceeded toward the address she said was her daughter's. I helped her into the car and took off, feeling like a Boy Scout.

But as a cab driver, I should have known better. When I helped the lady out of the car at her destination, I waited for her to reach into her cute little purse and pay the fare. Instead, she started scooting away, her walker rattling on the pavement.

"Ma'am," I said, "it's five-fifty." I was following her down the sidewalk as she continued to hurry away.

"Fuck you," she said, and continued on.

I couldn't quite believe it was happening. She was in a walker and thought she could get away from me.

And she was right. I followed her for about three-quarters of a block before I felt so damned silly that I just gave up. I would have paid *ten* dollars to get away from the situation. My naïveté about the suburbs had been corrected.

The next few fares were better. All of them were polite and quiet and the rides fairly long, bringing in enough money to make up for my runaway. If I could get a few more good runs, then a decent bar rush between two and three, it would be worth the trouble.

Then I got a trip to the airport—a thirty-dollar fare, and a guarantee that I would get another long ride because whenever you got sent to the airport you were put on the stand and picked up a fare from the incoming flights.

I dropped off a middle-aged businessman at the terminal and took a spot in the cab line. I was counting my money, thinking what a great night it was to be a cab driver, when my new fare climbed in the backseat. I didn't recognize him until he spoke.

"You willing to drive as far as Mill City?" the voice asked, the unmistakable, confident voice of Andrew Welch. I glanced in the rearview mirror without turning my head. Welch was wearing a tan herringbone jacket and white shirt. He had tossed a garment bag and small leather suitcase into the backseat before climbing in.

I nodded yes to his question, still looking straight ahead. "Terrific," he said. "Let's go."

I wondered what the odds were that I could drive for twenty-five minutes with this guy in the car, unload his luggage, take his money, and not have him recognize me. Probably pretty bad. But what the hell. I was given to unrealistic planning, so I would try.

I drove the freeway from the airport. Off in the distance toward the valley I could see the beginnings of a summer lightning storm. The distant reports of thunder reverberated in me as foreboding. I thought about turning around and saying, "Well, hello,

Mr. Welch," but instead stayed silent, having taken the course that I would pretend I didn't notice who he was if he happened to recognize me.

We drove for ten minutes without speaking, the silence only broken by the thunder, coming closer now, accompanied by bright flashes of lightning. Mist accumulated on the big windshield of the cab. I occasionally hit the wiper switch to clear it off.

"You know I recognize you, don't you, Scott?" Welch said at some point during our trip through the valley.

"Pardon?" I asked, still feigning ignorance. I turned my head to look in the backseat. "Oh, Mr. Welch, it's you. I'm sorry I didn't notice when you got into the cab."

"Bullshit," he said matter-of-factly. I wasn't going to debate him on the matter so I kept driving.

There was a sullen silence, then I said, "So, did you have a nice trip?"

"It was okay," he said. "Just a little business in Seattle."

"I hope it went all right." If I kept this conversation up much longer I was going to hire myself out as a flight attendant.

"It went well enough."

"Your friends, Jack and Diane, they still visiting?"

"No, they've gone home."

Welch's replies were a little too curt for my taste. I was keeping up my imitation of an insurance salesman; why couldn't he?

"So now I know another of your little secrets," he said, not helping at all.

"How's that?"

"Your cab-driving gig."

"Yes. Well, I have to do this kind of thing for a while—the newspaper job is part-time. I have to work my way up." I thought being long-suffering and noble was my best ploy.

"Well, it's a little detail that, along with the other things I know, causes a certain loss of confidence."

"Other things?"

"Like your time in a mental hospital and involvement in a murder in Spokane."

"Oh."

We fell back into silence again. I thought about Xanthia. I missed her already for the time in the near future when I would be forbidden to see her.

"You ever been in a war, Moody?"

"Sort of."

"Then you know what it's like. Under attack, in the trenches, on patrol."

"I know something about it. I didn't do a lot of patrols."

"But you know what it's like. How it changes you. You know the value of life."

"True."

"And you know what it's like to have a secret. Something you can't tell anyone—even your loved ones."

"I'm not quite following you," I said truthfully.

"I'm just feeling particularly old tonight, I guess," Welch said. "I shouldn't have had those drinks on the plane."

I waited. I felt he was leading up to telling me not to see Xanthia in some roundabout fashion.

"You know you're not a great candidate for my daughter," he said, disappointing me by not continuing to be roundabout.

I knew what he meant, but said, "Why not?" anyway.

"You have a daughter, don't you, Moody?"

"Yeah," I said, not liking this subject.

"Then you know how important it is to protect them."

"Yup." He was probably right, but I didn't like it. I always felt one down with Welch. I was his social inferior. He had lived his life right and been rewarded for it. I was a loser being ejected from one more club.

"You think you'll have a long life?"

"What do you mean? You think someone's going to kill me?"

"You do have a dangerous approach to life, but no, I mean, generally. You think you're going to have a long life?"

I decided not to tell him that I thought about death every ten seconds. "I don't know. I guess I hadn't thought much about it."

"You ought to think about it. The only thing that matters is that you love someone—genuinely. Doesn't matter how bad you are, or how phony you are with others, as long as you love *someone* truly."

I looked in the mirror at Welch, who was looking out the window at the lightning storm. He said he felt older, and in the flashes of lightning he looked older. I had usually thought of him as a very young-looking forty-nine, but tonight he reminded me of people who looked handsome or pretty in the darkness of a nightclub, but who aged fifteen years in the lights of the lobby.

After that I drove without speaking, hoping that Welch wouldn't speak again. I assumed, with some sadness and bitterness, that I had been exiled from the land of the Welches. I couldn't help thinking about Xanthia as we pulled into Mill City and I turned toward the lake and their beautiful house. As we neared it, I ventured, "So, are you saying you don't want me to see Xanthia?"

Welch looked at me in the rearview mirror. "No," he said, tiredly. "I'd like to, but that might just encourage her. She'll figure out what you are in time."

Somehow that permission was more of a blow than a prohibition. He handed me two twenties over the backseat and climbed out of the cab. Rain was coming down now as the storm reached a more serious phase. As Welch neared the door to the house, I began to pull away, heading back toward town.

I was holding the mike, just about to report in to the dispatcher, when I looked in my rearview mirror for another glance at Welch for some kind of morbid confirmation of this unpleasant encounter.

What I saw was not what I had expected. Instead of seeing Welch disappear into his house, I saw, in the flash of lightning and the dim glow of a street lamp, a struggle between Welch and another person. I stopped the cab and turned to look back the hundred feet or so. Without the lightning I couldn't see as well, but there was movement, an apparent skirmish, in the bushes near the front door. I threw the car into reverse and sped backward toward the house. The tires skidded sloppily in the wet as I stopped and climbed out. I looked toward the house, but saw nothing now. I walked nearer. I felt that I probably ought to climb into the cab, put it in gear, and get as far away from there as possible.

Instead, I took a few more steps toward the house.

Then Welch appeared, walking out of the shadow. At first I thought things were okay, but as he neared I saw blood all over his face, slashes diagonally across his cheeks and forehead. As terrible as these were, they were nothing compared to the huge slash at the base of his throat, oozing dark blood onto his white shirt, which was quickly turning red. I was frozen with horror, but I saw that Welch was laughing a barely audible kind of raspy, gasping laugh. He clutched at my denim jacket and looked at me, a giddy smile on his face. We were both soaked in the rain.

"Scott, thank God. You scared him away. I never expected help from you."

I was not looking at his face, but at the blood covering the front of his shirt. He looked down to see what was so fascinating me and began to realize his condition. He looked at me again. "I really thought," he rasped, "I really thought I'd live to a hundred."

Then he dropped, his hand still grasping my jacket, pulling with the weight of a steamer trunk. I went down too and became tangled with him as he began struggling, fighting to hold onto me as though I could prevent him from falling into some abyss. I knew his struggle wasn't with me, but with the claustrophobia of approaching death. I panicked and fought back, fought my way free, coming up sweating, covered in blood and rain.

He was still now. I looked down at him. I touched his neck to see if I could feel a pulse, but I was aware that I really didn't know how to do that. I ran back to the cab and called the dispatcher.

"Forty-one!" I said into the mike.

"Yes, forty-one," came the reply.

"I need an ambulance."

"What's happening?"

I was about to reply when I realized I wouldn't have to call anyone. Practically a fleet of police cars was coming down the street. I never replied to the dispatcher. I slowly dropped the microphone and climbed out of the car. I held my arms out at my side, not wanting to appear to be viewed as a truly bad guy by holding them in the air, but wanting to be sure they knew I was no threat. Officers swarmed around us.

I came into the office the next morning with a dark secret. It was like coming back from Vietnam all over again; it was something I didn't want to talk about. It was something I just didn't want to explain. I had done enough explaining all through the night and had eventually, I thought, been believed. I was a cab driver caught in strange circumstances. I knew the Welches, yes, but it was a coincidence that I had picked him up at the airport. There was no physical evidence to suggest otherwise. I had no knife. I had been released near dawn with the understanding that I would be questioned again. I had not heard Welch's fate, but was pretty sure I already knew it. I had not seen Xanthia, but heard "the daughter" mentioned a number of times by the police and understood that she had been taken to the hospital to be with her dad.

I had considered skipping work at the newspaper, going home to sleep all day, try to recover. The thought of being alone with the memories of last night, the thought of dreaming about them, helped me to locate my duty to the newspaper and complete my page as usual.

I arrived at work wearing the clothes I had changed into after a long hot shower at home to try to remove any trace of Welch's blood. I had been released in a jail jumpsuit after my clothes had been taken into custody by the police, to be examined for any sign that I had been more involved in Welch's death than I had told them. I was told I would have to return the jumpsuit some time during the week. It pissed me off that they seemed to think I would want it for a memento or that they thought my clothes were so crummy it would have been an improvement.

I found an empty desk, lit a cigarette, and began editing stories about the wheat crop prospects and promotional news releases from state senators.

Then I tackled the obits. These were always tough for me and more so today. There were only three. One of the three had died in his early fifties. They didn't say how. That was less than twenty years away for me. I wondered what it was I wanted to do in the next twenty years. It didn't seem very long. After Welch's death my own mortality seemed imminent. I considered calling the doctor and getting an appointment for a physical.

Ten minutes later Jan came running into the office, grabbed a desk, and began typing furiously. Five minutes later Billy arrived.

"Jan, did you get the story?" Billy asked. "I heard about it over at the courthouse. Did you get it?"

"Of course," said Jan, with a superior tone, as though it had been a stupid question. "I have lots of quotes from the chief and it's halfway written. The AP's going to pick this up."

Billy looked over her shoulder at the page she was working on. He ran a worried hand through his blond hair. "I should never have let you cover my beat two days in a row."

"Destiny," said Jan quietly, mentally composing her next sentence as she studied the last one. The brown copy paper waited patiently in the ancient machine.

Andrea walked through the door, nodded as I looked at her, and sat at her desk. She took out her notebook, put paper in the typewriter, and began working.

I turned my attention back to Jan. "What story is this?" I asked, sure I already knew.

"Murder," said Jan stonily, "most foul. Hell of a story."

I ignored her ghoulish humor. "Who was it?"

Albert, still poised over his *Quill,* peeked at Jan from the corners of his eyes.

"Welch is the guy's name."

"You know him," said Billy. "Xanthia's father. Lives at Three-twenty-four Larch Lane. Fancy house down by the lake."

Jan stopped typing. "Look, you fuckers," she said, "just keep quiet. I've got a good story here, and I want to write it." Jan bit her lip. Her typewriter burst into staccato activity.

Quietly, I asked Billy, "What happened?" I wanted to know what he knew—evidently nothing about me so far. I wondered if someone had been picked up during the night. I hoped so.

"I don't know too much," said Billy. "He was killed last night. All I've heard are informed rumors."

"What are the rumors?"

"I guess Xanthia was taken in for questioning. Some have said the cops thought she had something to do with it—not the actual murder, but planning it. She's been released now, though."

"Why would they think she was involved?"

"I guess some cops just make the assumption that family is involved unless they already have a better suspect. You know the Mill City Police Department; they suspect whoever's handy. I'm sure we'll be picked up before the day's out. They also questioned some cab driver. He's the better suspect in my opinion. I guess he said he had just brought Welch home from the Spokane airport."

"They suspect him?" I asked.

"*I* suspect him. I don't know about the cops. Welch was slashed with a knife; it would have to be someone pretty strong to confront him. I guess it was pretty bloody. Can you imagine? What a way to die. Give me a nice clean bullet wound any day."

"Who called the cops?" I asked, remembering how quickly they had turned up at the scene.

"A neighbor. Society-type citizen above suspicion. She saw Welch fighting with someone."

That cleared up one mystery, but it sure didn't solve the bigger one. Mill City was a pretty quiet place. I couldn't imagine this as a random crime. I hoped the police department would get a break, pick up some blood-covered guy walking the highway carrying a big knife. I would be more comfortable when they had the murderer under lock and key, convicted by uncomplicated, definite evidence.

I thought about calling Xanthia. I knew from my eavesdropping at the police department that she was safe, but I was worried about her, how she must be feeling. It was likely, however, that she was not home. It was likely that she would be sleeping, perhaps sedated after a long and horrible night. Still, I reached for the phone. Maybe I would try just once. Even if I woke her, she would appreciate the contact with someone who cared how she felt.

I was holding the phone, still trying to decide whether or not to call her, when three Mill City police officers walked through the swinging doors into our office. They must have been day-shift officers because I didn't recognize any of them from the night before. When they came in, they didn't have their guns drawn; but in the usual manner of cops, they looked like they were daring anyone to cause trouble.

"Scott Moody," one of them said.

I didn't raise my hand. I had been in the army and I knew better than to volunteer. But I didn't have to volunteer—everybody kind of volunteered me. They didn't really mean to; they just all looked my way.

"You Mr. Moody?" asked one of the officers.

"Yes," I replied, timidly.

"We'd like you to come with us, sir," said the officer.

"Billy, Jan, can you cover my page?"

Jan and Billy looked at each other. "I'm pretty busy with this Welch story," said Jan. She had hijacked Billy's story and wasn't letting it go.

"I'll do it," said Billy.

"Thanks." I grabbed my cigarettes and followed the cops out of the office. I began to see an image of myself, of my life and career, as a small plane, a little Piper Cub, buzzing down the runway of the Mill City airport, trying to get enough elevation to get above the trees at the end. It had lifted off the ground just high enough to clear the trees, but now it was veering to the right and plummeting into the ground in a ball of flame. I hadn't gotten very high before crashing.

As I passed her, Andrea gave me her questioning look. "Scott?" she said.

I looked at her and shrugged.

They put me into the backseat of a police car—returning me to the world of doors with no handles. This was not a world I had a lot of interest in returning to.

The officers delivered me to the main counter at the police department, a big, square brick building on the main street of town. The plump, mustached officer studied my face as though it were an Egyptian hieroglyph. Behind him a clerk typist chewed gum and rattled her Royal typewriter. The office we stood in was a small anteroom to the jail. Bulletin boards were filled with memos, duty rosters, and wanted posters. The carpet on the floor was unraveling and so was the officer across the imitation wood counter from me. He had probably been up all night beating prisoners.

"You're Moody?"

"Yeah."

"You were some kind of private eye in Spokane, Moody?" His name tag said Blaine. I had dealt with him before when handling the police beat for Billy. He didn't seem to like me.

"Was. I'm not now."

"Well, that's one of the things the chief wants to talk to you about."

As if on cue the chief walked out of his office with a coffee cup in his hand. Chief Ryder was a blond, mature version of Blaine with the same portly stance, chubby face, and mustache. He wore the two-tone brown uniform, the shoulder patch of the Mill City Police Department, and the star that was the symbol of his authority. He occupied the largest of a series of small offices opening onto the anteroom and front desk.

"How you doin', Moody?" he asked jovially. "I hear we had to bring you in for questioning on this Welch thing." He said it as though we were chatting about the most casual of subjects, like the purchase of new tires for my car. Which, as it happened, I needed. "I hear you were there when it happened, drove him home in a cab or something?"

"Yeah, I drive a cab nights."

"Well, you know the little gal, too, right?" the chief said. "The daughter?"

"Yeah, we're friends."

"More than friends is what I hear."

"We're dating," I acknowledged.

The chief walked across the room to a metal coffee pot, pulled the lever over the plastic spigot, and filled his cup. "We also got some surprising news about you when we ran your name past some people in Spokane."

I knew what was coming now.

"I didn't know you had such an interesting past—involved in another murder. You were dating the victim's wife—while they were still married."

"It was a little more complicated than that."

"It always is," he said, smiling knowingly. "Tell me about it." He motioned me into his office with the coffee cup. "Blaine, bring the boy a cup of coffee and send in LuAnn. We'll want to take a few notes." He looked at me. "You don't mind, do you, boy?"

"No, I don't mind," I said, feeling a noose tightening around my neck.

We talked, and while I answered the questions, I learned things too. The most interesting thing that came out of the conversation was the implication by the chief that Welch had spoken to him about me sometime during the past week. Welch had intimated there was a cloud over my head. This was part of the reason Ryder had decided to bring me in. Welch had probably been overly protective of Xanthia and had investigated me. He had picked a bad time to be protective, but it was a little too late for me to hold a grudge.

I left the chief's office two hours later after having gone over the events of the past twenty-four hours in detail. I drove toward the offices of the *Sun,* but stopped a couple of blocks short, pulled to the curb, shut off the engine and promptly fell asleep.

I was back in the pyramid. This time I was deep in some large, inner chamber where torches provided a dim light, illuminating a large, multi-colored sarcophagus. From somewhere outside I heard the distant, powerful report of thunder. I could barely move because I was wrapped up in something. I was being carried, prone, with my feet sticking out ahead of me. I began to panic because of the claustrophobia induced by my position. I tried to escape the grasp of my Egyptian guards. They were all evil, wanting me to suffer, knowing that I would be put into the sarcophagus and then it would be sealed forever. I began to thrash against my captors, to throw myself back and forth, not sure what this would accomplish because I would still have been wrapped in the cotton of a mummy about to be entombed. Then I noticed that I was in pain. My head hurt, and also my shoulders. The reason for this became clear when the pyramid evaporated and I found myself in my Pinto on a hot July day, wedged between the driver and passenger seats with my head and shoulders now protruding into the back seat. I struggled free, threw open the door and got out of the car. I stood there shaking, like I had just crawled out of a pit full of snakes. I lit a cigarette, smoked it, and lit a second one. Then I headed to the office.

# Four

By the next morning I had recovered from my ordeal somewhat. I had in fact not only risen above the fear and depression, but reached that slight elation caused by surviving a close call with death. I had explained the events surrounding Welch's death to the other reporters, including Andrea, and was comforted that they believed me and sympathized. I had not heard from the police department for nearly twenty-four hours and I was trying to stay in complete denial about the effect of this event on my life. I was about to leave the office for my appointment with Frosty Shields when I got a call from Xanthia. I didn't recognize the voice.

"*Daily Sun,*" I said, "Scott Moody speaking."

"Scott Moody?"

"That's right. Aka Scott Moody. What have you got? A church announcement?"

"This is *Xanthia.*"

"Oh. I'm sorry. I'm so distracted I didn't recognize your voice." I held my two fingers in the air and made a scissors movement with them in a signal to Billy. He tossed me a cigarette. I had run out of my own an hour ago. "Are you okay? I was going to call you today. I didn't call earlier—I thought you'd be with relatives. I thought you'd need time to recover."

"We can talk."

"I'd like to talk about it tonight," she said.

"Sure. I won't be free until about seven. I'm working late on an interview." It was a rare night off from cab driving. In normal times I would have already arranged to see her on my night off. The events had thrown me off my stride, like a deer in the headlights.

"Seven would be okay, but I don't want to meet at my house. I'm staying with a friend. It would be nice to meet at the beach—it's beautiful in the evenings now."

I found myself wishing her father's death was not an issue for us. I much preferred the simple notion of a date instead of the recurring specter of her murdered father and the chief of police. "I'll be there," I said.

"See you then."

"Good-bye."

I hung up, puckering my lips as I thought about Xanthia. I stopped thinking about her when I noticed Andrea eyeing me. Was that a look of jealousy on her face? I made eye contact, but she returned to her work.

I picked up my notebook and pencil, heading out of the office for my interview with Frosty Shields.

I had made up my mind that I wasn't going to do a series on this story. One time with this subject was enough. I would do one long interview with the old man and end it right there.

Frosty Shields lived over on Hemlock in a wooden house he may have built himself sometime during the 1930s, during the heyday of the Depression and the New Deal. A dusty '53 Buick took a deserved rest in the driveway. An old wooden garage grayed in the sun. It was open and I could see inside it two crosscut saws, carpenter tools, and a few racy calendars from the forties—back before women's lib.

The voice at the other end was straining for composure  don't have relatives," she said. "But, what I wanted to ask abc  why I called . . ."

"Yes?"

"I heard you were . . . *there.*"

"Yes," I said, trying to maintain my own composure. "It w  a weird coincidence . . ."

"At this level it's not coincidence—it's like . . . *fate!*"

"I wouldn't argue with that."

"You're a cab driver?"

"I drive nights. My job at the paper is only part-time, it won'  pay the bills."

"You picked him up at the airport?"

"Yes, he was coming back from Seattle."

"This is all so strange, I mean, his death, you being there  when it happened."

"I feel the same way."

"I'd like to talk, Scott."

"Sure. I'd like to see you. I want to know you're okay." I  sucked in a large draft of smoke. My lungs ached, but the other  ache in my gut had nothing to do with smoking. My memory of  Welch's death and of the chief's possible suspicions had re-  turned. I also worried about being expected to provide emo-  tional support. I could take it, but I couldn't dish it out. I had  enough trouble getting through a day at Disneyland.

"Scott, are you still there?" I grunted assent. "Part of the rea-  son I want to see you is kind of business," Xanthia said.

"Business?"

"Yes. I read in the paper that you had been a private investi-  gator. I want you to do something for me."

"I'm not a private investigator anymore. I wasn't very good  at it."

"Please, Scott."

I pulled in behind the Buick, waited for the overheated Pinto engine to stop dieseling, and climbed out. I carried my notebook and pencil up to the cedar-shake house, which was overshadowed by a giant ponderosa. There were also a few firs and white pines that hadn't quite reached the magnitude of their neighbor. Frosty could have made a good income just by logging off his front yard.

I knocked on the white door and looked around at the mounds of needles covering the lawn. The house and yard weren't that unusual in Mill City, which tended toward the woodsy.

Someone jerked at the door, but it didn't open. I heard a muttered, "Well, goddamnit!" and more fiddling. At long last the old portal shuddered on its hinges and opened. The curious eyes of Frosty Shields gazed out at me. He was about five-nine, but I imagined him much larger in his youth. His frame was crooked from years of labor and the toll of age. He wore black logger's work pants with suspenders and his feet were clad in old-fashioned brown slippers. A long-john top covered his upper torso despite the August warmth. He had a full head of white hair. He was a handsome man for eighty: square face, deep-set eyes, straight, prominent nose. His eyebrows were two beautiful bushy caterpillars above his eyes.

"Howdy, young feller," he said, but continued to stare at me as though I were a feller from Mars.

"Hello. Are you Mr. Shields?"

"I was never *Mr.* anybody. My name's Frosty. Jesus, friend, what did you do to your nose?"

I ran my finger lovingly over the curves and turns of my proboscis. It was the Lombard Street of noses. "Fist fight," I said, figuring most loggers would approve of that. When asked about my nose, I always lied. A beating in a mental hospital was an unattractive explanation.

"Musta been a lollapalooza," he said with a grin. His voice had a grating rasp "Well, I'd invite you in for some coffee, but I don't know who the hell you are."

"Scott Moody. I called you from the newspaper. I wanted to do an interview."

"Oh, yeah, newspaper feller. Well, come on inside. What I got ain't catching."

He opened the door wider, extending a gnarled hand in welcome. I walked into the 1930s. The room was hot, and for a moment I thought the old wood stove in the corner was going. An ancient brown rug covered a floor that creaked and squawked as I crossed it. I waited by the dark brown couch for Frosty to be seated in a rocking chair nearby. He fooled me and didn't sit in it.

"Coffee?" he asked, walking by me toward the kitchen.

"Sure, I'll have a cup." I treaded air, a hummingbird looking for a place to light, while he filled an old tin pot with water and placed it on a gas stove in the kitchen. I glanced around the room, aware of something odd in Frosty's house. I had expected him to be a logger, for his house to be old, for his manner to be woodsy. I wasn't prepared for that Mill City rarity—a book reader. The walls of Frosty's living room were covered with thousands of dog-eared, well-fondled volumes resting on time-worn, planed pine shelves. They filled the room from floor to ceiling, except for the bare spots over the doors and windows. While Frosty banged around in the kitchen, I browsed the shelves and found the selection surprisingly eclectic, from Louis L'Amour to Carl Sagan, from Chaucer to Thorstein Veblen—anything, apparently, he could get his hands on.

"Quite a library you've got here," I called out to him.

"Oh yeah, I got a book or two," he said, and a moment later appeared in the doorway to the kitchen, his eyes shining, a delighted smile on his wrinkled, white-stubbled face. "Most people don't think much of it though," he added wryly. "I met an old gal last year and invited her over here—first one I'd let in the place since Martha died. We were sitting over here at the couch and things were going fine and suddenly she looked up and said, "You have so many books!" with this high voice, like a minister's wife who had just discovered her husband was screwing the whole congregation. I thought she was gonna have a fit right here in my living room. I guess she figured I was doing things to excess. That kilt it right there. No nookey for me." Frosty chuckled and disappeared into the kitchen before I could ask if I could quote him.

I continued to paw through his literature until I came upon a book written in 1912 called *Old Age—Its Cause and Prevention*. I pulled it off the shelf as he came back into the room carrying two age-stained mugs full of coffee.

"That book is just so much bullshit," he said with disgust. "I did those exercises for ten years—and look at me. Don't look a day over eighty."

"You look pretty good for your age," I said, trying to ameliorate what I felt to be the poignancy of the moment. I shelved the book.

"You mean I don't look bad for a guy who's going to die in a couple of months." Amazingly, the twinkle was still there.

"Is that how long they figure?"

"More or less. Two months, maybe six months. Hell, I get so many transfusions I ain't working on my own blood now." Frosty limped over to the rocking chair and sat down. He seemed in a reflective mood as he held the hot coffee in his wrinkled old hands and sipped it. He smiled as I sat across from him on the couch, shook his head with pleasure. "I still make the best goddamn coffee," he said with satisfaction. "Martha couldn't have done better. I had a couple of eggshells left over from breakfast; I always put them in to take the edge off."

I sipped the coffee and agreed with him. "Good coffee. What kind is it?" I felt like I was in a commercial.

"Frosty's coffee," he said with a grin. "Hardly matters what kind you get so long as it ain't the cheapest in the store."

I tried turning the conversation back to the subject of the interview. "I don't know exactly how to phrase this," I said. "I want to ask you a question kind of point blank."

"Spit it out, kid. I'm too old to break your nose." Frosty sat back in his chair, reached for a bag of Bull Durham and papers from his pants pocket, and proceeded to roll a cigarette.

"How do you feel, knowing that . . . I mean, finding out that . . ."

"I'm gonna die?" He pulled the bag shut expertly while holding the filled paper in his left hand.

"Yeah."

"Hell, I don't feel good. Kinda like having a pretty girl kick you in the nuts."

Boy, was it going to be hard getting quotes for this.

Frosty took a kitchen match from his pocket, struck it on a well-worn part of the chair, and lit his cigarette. It burned unevenly. With a shaky hand he brought the match up to his mouth and blew it out. "How do *you* feel about dying?" he asked. He drew on the cigarette. I lit one of my own before I answered.

"I don't think about it," I lied. "I just want to put it off."

"It don't get put off forever," he said, balancing the ashes on the end of his cigarette until he had reached the ashtray.

"I'm beginning to figure that out." I was thirty-six now, and it seemed I hadn't been around very long. Life didn't seem the grand, everlasting gift it had at eighteen. There was hardly time for a mediocre career, much less a great career, or two or three of them, or a lifetime with a family. It was more like a three-day weekend spent rising and eating and whiling away the hours at whist; then, suddenly, it was Monday and the Grim Reaper was asking you to join his carpool. Or, maybe, he would jump out of the dark and stab you.

"You get it figured out, you let me know," he said, chuckling. " 'Course you'd better hurry."

I looked at my watch. It was getting late in the morning and my page would be due soon. I would have to do something with this interview and get back to the office. Obviously I wasn't going to be able to finish this story in one sitting the way I had wanted to. I decided to start the story with a profile of his life.

"You spend all your life in Mill City?" I asked Frosty.

"Nah, back in the twenties I was a literary agent in New York."

"What?"

"Hell, I'm only kiddin'." He laughed, his tongue tucked into a corner of his mouth with pleasure. "I wanted to do lots of things, but I ended up as a gyppo logger most of my life. Raised a little family with Martha and don't understand a one of them now. They all live around here and they come to visit me and watch after me. I love 'em, by God, but I don't understand them. They took all my worst traits and Martha's as far as I'm concerned." He looked at me significantly, placed the cigarette in the corner of his mouth. "And there just ain't enough time to do it over again."

We talked about other things for a while; then, just as I was about to walk out the door, Frosty asked, "Say, did you hear about that feller got himself killed the other day?"

"Yeah, I did." I heard and I saw. I had half an urge to tell him that I was a witness, that I saw the death, if not the murder. Such events, I knew from my Vietnam experience, had a peculiar effect, making you feel that you wanted to share the drama, while at the same time you were appalled by your own willingness to brag that you had witnessed a tragic event.

"I knew him. He was a nice feller. I talked to him a lot of times. Hell, I knew him since"—Frosty stared off to a corner of the room remembering—"1965."

I recalled seeing Frosty downtown, not knowing who he was,

but noticing him as he was like a lot of the older people, wandering around during the day looking for conversation. But in 1965 he might have still been working.

"I never met a young fella who knew as much as he did about the Great War," Frosty said.

"The Great War?"

"World War One. It was 'the Great War' until we had the Second World War," he said. "I was in it. Welch and I got to talking about it, and I tell you I never knew someone young like that who knew as much about it. I tell you it was like talking to one of the other guys who was in it with you."

"Is that right?"

"That's a fact. One thing that surprised me was when he started talking about the 'dizzies.' "

"Dizzies?"

"Yeah. Like you, most people don't know what they were. It was a kind of trench during the war. You see, once we were dug in at a particular spot, we had a number of different kinds of trenches. The fire trench, or front-line trench, was the most common; it spread out horizontal to the front, so you could fire at the enemy."

"I'm with you so far," I said, though I wasn't quite.

"Another kind of trench was the communication trench. It was perpendicular to the fire trench. It was there so you could get from the fire trench back to the rear."

"Okay, I follow. That way replacements or someone with a message could get to the front line without getting shot. But what the hell are dizzies?"

"First, you gotta understand the problem with the communication ditch," he said, slowing me down, "because the communication ditch is a straight line, from the enemy's point of view. It is vulnerable to being enfiladed."

"Enfiladed?"

"That means someone can point a machine gun right down its length and shoot everyone in the ditch. You get a bunch of men heading toward the rear, and someone shoots down the length of the trench and you can kill every man jack of them."

"So what are dizzies?"

"You didn't see them on every communication trench, but on some they put in a dizzy. A dizzy was where the trench split and went both ways around a kind of circle and then joined up on the other side. They called them dizzies because if you wanted to you could go into a dizzy and just keep going in circles."

"I see what you mean about most people not knowing much about dizzies."

"Oh, hell," he said with disgust. "Most people don't know anything about war—that one or any other. They don't seem to know that that's why most veterans don't want to talk to them; they're too fucking ignorant."

"But Welch *did* know about this?"

"Yeah. Surprised the hell out of me. He owned a restaurant or something, didn't he? How the hell did he get to know about that war?" Frosty scratched his head like he couldn't figure that one out. "But he and I talked about a lot of other things. He seemed real interested in the old times. I'm gonna miss him. Funny thing how a guy as old as me is still here today and a guy as young as him is gone."

I nodded at the irony, waved, and walked out to my car.

It was near noon before I got back to the office, my notebook filled with chicken scratches I would have to use sparingly to get a printable story about Frosty Shields. I didn't like what I would have to do—take a slant at the story that made him come out a man who had taken a positive attitude toward his fate and hope for the future, for an implied afterlife that may await. Anything else wouldn't wash well in Mill City or with my publisher. In any event the story would have to wait to be printed. I didn't want one to run without knowing what the next one would hold. I had decided to do a series after all, and it would be a stronger series if I wrote it all at once and integrated them.

I filled my page with business news and building permits. I was about to finish and get out of the office early to catch a quick interview for the arts and entertainment page when Andrew Welch's obit came across my desk. As usual, it had been submitted by a funeral home, the Quiet Hours, a stately, pillared Southern mansion-style building overlooking a plantation of marble and granite slabs. I quickly wrote an obit from the source material, ignoring its personal impact when possible. Andrew Welch was forty-nine when he died. He had lived in Mill City for twenty years. I detailed a little of his life since his arrival, that he was a prominent businessman, involved with local civic organizations, a small pillar of one of the town's currently important industries—tourism. There was little information about him prior to 1960. It simply said, "Mr. Welch moved to Mill City from Seattle." His exploits prior to that time couldn't have been too impressive. He had been thirty on his arrival, just a kid, younger than I. He was survived by one daughter, Xanthia Welch. I slugged the story and tossed it into the typesetter's basket. I took a sip of the cold coffee on my temporary desk.

"Someone else has work to do," said a voice behind me. It was Jan the Barracuda.

"Sure," I said, with an air of resigned indifference. The weight of the past couple of days was showing. I was thinking more about death and less about work and a future. I kept touching my chest just to feel my heartbeat. It was becoming another fixation.

I rose, pushed the chair back, and gathered up my materials. I stuck my dead notes in a drawer set aside for that purpose and kept my notebook with me. I picked up my camera. I would need a picture for the next story, and on a small paper like this one we were all expected to double as photographers. Jan pushed by me hurriedly. She was still on her murder story.

"Scott," someone said.

It was Andrea, looking at me with concern.

"What?" I paused at the opening to the cubicle.

She rose, walked past Billy. She looked at me. "You got a minute?" she asked.

"Sure."

She pointed toward the front of the building and I headed that way. Billy and Albert Swallow gave up eavesdropping and went back to work.

We walked out front.

"How are you feeling?" Andrea asked.

"I'm a little down."

"Jan gave you that obit. She thinks she's some kind of bigshot now she's on this murder story. If she was smart, she'd know you could help her get an interview with Xanthia."

"No. She's right. I wouldn't help her anyway. I don't think I'd put Xanthia through that."

"You're going to see her tonight, aren't you?"

"Yes."

"You like her?"

"Some."

This was an interesting conversation. Andrea was showing more concern about my love life than usual, and I hoped it was because of a renewed interest in our relationship. Still, for the moment I was ambivalent about such things. What difference would it make? We would all be dead soon.

"I don't know if she's good for you," she said. "I don't think she understands you. I can see the sexual attraction, but you're different types. You're kind of a funny, cynical guy. She's into all this spiritual mumbo jumbo, very serious."

I didn't say anything. I didn't feel like making a joke. And besides, I was thinking about death.

After a moment, realizing I wasn't going to reply, she said, "Anyway, I hope you're feeling better. I care about you and how you're doing."

"Me too," I said, then, "I mean, I care about you and how *you're* doing. You still seeing Buck?"

"I don't like the way you say his name." She fumbled through her purse. "Have you got a cigarette?"

"Yeah." I handed her one and lit it for her. As she puffed on it, looking at the ground, I studied her eyebrows, perched at the edge of a strong, flat forehead. They were full eyebrows, auburn like her hair. They weren't eyebrows that had to be painted on, and yet they weren't too much. I thought about Frosty Shields's eyebrows, overgrown sagebrush eyebrows, but just right for him. I wondered if it was peculiar to love people for their eyebrows.

She smoked her cigarette for a minute as we stood silently surveying the street, watching the passing cars. Then she said, "I've got to get back to work. Take care." She threw the cigarette over the curb and walked back into the building without looking at me.

# Five

The beach was quiet as it neared sunset. I sat at a bench facing the water, shielding my eyes from the glare of the sun. Down the way, the lifeguard snored in her tower and a few old ladies swam for their health in bathing caps and old-fashioned one-piece suits with frilly middles. There was nothing to do, little to watch. I hoped Xanthia would be on time. Outer peace, like inner peace, is a phenomenon with which I have limited experience.

A few minutes later I saw her, approaching gracefully on her ten-speed bike. She walked with her bike to the bench. She was wearing her customary summer outfit of long cotton skirt and tank top. Her feet were bare. She was gorgeous.

"Hi, Xanthia."

"Hi." She smiled as she neared and lowered her bike to a resting place in the grass. She came over and sat down beside me.

She put her hand on my shoulder and we kissed. I remembered how recently I had been able to touch her anywhere, and I longed for that privilege.

"Are you okay?" I asked.

"Not really." Xanthia let go a burst of sobbing and fell into my arms. I hadn't expected this. I don't know why, but I hadn't. I held her and tried to keep from crying myself. After a minute or two, she moved away.

"It was so senseless. And these cops are so stupid. The kind of questions they asked made me feel like they thought I had something to do with it." She began to cry again and I held her. I let her cry it out without saying anything. I enjoyed the warmth and closeness and the smell of her hair and felt guilty for taking pleasure from such a somber moment.

She sat up and took my handkerchief, which for once was clean, and wiped her nose. Tears streaked her face, but had not marred her makeup because she didn't wear any.

Then she reached into her purse, took out a handmade leather wallet with flowers tattooed on the outside. She opened it and pulled out a check. "This is for you," she said.

I looked at it. The amount was five hundred dollars.

"For what?"

"A retainer. I know you're my friend, but I don't want to take advantage of you."

"What do you expect me to do?"

"Find out who killed my father and why."

As I thought about her words, I realized I had blocked the meaning of our relationship for the past couple of days. Welch's doubts about me, combined with his gruesome death, had scared me away from feelings of love for her. Now, Welch's concern seemed to be moving into me, transferring itself, like the burden carried by a sin eater. Tears welled in my eyes. Even if I had not loved Xanthia, even under greater threat, I would have been moved to help her. I was afraid, but I would not be able to prevent my inclination to rescue, to protect. I was incompetent, but she wanted me. I would try to live up to her expectations. Still, I made one more effort to deflect the request, to make sure it was really necessary.

"I feel terrible about your father's death," I said, "and I'd like to help you find out who did it. But you know it's very hard for a private individual to learn what the police can learn."

Xanthia's mouth tightened; her eyes shone with anger. "I

know just how competent the cops are in this town," she said. "I want you to look into it because I don't think they're going to do anything. Other than maybe arrest me."

"I'm a correspondence school detective," I told her. "Not much of a recommendation."

"You're bright; you're not afraid," she retorted.

Not afraid? I was afraid of pretty much everything. "Take this back," I said. "I'll check into it a bit, find out what the police are doing, but I don't want any money from you."

"It's not like I'm poor. My father left me money. I won't miss it."

"I don't have it coming," I said. "I can't guarantee you anything."

"Keep it. Don't cash it if you don't want to and give it back if you can't help." Her voice was gentler now.

"I'll see what I can find out. I would like to know as much as anyone. But I think I have to be a little careful. Unless I think I can really accomplish something, it might be counterproductive to become involved in this. You and I know, of course, that I had nothing to do with your father's death; but if they don't develop some leads, they might revise their opinion on that. Cops need someone to focus on, and they don't have too much patience in looking for a suspect."

"I can't imagine why they would suspect you."

I shrugged. "Surely you've heard more about my past by now."

"Yes, but it certainly doesn't make me distrust you."

"You are the exception," I said, "especially since I was at the scene."

She looked at me as I said this, and her eyes suddenly filled with tears. "I need to know . . . what he said."

"His very last words?"

"All of it, but those especially."

"He thought he was going to live to a hundred."

She looked at me, puzzled.

"When he saw how badly hurt he was, I think he knew it was fatal. He said something like he was surprised, that he'd thought he would live to a hundred."

"I thought so too," she said, barely able to speak for the emotion. "He took such good care of himself." She burst into sobs again. Then the tears subsided. After a minute she asked, "What did you talk about before that? You brought him in from the airport, right?"

"Yes. We were together for about half an hour."

"What did you talk about?"

I didn't like where this was going. "We talked about his reservations about me as a suitor for his daughter."

"Oh."

"He knew about my mental history."

"Did you argue?"

"No. It was a civil conversation. He didn't even forbid me to see you; he said it was up to you."

"That was like him. He was always very fair to me." She seemed consoled by this news, by gleaning a good opinion of her father out of this conversation. I wasn't so happy. I felt that I was the low-class loser who had been allowed to continue seeing his daughter as a matter of patrician largess.

We sat there for a time; then without a word we got up and began strolling toward town, Xanthia pushing her bike.

"There were so many things to do after his death," she said as we walked. "They just hit you with everything at once. I had to identify him, you know." She cried again and turned away. After a moment she continued, "Then I had to fill out a thousand forms and see my lawyer and the undertaker, and all the time I just had this ache in my gut, this knot that I couldn't untie. I miss him so much, Scott. I was so close to him. He was everything to me."

"What happened to your mom?"

"She died when I was born. I never knew much about her."

"That's too bad. My mom died when I was little, too."

She looked up at me. "Yeah?"

"Yeah. When I was three. I don't remember anything about that time except that when I think about being three it feels happy. After that everything seems out of kilter."

"I never felt anything was right," she said. "Things were out of kilter from the beginning. It's just not right to start out with no one but a father for family."

"You have no one in Seattle?"

"How'd you know we were from Seattle?"

Boy, was I stupid. "I did your father's obit," I admitted. "It mentioned that's where he came from."

"Oh." She shrugged. "It's okay. It's your job. Anyway, there's no one in Seattle. I asked my dad about it a dozen times. He often goes to Seattle on business, I mean, he used to go, but he seldom took me along, never introduced me to anyone." Tears formed in her eyes. "I have an aunt. She lives somewhere in the Southwest. She visited a couple of times when I was a child. I've been looking for her address among my father's things, but I haven't located it so far."

I touched her shoulder as we walked. Her shoulder was warm and firm.

We strolled into town. Xanthia locked her bike up, and we had dinner at Green Planet, a health food restaurant where I wasn't allowed to smoke. Afterward we wandered around town for a while; then we sat at a bench in a small city park and embraced and looked at the stars.

I left Xanthia in my bed the next morning. I felt a little guilty because I was comparatively cheerful and confident—in spite of what had been happening. Usually, unfortunately, my moods were like that—totally disconnected from any logic.

I dropped by Allison's playground, then went to work. I edited my copy and filled my page with a story and pictures I had been saving for a long time. It was about a local woman who taught yoga. I thought it would be inspirational for the locals and a change for their religion page. I thought they would find it interesting that they had a woman in their midst who thought she could extend her life by regulating her body temperature through yoga.

Afterward, I had another appointment with Frosty Shields, but first I wanted to fit in a quick visit to the woman who had called the police the night Welch had been killed. Her name was Allbright. I knew nothing about her except her name. I had heard it at the police station while officers discussed the case.

I escaped from the office by early afternoon and headed for her house. In front of the house, a narrow boat dock stretched out into the calm waters of the lake. As I pulled into the driveway behind a tan Jaguar XJ6, I noticed a woman on the end of the dock looking around the lake with binoculars. I went around the side of the house and walked down the pier toward the woman. The day was overcast, calm and warm though the lake breeze was cool. It was nice. I was in the neighborhood where I had witnessed a brutal murder and I was actually enjoying myself. You could never tell when that might happen.

The woman didn't notice me. She kept searching the lake shore with her binoculars, scanning left and right until something caught her interest, then pausing briefly to study it. When I approached, she was looking toward Andrew Welch's A-frame home, a scant hundred yards off. She was a blonde woman, mid-forties I guessed, her hair tousled from brief gusts of wind. She wore a light turtleneck and brown cotton jeans. She had the casual, down-home elegance of wealth, from the gold watch glinting in the sun to the gold bracelet on her graceful ankle. As I neared I saw the reddish scar around her left jaw snaking up toward her ear. It was a surprisingly ugly scar and seemed to have affected the shape of her face on that side so that there was a clear disparity between the beauty of her right side and the distortion of her left. And it showed through despite an ample application of makeup.

"Who are you?" she asked sharply. "What are you doing here?"

She was afraid of me. I wasn't used to that in Mill City. I felt like a burglar caught in the act.

"I'm a newspaper reporter," I said. I didn't use my name since it was in the newspaper and I didn't want her to know I was one of the people she had seen the other night.

"I've already told the newspaper all I'm going to—all I know," she said. She seemed less afraid, but anxious to get rid of me. The binoculars were still gripped tightly in her left hand, held half at the ready.

"I work for the *Daily Sun,*" I explained, "but I'm not here in my capacity as a reporter. I'm also a private investigator and I'm looking into Andrew Welch's death on behalf of his daughter, Xanthia."

"Show me some identification," she said. She finally let the binoculars drop, and they swung from the strap around her neck. Her blue eyes glanced around the shore nervously as though she were expecting onlookers or gossips to notice our exchange. I handed her one of my old cards from my brief tenure as a PI in Spokane. Maybe she hadn't paid much attention to the newspaper stories because she didn't say anything or act like she recognized the name.

She handed the card back to me. "What do you want?"

"Just to ask a few questions about the other night. It won't take very long. Very routine kinds of questions."

"Well, all right. Let's go into the house." She started toward shore and I followed her.

"See anything interesting?" I asked her.

"What? Oh. Not really. I just like to take advantage of this beautiful view along the lake."

"You were looking at the Welch house when I arrived," I said.

"I've, uh, been kind of keeping an eye on the house since Andrew was killed. I just thought I might see something or someone."

"Good idea."

She smiled self-consciously. "*I* thought so."

Inside the house the randomness of the placement of her possessions gave the impression that Mrs. Allbright had not yet settled into her life in Mill City and I wondered how long she had lived here. I had assumed she was a long-time resident, but the look of the house said otherwise. The style of the interior was stark and modern, but the effect was softened by handicrafts from around the world, strewn about haphazardly as though only recently received. There were tapestries from South America, sculpture and pottery from the Middle East, and an Iranian rug. In the middle of the far wall was an unadorned, small fireplace, cleaned, apparently unused for some time.

"I've forgotten my manners," she said as we entered. "Would you like some coffee or tea? I have a nice hibiscus."

"No, thanks," I said. The very thought of a nice hibiscus made me nauseous. "I'll just make this very brief."

"Well, then, have a seat."

I sat at the end of an enormous leather couch and took out my pencil. She sat in a matching chair, her hands folded and kneading nervously. I wondered if she knew how many cows had died for her furniture.

"Looks like you just moved in," I said, hoping to start the interview low key.

"Oh, does it? I've been here for months."

"Where did you move from?"

"San Francisco. Excuse me, but this doesn't seem to have much to do with what happened the other night." Despite her apparent nervousness, she was hard to intimidate. She reached over to a small sterling silver case on the handmade wood table near her and lifted the lid. Inside were cigarettes standing politely on end. I noticed as she took one and lit it that they were English Ovals.

"You were a witness so I was trying to learn a little of your background."

"I'm sorry, but I'm a very private person. I haven't lived here very long, but I'm a very respectable lady. I'm planning on starting a business and living here permanently."

"No offense intended," I said.

"I just had the bad fortune to happen to see someone being attacked," she said. "I hope I never have an equivalent experience."

"How did you happen to see what was happening?"

"It was a strange night—the rain and lightning. I was out on my deck with my binoculars. I noticed something going on over there; then I saw the taxicab, and someone struggling with Andrew Welch."

"What did he look like?"

"I couldn't see well. He was taller than Welch, dark-haired. I think he had a mustache."

It sounded like she was describing me. If that were the case, what had the police made of it? Did they believe me, or were they merely giving me rope to hang myself?

"Did you see anyone near the house before the murder or since?"

"No one—except for a lot of police officers during the past few days." Her face was softer now, less nervous, less obstinate. She was quite attractive for an older lady—on one side of her face anyway. She was looking at me, examining my face, too. Without warning she got up, went to a table where there was a stack of newspapers. She shuffled through them and read for a minute. I tried to think of a question to distract her from this activity, but my mind was blank, as it often is.

"I thought I'd heard your name," she said, tossing the newspaper down again. "I don't know what you're up to, but I want you to leave."

"I was at the Welch house that night, but I had nothing to do with the murder—I merely happened to witness it. I was hoping that you might have seen the person who did it."

"Please leave."

"I'm sorry, I didn't mean to upset you."

"But I'm afraid you have. I'd rather not continue this." She crushed her cigarette in a crystal ashtray and rose from her seat.

I stood also. "I'll go then," I said, seeing no other direction to take the conversation.

"I wish you would."

We both walked toward the back door. I paused at the exit. "Thanks. Sorry to have bothered you."

Outside, it was still a pleasant day, but I wasn't having fun anymore. Now I was going to talk to Frosty Shields. Events seemed to have conspired to ruin my mood. As I walked away I heard the door slide shut and lock behind me.

Should I pursue this further? How? Do a search of the Welch house?—if I could get in now that it had been designated a crime scene. It wasn't likely the cops would allow me that privilege. I looked around the neighborhood. There were five or six houses within viewing distance of both Mrs. Allbright's house and Welch's. I could do a survey, ask the neighbors about anything they may have seen, confirm or refute Mrs. Allbright's story. Perhaps the cops had missed a possible witness, someone who might have seen a stranger in the neighborhood. For now, however, I would have to return to my life as a reporter—pretend things were normal. As I was cranking up the Pinto, which took a good two minutes, I thought about her name. If she was Mrs. Allbright, was there a Mr. Allbright? Had he been in the house that night? Maybe she was divorced. Or widowed. Oh well, it probably didn't matter.

As I backed out of Mrs. Allbright's driveway, I noticed one more anomaly to give me something to think about—as though I needed more. Mrs. Allbright had a big Harley chopper parked near her garage door, partially obscured by the Jaguar. Somehow it was an unlikely image, Mrs. Allbright revving the throaty engine of a Harley and riding the road in black leather.

I buzzed off toward Frosty's house. Even though he was dying, I would have more in common with him. I had associated with rich people under all sorts of circumstances, but the intelligent poor suited me better.

When I got to Frosty's I noticed that the old Buick in the driveway had been washed, and I wondered if he had taken it out for a drive. I hoped so. Little pleasures become important when your skills and abilities begin to atrophy. I had been through it, knew what they meant.

I parked, walked up to the door, and knocked. I glanced around at another car, a Datsun station wagon parked at the curb. Frosty had other visitors. I knocked again, this time a little louder.

"I'm comin', you bastard, just hold your goddamn horses," I heard Frosty say.

"You watch your language," said a shrill voice.

"Goddamn four-eyed bitch," Frosty said, as he struggled with the door. He was beginning to shock even me.

The door came open hard as usual and Frosty squinted out at me from under his bushy eyebrows. I thought I saw a look of fear as well as defiance when he first stared at me. Then he said, "Oh, it's the feller with the crooked nose," matter-of-factly. "Well, hell, it's open house. You may as well come in, too."

He walked away from the door, which I guessed was his form of invitation. I went inside where I could smell the strong aroma of Pine Sol and ammonia. Frosty, walking away from me, was wearing his customary black logger's pants and suspenders and a heavy wool shirt. I wondered what the hell he wore during the wintertime. He was leaning on a crutch as he walked.

"What happened to your leg, Frosty?" I asked solicitously.

"Oh, I hurt the goddamn thing again! Every goddamn thing is going wrong," he said petulantly.

"Frosty, you stop complaining," the shrill, disembodied voice said. It seemed to be echoing from the kitchen, where I heard some occasional banging and thumping of utensils and pots.

"What's wrong, Frosty?" I asked, hoping to open him up and let him get some of his anger out.

"Shithouse mouse, everything is screwed up," he said. "Then, to top it all off, they have to send this bitch over here to clean up after me."

A brown-haired, plump woman in her late thirties appeared in the doorway. She fixed Frosty with a searing stare. "You stop complaining, Frosty Shields. You're just an old sinner and you won't get any sympathy from me." She glared at me as if to include me in her condemnation, then disappeared back into the kitchen. She didn't seem in the least curious about who I was.

After their encounter, Frosty gave me the first smile of the day as he sat on the couch and pulled the familiar pack of Bull Durham from his pocket.

"Goddamn, I irritate her," he said, grinning. "She's been tryin' to make a Christian out of me ever since my kids hired her to clean up and check on me." The grin was brief, replaced by a tremulous pout.

I stood in the middle of the room looking at Frosty, seeking a clue to his real mood. As he was licking the paper to his cigarette, his lips quivered and tears came to his eyes. He let the cigarette drop and put his face in his hands and sobbed. His shoulders shook.

"What is it, Frosty?"

"Shit. Jesus, man!" he spat. "Leave me alone! Goddamn bastard, but I feel like a fool." He straightened up and took a red print handkerchief from his pocket. He wiped his face, sniffed some, and stuck the handkerchief back in his pocket. He waved his hand at me, gesturing me toward a chair. "Stick around," he said. "I'm not always crazy. Wait for this goddamn bitch to leave." He reached down and picked up the ruins of his cigarette, poured some more tobacco, and licked the paper. He expertly rolled it into a tight tube. He lit it with a kitchen match from his pocket.

"Sally, you about through in there?" he asked loudly.

"I'm leaving, I'm leaving," Sally said, passing through the living room with a large bag full of cleaning supplies. She gave him one last angry look as she walked toward the door. "You could help if you'd be just a little neater," she said, then jerked the door open and marched out. The door slammed behind her.

"Jesus, it's a relief having her gone," Frosty said.

I took a seat in the old rocker, lit a cigarette, and rocked awhile. "Having a rough day, huh?"

"Those bastards better not come back, by God. They just caught me when I was feelin' bad. They come back, and by God I'm gonna find my old four-ten and blow 'em a new asshole."

"What bastards?"

"Oh, that pair that came by here earlier today. Goddamn 'em. Tryin' to scare an old man." Frosty's cranky expression changed to a tremulous pout.

"What happened? Who tried to scare you?"

Frosty stiffened his chin, as though he were impatient that I didn't understand and was going to make it perfectly clear. "Some man and this woman came to my house earlier today and asked if I was any relation to Andrew Welch."

"Why in the hell would they think you were related to Andrew Welch?"

"Goddamned if I know. But the guy was a real big guy, mean,

and he pushed right up against me and said, 'You sure you're not related?' like I was lying, and like if he found out I was lying he was going to hurt me or something. If I was younger I would've kicked his ass, but I guess I'm just an old man and can't defend myself no more."

"What did they look like?" I was dying to know who these people were. They could provide the police somewhere to look besides at me. I thought about Jack and Diane from the other night. Could they be the couple?

"I don't know. The man was big. Had a beard. The lady—just a *lady*. I told them half a dozen times I was only a friend of that Welch feller. They said they'd seen me talking to him and they wanted to know if I was his uncle or his dad or something. I told them he was just a guy I talked to now and then. I talk to a lot of people."

I put my hand on his shoulder. "I'm sorry they bothered you, Frosty. It's a pretty bad way to start the day."

"It's a goddamned waste of my time, and I ain't got many days left to waste." Frosty picked a stray piece of tobacco off his wrinkled lower lip then puffed on his cigarette. "I only wanted a couple of more months of feeling good."

"Well, I hope you get it," I said.

"Hells bells, I ain't got much chance of it now." His lower lip quivered.

"Why?"

"Oh, the goddamn doctor won't give me any drugs—chemotherapy. Hell, that's the only chance I got of licking this crap."

"You really think it would do you some good?"

"I don't know. Without it I ain't got a chance. I know it'd be rough. I'd probably lose my hair, be sick as a dog on a merry-go-round. But hell, it might help. But no, *I* can't have it. He says I'm too old. Just too goddamned old." Frosty massaged a wrinkled forehead with a gnarled hand. "Hell! And here I thought I had a long time yet. Just a few months ago I was figuring what I'd be doin' to keep entertained for a few more years. And I got a lot of books I want to read!

"Funny thing is, I always figured I'd go in the woods like Shorty and Whitey and Jimmy Smith—get rolled over by a log or burnt in a goddamn forest fire. Now here I am, just wastin' away like a little old lady."

"You ain't no little old lady," I said, falling into his vernacular.

"I know I ain't no little old lady," he retorted, brushing aside my attempt at camaraderie. "Don't tell me things I already know. I thought a writer feller like you would be smarter than that." Frosty scowled and looked off toward the kitchen, resting his hand on his chin.

I sat there a moment, feeling stupid, trying to think of something that would improve things. "Somebody washed up the old Buick," I said.

"*Somebody* didn't wash up the Buick. *I* did, you goddamn ignoramus sonofabitch. Pretty soon you're going to start telling me the story of the goddamn birds and the bees."

"Want to go for a spin?" I asked. He looked at me. He didn't grin, but he didn't pout either.

"Hell, I'm not allowed to drive anymore. I just get to wash the goddamn thing and keep it up so some chickenshit sonofabitch will buy it for peanuts when I'm gone. All I get to see anymore is this house and the damn hospital."

"I'll drive," I said. "She looks like she could use the exercise."

"If a beer's included in the deal, you're on," he said, not smiling, but looking a hell of a lot more alive.

"How about a drive over the Denton Bridge and a beer at the Blue Lantern?"

"Blue Lantern? I ain't been out there since the fifties. Hell, we used to dance up a storm out there. Just give me a minute."

Frosty limped over to a closet and took out a light wool jacket. "My circulations no good at all anymore," he explained.

A few moments later we were cruising through town in the old black beauty. Frosty was sitting up, looking all around, and I was enjoying the quiet purr of the old car. Frosty got a local country western station on the radio, and I put up with it because I was having a good time.

I headed across the Denton Bridge, a half-mile straight stretch across the lake. It looked like a Tinkertoy project, with wooden pilings sticking up every twenty feet. I got Black Beauty up to eighty-five.

"Goddamn," said Frosty, sticking his face out into the wind and braving the insects. "Well, goddamn!"

I turned off on a county road the other side of the bridge and snaked along a crooked forested highway to the Blue Lantern, a roadhouse in the old style, with sawdust on the dance floor and half a dozen old heaps parked out front in a gravel parking lot.

We went in, Frosty limping along with his crutch, and took a seat at the bar. We sat there for half an hour drinking a bottle of Miller each. I asked Frosty a couple of times if he could remember any details about the couple who'd visited him, but he was short-tempered and had lost interest in the subject, so we ended up chatting with a corpulent, frizzy-haired wench of a barmaid who claimed to own the tavern and kept trying to get me to tell her what had happened to my nose. I finally said I'd been billy clubbed by a gay cop in Scottsdale, Arizona. At that Frosty damn near fell off his stool.

Then we headed back for town and on the bridge the speedometer climbed to ninety. I hadn't done anything like that for years and it showed because I wasn't looking out behind me. We had just passed a sign that said SPEED ZONE AHEAD when I noticed the blue and red lights of a county patrol car behind me. I pulled over at the end of the bridge and waited. The officer who got out of the car was Patrolman Blaine. Frosty said, "Good thing we don't have an open case of beer in the backseat."

When we returned to Frosty's house, I had a fresh traffic ticket and Frosty's words, "That guy don't seem to like you," to ponder.

"How about another drive some day soon?" said Frosty, as I was about to leave.

"Sure," I said, "but let's take my Pinto. I can't get it going fast enough to get a ticket."

Frosty chuckled. "Okay."

I was late getting back to the office, and I hadn't taken a single note on Frosty's story.

I was just getting back into the grind, had turned out a couple of stories, and was ready to go home for a nap before driving cab when I got a phone call from Xanthia.

"Scott, I want you to find out something for me," she said when she came on the line. She offered no endearments nor love chatter, which would have been nice and might have been overheard by Andrea—sitting across the desk from me. I thought about the couple who had visited Frosty and wondered if Xanthia would have any ideas on who they were.

"I'm looking into it, Xanthia," I said. "I haven't come up with much, but I'll have more time soon. Actually, I might have a few questions for you."

"It's not about my father's death," she said. "I want you to help me find out something else. I want you to find out who my father was."

"You know who your father was," I answered, startled. I felt a little like I was living inside an M. C. Escher print.

"I don't think so," she said calmly. "I got a call today from my lawyer. My father left me an estate worth seventy million dollars."

I spent the weekend driving cab and sleeping. It was a quiet moonlit Monday night before I saw Xanthia again. I trudged from my car to Xanthia's house carrying a small briefcase. It contained a copy of the autopsy report, my notes on the case, and the advance Xanthia had offered me. I had not yet cashed the check.

Xanthia had moved back into her father's house a couple of days earlier and had suggested the meeting tonight. She wanted me to look at some things. Then I was to help formulate a plan to discover her father's past and thereby something about her own genesis. It was a surprise when I arrived and she was in the bathtub soaking in water mixed with Kama Sutra oil. She had left the deck door partially open, and when I knocked, she called for me to come in. It seemed a mighty brave thing to do after her experience of the other night; she seemed to be inviting the shower scene from *Psycho*.

When I went into the bathroom, I was prepared to tell her she should lock her doors, but the sight of her lovely breasts distracted me. Instead of lecturing her, I gave a kind of grunt.

"You're usually more eloquent than that," she said, sponging a bronze shoulder. The water descended and trickled off a pink nipple. Her long black hair hung in the water behind her.

"I'm usually not caught off guard in this way," I said, taking a seat on the stool a few feet away. To add to my present preoccupation, all the porcelain in the bathroom was labia pink and there were prints of Japanese erotic art.

She raised her eyebrows and her brown eyes stared at me suggestively. Her eyebrows were strong and black and at any other time would have been my idea of her most attractive feature.

"How come you're in such a good mood? I thought it would take you longer to recover."

A troubled look crossed her face. A little guilt just for feeling good, I thought. I had said the wrong thing. "I don't know. It might just be an emotional remission. I *am* thinking about all the things I can do now. Father's gone and that can't be helped."

"You're alive and life goes on."

"Not just that. I can do so much for other people. There are so many things that need to be done. Like a friend of mine who is developing a wind generator and now I can help him. And I can promote my beliefs about how diet and exercise and yoga can improve and lengthen life."

I sat there, looking at her, but not listening to her.

"Do you want to take a bath?" she asked.

"I'm not that dirty," I told her, kicking off my shoes.

After weathering a couple of storms in her tub, I found myself physically and emotionally well scrubbed and sitting on the shag carpet in her living room. I was wearing a borrowed robe and was poring through a box of records she had pulled from various desks, safes, and hidey-holes. I was having fun, lounging with a beautiful woman in a fancy house. Still, the scene had its ghoulish aspects, and I was having flashbacks to the time when I was crazy and believed in life after death. I half-waited to hear the voice of her dead father. To add to the eeriness, the room was dimly lit by a small porcelain lamp, candles, and the moonlight coming in through the huge A-shaped window overlooking the lake. The moon reminded me of my crazy nights, too. Lunatic is a term not given casually; I had had a personal relationship with the moon at that time. Tonight, it was like a huge eye watching over us as we sifted through the records of a man's life.

As we did our investigation, I told her about Frosty Shields and his visitors. The story shocked her, but she had no clue about the couple's identity, especially since Frosty was so vague in his description. We discussed it, trying to figure it out; then, having failed to come up with any useful ideas, we settled into sorting through her father's papers.

"You should report it to the police," she said, as a final thought.

"I did, but Blaine took the call. He asked me for details, but I got the impression he thought I was trying to throw them off my scent."

She looked at me with the expression that told me of her disgust with the local police department.

We continued examining the papers and mementos. "So far, I don't see anything that unusual," I said, after we had worked at this for a while. "Your father's birth certificate seems in order. Born in Astoria, Oregon, in 1930." I put the paper aside for future reference. "And here's a military record. Served in Korea— Purple Heart." I put the paper down with the birth certificate and thumbed through a sheaf of legal documents, mostly deeds and records of purchases. Xanthia was wearing a cream-and-brown-colored velour robe. She was sitting at the sofa, her wet hair hanging down as she searched through another stack of records.

"I saw those before," she said, "but they're the only records I have of him before 1960, except for a few financial records. What I want to know is where would my father have collected seventy million dollars? I knew he had money, but I didn't expect anything like that. He has property everywhere. And stocks— AT&T, Ford, Xerox, General Motors. We have liquid assets of over thirty million dollars."

I was surprised this lady was speaking to me, much less sharing her bathwater.

"Well, what do you think, then?" I leaned back and lit a cigarette. I wanted to forget about Andrew Welch. He made me feel too mortal. I also felt a little guilty to be smoking here. Xanthia was allowing it even though her father never had. His house was equipped with all sorts of electrical air cleaners so that the air of the house would be cleaned of "free radicals" and other chemicals that would possibly harm him. "Do you have any guesses?"

"No, I don't have any idea. But I don't think he was using his real name. Which makes me wonder: What is *my* name? I wonder if he ran away from some past life. Maybe I have a mother and siblings. Sometimes I wonder if he was a witness or something and they changed his name."

"People in the witness protection program seldom accrue seventy million bucks. They're lucky to keep anything."

"Well, then, maybe he was a crime boss or something, and he had to run away."

This was pretty wild speculation by a daughter about her father. "That doesn't seem very likely. I knew your father, remember?"

"I guess I don't think so either, but something has to explain this."

I reached into the box and came out with a handful of old black-and-white photographs. They were dog-eared and faded. "What's this?" I asked.

"I don't know," she said, not looking up. She was studying a deed, perhaps trying to decide through all the legalese what kind of property it was and where it was located.

I looked through the photographs. They were pictures of a variety of young men, children, women. One picture was of an old man in the white shirt and bow tie of the turn of the century. He was standing beside a grand white house and grimacing at the camera. I turned it over. JOHN STYLES, 1909, was written in very old ink on the stained back of the photo.

I handed Xanthia the photograph. "Do you suppose this could be some relative of your father's?"

She looked at it. "I don't know. Father never spoke about his family or my mother or anyone. That's why I'm suspicious. I suppose he could be a relative. I just wouldn't know."

She handed the picture back. I put it aside and looked at the other pictures. In one, a group of young boys was standing, restraining their mirth, trying to pose for the camera. The writing on the back said, LITTLE MATTY, GRAHAM, AND BOBBY GREENE. There was no date. I put the entire stack of photos with the birth certificate and army record. Then I dipped into the box once more and came up with a fat manila envelope. I unwrapped the string tie holding it and opened the flap. Inside I felt some fat bundles, but the envelope was too tight for me to get my hand firmly around them. I turned the envelope upside down and shook it. After a moment or two, several large packages of money hit the floor, followed by a key and a small envelope.

"Xanthia, I hate to tell you this, but you just inherited some more money."

"Oh, God," she said. "Where did he get it all?"

"I don't know, but you'd better check the mattresses and the walls," I said. "Your father collected the stuff."

We counted the money—forty thousand dollars in fifty-dollar bills. Peanuts to the Welch clan. Then I looked in the little envelope that was with it. Inside was a slip of paper, a government form. A post office box number was stamped at the top of the form.

"A P.O. box," I said. "Perhaps this will be of some help. I don't know where Wedgewood Station is though. They don't give the city." I put the slip back into the envelope and tossed it on top of the other documents—things I was putting aside for research into the history of Andrew Welch. I looked at the key. It was a door key of some kind. I studied it for a moment, then Xanthia spoke.

"I want you to go to Astoria," Xanthia said. "I want you to look into my father's birth certificate and find out if you can learn anything about his life there—who his family was. Maybe he inherited the money."

"I can't just take off anytime I want," I told her. "I have a job." And a daughter. And an ex-wife. And neurosis.

Xanthia reached for a business checkbook sitting on a teak coffee table nearby. She pulled out a check and handed it to me. It was made out to me in the amount of five thousand dollars. The note said: "Advance on Services Rendered." At my present rate of pay it would take me six months or more to earn that.

"You sure know how to bribe someone," I told her. "But I can't possibly take this." I thought about how many child-support payments this would make. I was still behind. It would help Andrea, and it would help Allison. She still had poor clothing; it was mid-1979 and the hippie days were almost over. Soon people would expect your children to be well-dressed—even in Mill City.

"But, Scott, I don't have anyone else who can help me."

"Hire a real private detective. There are probably some good ones in Seattle, maybe even in Spokane." I wanted to be her hero, but in her best interest I was really trying to protect her from my services, from my incompetence.

"But I don't *know* them. I don't trust people I don't know."

"Sometimes you can't trust the people you know either," I told her.

"Scott, it would be a big help. I could give you more money."

"You're way over my ethical limit already," I said. "The problem is that I'm not that good at this type of thing. I really didn't train for it properly, and the only experience I have is a disaster of a case that nearly got me jailed."

"In Spokane?"

"Yeah. I put a guy in a coma. There's still a chance that his family is going to sue me one of these days—especially if he ever dies." I hated to even think about the man in the hospital bed in a coma.

"You don't have to do the actual investigation," she offered. "You could hire private detectives. Just supervise things for me; make sure they're doing things that will help me."

"I don't know. I'd have to arrange for a leave of absence. I'd have to leave town to hire people—to follow up on some of these leads."

"Couldn't you do that? I'm sure they'd give you a leave of absence. Your daughter would be with your ex-wife; she'd be fine. And you could give them some of the money."

I lit another cigarette.

Xanthia moved to the sofa. "Sit here," she said, motioning me to the spot in front of her. I put out my cigarette and did as I was told. I sat on the carpet in front of her, leaning against the sofa and feeling the touch of her bare legs on my arms. She leaned over me and massaged my shoulders as her face touched my neck. Her robe had fallen open, and I could feel the softness of her breast on my back.

"It won't take long, really, Scott. And it would be of so much help to me. I really want you to be part of this. I admire you so much, and I like being with you so much. I want us to share this. You'll earn the money by helping me, really. And it'll give us a chance to be together more."

She continued, but she had already won me over. I had decided days ago, when she first asked me, that I would help. Money made it possible, but much more than the thought of having the money was the thought of having a wonderful woman like Xanthia really love me. I would be helping her. She would be thinking about me all the time, and I would be thinking about her. And when she thought of me, she would be thinking of a wonderful heroic man. Not a weakling and a loser.

I took the key I had been holding, the one that had fallen out of the envelope with the money, and put it on my key ring—

in case I should run into its lock. "I'll ask the newspaper if they'll give me a leave of absence," I said. "It's the only way I can consider doing this."

"You'll be wonderful, Scott. I know it."

Late the next morning, I was planning to arrange a meeting with the publisher and Albert Swallow. I was going to ask for a leave of absence. It was like asking the pope for a fornication license, but I would do it and then we would see. Getting away from the cab company would be no problem. And unfortunately, they would be quite willing to hire me back.

The office was as quiet as usual—about the decibel level of the inside of a jet engine—with layout people creating mayhem on their side of the partition, while Jan the Barracuda and Billy fought over who had the right to some new story on the police beat—another death, this time a manslaughter with the accused party in custody. Andrea quietly made phone calls and collected notes for a city-planning story. I was on a spare wooden chair near Albert Swallow's desk, trying to whisper my request to him and still be heard over the din of the argument and the typesetters. I had expected him to be reluctant, but he surprised me with his willingness to arrange a get-together.

He soon ushered me into the front office occupied by Norman Teane, the publisher. His office was used for conferences with local VIPs and therefore was the only area in the building that showed any class or spared expense. Norman's wife, Theda, had supplied the office with plants and bamboo curtains and prints of clowns. The large desk was simulated walnut and the chairs were brown Naugahyde. I sat on a leatherette couch as Albert took a seat in a matching chair, puffing vigorously on his pipe and looking worried. I wondered what he could possibly be worried about.

Norman sat at his desk, ignoring both of us, signing papers and making phone calls. Norman was a fat, greedy, little bastard. He was in his forties, had been a printer all his life, and had now ended up printing a newspaper. He had a face that showed all the character of the moon, except that the moon is not shiny from sweat and grease. Tiny little eyes peered out from puffed slits in his face, and a button nose provided the only relief from an otherwise flat facial topography. He was wearing a brown leisure suit. This was one of those wonderful 1970s creations. It was a way to be casual and still be a tightass. The suits were ugly and the colors were terrible, but they were comfy—unless there was a nuclear attack and then they would melt like Cheez Whiz because they were polyester.

Teane finally looked up from his paperwork. "Now, what's this about?"

"I'd like a leave of absence, sir," I said, doing my best Oliver Twist imitation. "I have some unavoidable business I need to take care of. I don't expect any pay; I would simply like my job back when I return."

"A leave of absence, huh?" Teane popped a codeine cough drop into his mouth. "Why do you need a leave of absence?"

I explained the situation as best I could, keeping personal relationships and money out of it. I told him it would take about a month. When I had finished, Teane was looking at me skeptically. Albert was waiting to read Teane's face before forming an opinion.

"Well, as it happens, I won't be able to give you the leave of absence. But Albert and I have been talking about making some changes around here. This request and the arrangements you've made will help facilitate those changes."

"I don't understand."

"We're going to let Jan take over your page. You were doing okay until recently; you've become a little unreliable. Among other things, we know about these little naps you take between assignments. We think you need some time to sort things out and decide whether or not you really want to be a reporter. And Jan does a bang-up job."

"I see." I touched Xanthia's check to make sure it was still there. I would need it now. I had no respect for Teane and little for Albert, but it hurt to be rejected, even by these two.

"One good thing," said Teane.

"What's that?"

"You don't even have to finish your page for today."

When I returned to the newsroom, Andrea came up to me. She had an angry expression. "Are you taking a leave of absence?" she asked. She had evidently overheard me talking to Albert.

"That's what I asked for," I said.

"To do something for Xanthia, I suppose."

"Well . . ."

"Goddamn you, Scott. I thought you were through with this detective crap—and Xanthia. How are you going to see Allison and . . ."

"Look, I was going to ask for a leave of absence, but I got fired instead."

"Dammit, Scott," Andrea said bitterly. She started gathering her notebooks and tote bag for an exit.

"I'd like to see Allison tonight," I said quickly. "I'm leaving town for a while starting tomorrow."

Andrea said angrily, "You can see her. You are her father—even if you aren't the best she could have." With that bit of venom she walked out of the office.

I stood there feeling bereft and foolish. After a few moments Jan asked me to explain my schedule for putting out the page. She was polite as pie.

I dropped by Frosty's that afternoon so that I could say good-bye and let him know I hadn't forgotten about him. He was pissed at me also.

"I thought we were going to take another drive here pretty soon," he said, an angry scowl on his face. "How long are you going to be gone?"

When I told him, he said, "I hope I'm alive until then. That's just the way my goddamn life is going."

I tried to make him feel better, but he told me I'd better get going or I might be late.

I headed home and packed a few things, threw them into my Pinto. I called the cab company and told them I wasn't going to be able to work for a few weeks. Then I went downtown for dinner. When I was finished, I drove by Andrea's.

"You can visit her the rest of the evening," Andrea said coldly, "since you'll have to leave tomorrow. I'm going out." And shortly thereafter she left.

The time with Allison was pleasant. We wrestled and played and talked and watched TV. But when it came time to go to bed, she was in a crabby mood and didn't want to go to sleep. I tried to reason with her for a while and then she became mad and started sassing me. She started to get out of her bed, insisting on going back to the living room to watch TV. I put her back in the bed and told her she had to go to sleep. She cried intensely, and through the tears and sobbing she said, "I never, EVER want to see you again."

"I'm sorry that you feel that way," I told her, "but you have to go to sleep. It's bedtime."

She curled up in the bed and turned her head toward the wall. I walked into the living room holding my breath.

Andrea came home a little after ten. I tried to talk to her, but she just said, "Good night, Scott," and waited for me to leave. I got into my car and went home.

I woke early in the morning, dressed, and headed out on the highway, my briefcase full of papers, my suitcase full of second-hand clothing.

# Six

The freeway to Seattle was long and dead. The sagebrush and marmots of the desert lands in central Washington passed in stoic silence. I felt like a fool on a fool's errand, a fool without strong family ties or mental health. Still, a fool well paid for a change.

The Pinto droned along, a noisy little bumper car.

I struggled with the tactics of the case, with my errands to be run in Seattle and Astoria. But my mind wandered as I began to notice the corpses of numerous Pintos along the road.

A baby blue Pinto had been abandoned near Vantage, a pink slip on the antenna like a toe tag on a corpse in Vietnam. Another Pinto took a rest on the roadside near Ellensburg, a bronze one with a tire removed, the car perched precariously on a block of wood like an accident victim in traction.

Just before Snoqualmie Pass I saw another one upside down in a ditch, doing a dead cockroach imitation.

I told myself that it was merely coincidence, caused partly by the vast numbers of Pintos that had flooded the country. Still, I listened ever more carefully to the buzzing of my engine.

Hundreds of fancier cars zoomed by—Lancias, Porsches, 280Zs—climbing a social ladder I had not reached but thought about now that I was dating a wealthy woman.

As I came over the pass toward Seattle, I began to relax about the car. My thoughts turned toward dealing with the traffic of the city. I had been in Seattle only a few times, and the experience had not been that pleasant. It was a comparatively aggressive city, with drivers who seemed to hate each other. I didn't mind hating them, but I didn't like the idea of them hating me back.

But as I approached North Bend, a suburb of the big city, a small explosion shook the car and a blue-black cloud from the exhaust pipe filled the highway. I pulled over as my Pinto gave its death rattle.

It took me an hour to get a ride; then I had the car towed. It would take five days to repair it at the local shop, and I didn't have that kind of time nor did I want to spend the money on an engine overhaul. I sold it to a wrecking yard and caught the next bus into Seattle.

I got in late that night and stayed in a tacky motel downtown, then spent the next day roaming through the used-car lots. I was intent on getting a practical car; but when I saw the second-hand brown Saab sitting elegantly in the lot, it drew me deeper and deeper into its web. It was cheap for such a nice-looking, second-hand car, and I paid a large down payment with traveler's checks. I didn't even want to know the interest rate I was being charged. With my credit rating, I knew I was getting the money from a loan shark.

I threw my briefcase and suitcase into the backseat and drove off, worried about the money, but at least I had climbed a couple of rungs on the social ladder.

In a phone booth I checked the yellow pages for detective agencies. I wanted someone cheap, so I avoided those who had paid for spot ads. I settled on Ira Sugarman, Investigator, a man with the smallest listing and a Capitol Hill address. I held Andrew

Welch's birth certificate and dialed the number. The phone was answered instantly.

"Ira's the name, sleaze is my game," said the jovial voice on the other end.

"My name is Scott Moody," I told him, "a private detective from east of the mountains. I need to find out if a man I'm tracing has a criminal record."

Ira paused. I could hear the slurp as he took a drink of something. He smacked his lips. "I got a guy who can check into that for me—probation officer. This a cash deal?"

"Could be," I said.

"I hate that plastic money," he said, confidentially. "I don't have the accountants for it." More slurping and smacking as he bit into something. I was getting hungry.

"When can you get the information to me?"

"When can you get me the money?"

"I've got it."

"Give me the name and two hours."

"You want me to drop by your office?" I looked at the listing. No address was recorded.

"No," he said quickly. "How about we meet? I suggest the Doghouse—great atmosphere." He gave me directions, then said, "Try the spaghetti smothered in chili." I hung up, wondering whether I had chosen my detective correctly.

I found the place easily enough. It was a grand old greasy spoon spawned by the needs of down-and-outers—cab drivers and drunks. It was dimly lit and badly in need of redecorating, lined with rows of booths equipped with the old-style music selectors you used to see in every restaurant, machines with all the great hits of Conway Twitty and Ronnie Dove. The waitresses were all over fifty, most over sixty, and looked like their varicose veins might blow out in the middle of the lunch rush. I passed a seedy-looking midget eating fried chicken and took a seat in a small booth. When my waitress, a cross between Ma Kettle and Dr. Frankenstein's assistant, arrived, I ordered the spaghetti smothered in chili and waited for Sugarman.

The hour was up and the better part of another had passed when I saw a heavyset man of indeterminate age wandering up and down the aisles between booths, leaning over from time to time to ask a question of some solitary diner, then nodding and moving on. He was somewhere between thirty and forty, but it was hard to set the age closer. His clothes were conservative early 1960s—narrow-legged, cuffed, olive drab slacks, black shoes, a dark blue sports jacket with narrow lapels, and a blue shirt. To accent this nice mix of colors, he wore a light blue necktie with a chartreuse bowling ball knocking the pins in every direction. On his head perched a black porkpie hat that looked too small for him.

His face was round, but pleasant, if a bit hairy. He had heavy black eyebrows and dark Mediterranean skin. His hair was cut short, but was greasy from too little shampooing. He was carrying a green steno pad. I realized no method had been established for our recognizing each other, but I suspected I had just located one Ira Sugarman.

I let him work on the problem until he finally passed me, heading toward the booths at the rear. He looked at me and said, "Moody?"

"Sometimes," I responded.

"How droll," he retorted. He began walking away.

"I'm Moody," I said. "Are you Sugarman?"

"That's right," he replied, returning. He tossed his notebook onto the table, removed his hat, and placed it on the seat. Then he scooted in. He had trouble avoiding a bruise to his belly in that motion. "That was very cute," he said, when he had settled in. "Do you have any more quick rejoinders or would you like the information?" The words were sarcastic, but he spoke them with a smile and good humor.

"To business," I said.

"How was the spaghetti?" he asked, looking at my empty plate.

"Better than expected."

"I'd better have some before I go on. I'm feeling a little undernourished." He motioned to the waitress, who dragged herself over and took his order. Then he turned back to me. "Don't you love this place? The real thing."

I shrugged. "It's okay. Did you learn anything about my man?"

"Indubitably. Now for the really important question. Do you have the money?"

"We haven't agreed on a price, but I can meet it."

"Fifty bucks," he said. "The information's worth it."

I didn't know whether it was or not, but this was the big city and I wasn't going to beat him at his own game. "Sure. Fifty bucks. What have you got?"

Sugarman delicately took a sip of the water the waitress had delivered, then brought his notebook in front of him and turned through a few pages. "Andrew Miles Welch," he said, "was arrested on June 19, 1952, for armed robbery. This little adventure took place at a haberdasher's in Vancouver, Washington. For this deed he received two years' rest at a sanitarium in Walla Walla. I have here his home address of record." He passed the notebook over to me. I gripped the page in my fingers in preparation to tear it out.

"May I?" I asked.

"As you wish."

I removed the page and returned the notebook. This criminal didn't sound like the Andrew Welch I knew, but then who *was* the Andrew Welch I knew? I had wondered if there was a criminal record because I'd speculated his money had come from crime. But I had not expected this type of crime. This crime was ridiculous—the robbery of a haberdasher's? I tucked the paper into a pocket of my jacket and pulled out my traveler's checks.

"For another twenty-five dollars I can provide you with a hard copy of the criminal record," he said, "complete with fingerprints and description."

I paused in writing out the check.

"Okay. I'm on my way to Astoria now, but I'll get it from you on my way back through town."

I handed the checks to him and he scrutinized them thoroughly. I thought he was going to bite them. "Ah, good old American Express," he rhapsodized. "Karl Malden would be proud." He placed them carefully into a beat-up old wallet and put it inside his jacket. He noticed the waitress coming in our direction. "Now for some repast," he said, tucking a napkin into his shirt above his tie. The waitress delivered a huge order of spaghetti and plopped the ticket onto the table.

"I'll pick up the check," I told him.

"I thought you'd never offer," he said, stuffing a shovelload of spaghetti into his mouth.

I escaped Seattle by early afternoon and headed my new car south down the freeway. I slipped around Olympia, then sped down the smaller forested highways to Highway 101 and Astoria.

I had been a child the last time I had seen this coastal town. It seemed much crummier than I remembered it, a poor, run-down fishing town with paint fading on the buildings and the locals running around in decrepit, fish-stained pickups and battered old cars. As I came off the toll bridge and wound my way through town in the spotless Saab, I almost felt like out-of-town aristocracy, the type the townies would ridicule and discourage from buying property.

I checked into the small motel I had contacted. It was a rambling affair built along the highway among the heavy, wet foliage that covers the coast. Everything seemed damp, including the bedding and the electric heater. I turned the heater on when I headed for town, hoping things would dry out by evening.

I couldn't get into the courthouse for records and the high school was closed, so my checking would have to wait for the following day. I roamed around, had a couple of beers, and stayed out of fights. When I got back to the motel, it was like a steam bath. All the moisture had left the bed and the walls and the curtains and now resided in the air. All I needed to do was to toss a little mentholatum around on the floor and I would be living inside a vaporizer. I woke several times during the night wondering if someone were suffocating me. After smoking a cigarette and feeling my heartbeat, I managed to get back to sleep each time. By morning I felt like I had slept in a puddle. I had done that a couple of times, so I knew what it felt like.

I got up, had breakfast, and went to the courthouse, hoping to find a duplicate of Andrew Welch's birth record. I went through the normal bureaucratic struggle and emerged a mere two hours later with an exact copy of the document in my briefcase. I had found Andrew Welch's hometown.

My next stop was the local high school. The main office was open even though it was summertime. The building was old, like the town, and covered with the stains of age.

I walked through the front door and looked around until I found the janitor, a slouching old man in Big Mac work clothes who was mopping the long hallway. He eyed me with interest, as though he were "the Man in the Iron Mask" and had not seen a visitor for twenty years. When I requested directions to the office, he gave them cheerfully and said, "You ask Mrs. Fogarty. She'll tell you anything you want to know."

"What is the meaning of life?" might have been my first question of such a knowledgeable person.

I finally found the office and Mrs. Fogarty, the superintendent's secretary. She was middle-aged and spreading. Her wool-imitation polyester dress covered what used to be curves and had now become mud slides. She adjusted her graying hair as I strolled into the room and stared pleasantly out of gigantic rimless glasses, her only stylistic concession to youth. She was probably trying to appear more *with it* for her juvenile charges.

"Can I help you?" she asked.

"I'd like to look at some old annuals," I said. "I'm trying to establish someone's identity." I explained my ostensible function in life and presented her with a card. She looked impressed and possibly sexually aroused. This must be a very boring town.

"What year?" she asked, her voice a murmured whisper, her eyes brimming with excitement and wonder.

"I guess about 1948, perhaps the couple of years before and after."

"We have those right over here," she said, leaving her desk with a swirl of her elephantine hips. She rummaged through a shelf of school annuals called *The Zephyrus* until she said, "Here it is," and handed me the one for 1948. I took a seat and quickly thumbed through it until I reached the seniors and looked under the Ws. No Welch was listed.

"Let's try the next year," I said, and she promptly handed it to me. No Welch again. We continued this search until I found him in 1950. He had finally graduated from high school at age twenty. No one could fault him on persistence, but it couldn't be said that he had been an academic *wunderkind*.

I studied the picture and compared it to one of Welch. The resemblance was not close. It had been a long time, but one expected some similarity to persist through the years. The Andrew Welch in the yearbook had hair that was slicked back and greasy and the face was round, which had never been the case with the Andrew Welch I had known. The Astoria Welch also wore glasses.

I pointed at the photograph and asked the secretary, "Did you ever know this man?"

She looked at the name and the face. "I think so. Yes. He was older than me. I went to school with him . . . I knew him. But, of course, he's dead."

"How do you know that?"

"I read about his funeral," she said, wide-eyed and a little defensive.

My eyebrows went up. "When?"

"God, I don't remember. Sometime in the 1950s. He died in a car wreck. He was a little wild, you know. I don't know why you'd be looking for information about him now."

Puzzled, I handed her the photograph I carried. "Do you know *this* man?"

She looked at the picture. "I don't think so." Then she observed, "He's very good-looking."

"He's dead, too," I said.

"Aren't they all."

I rubbed my mustache and looked at the picture of Andrew Welch. Not Welch anymore. Who was he? Had he known the Astoria Welch? Had he read of Welch's death? Was he someone Welch had worked with? If I could just keep this all straight and think. Did I have *any* clue as to Xanthia's father's real name? I guessed I would still call him Andrew Welch. I had to call him something. Maybe I should call him John Doe.

I did have the names on the photographs from his home. Maybe I would work with them.

I thanked Mrs. Fogarty, who gave me one last longing glance and I suspect was about to ask me what had happened to my nose when I escaped. I headed back to the courthouse—this time to look at death records.

I found him just before closing time. The Astoria Andrew Welch had died in January 1954 of "shock, trauma, and severe cranial damage" resulting from a head-to-head confrontation with a wayward Madrona. The death had been termed accidental, and I had no reason to believe otherwise. I considered dropping by his home of record to see if anyone knew anything about him or the usurper of his good name. First things first, however, and I went out to get drunk. I don't know why I decided to get drunk; the urge just took me. I hit the Anchor, the Lantern, and the Hold before I drove my car back to my motel. I bumped gently into a tree in the dirt parking area, swore, and careened to my bed, where I fell asleep in a puddle of drool and Oregon's environmental sweat. I had eaten no supper and it was not yet seven o'clock.

Imbibing alcohol in such quantities wasn't the smartest thing for me, a refugee from one of Montana's few mental institutions. I had made this mistake a few times since my release, more frequently as the date of my "recovery" receded into the past. This night I began to have vivid, almost waking dreams of battles with dead souls wielding huge swords of light. Psychotic fantasies are similar to dreams, but more intense and don't always recede with consciousness. A brilliant flash of light, a mental quasar, woke me at about ten and sent me screaming toward the ceiling. I looked around to see if my pursuers were in the room. I was suddenly terrified by the dark and turned on all the lights. Then, realizing that the terror was within my own mind, I became even more upset. I resolved again never to drink large amounts of alcohol. Nameless terrors, shapeless and omnipresent, are not my idea of fun. Long ago I had named my internal enemy, though I was only occasionally upset enough to use the name I had given the confused and dangerous personality who resided in my subconscious. I called him Ralph.

"Knock that shit off, Ralph," I said to calm myself.

It did calm me, but not enough. I was jumpy. I checked the lock on the door—not yet able to distinguish outer danger from inner danger. Outside, creatures formed and transmogrified in the darkness. I turned on the TV and quickly took a shower. Then I took my Thorazine. It had never had an immediate effect, but just taking it reassured me. Then I looked at the phone.

I should make contact with home, I thought. I could call Xanthia and inform her of my confusing findings and plan a course of action. I could also call Andrea and try to patch things up. When these tremendous fears held me, it seemed all the more serious that there were conflicts or unresolved feelings with people I loved.

I sat at the chair by the phone and dialed. It took me three tries before I did it correctly, and I waited for the ring.

The ring was truncated and broken and was quickly replaced by line noise and the sound of switching. Then a recording said, "This line is out of order. This line is out of order." I listened for a few moments, disbelieving, then hung up. I tried to remember what Xanthia's friend's last name was. Ursula . . . Cox? Ursula . . . Andress? Jesus. Ursula . . . Croft. Croft. That was it, or close. I dialed information and thankfully she was listed. I dialed the number and again waited for the ring. It had barely started when the phone was picked up.

"Hello."

"Ursula?"

"Yes?"

"I'm Scott Moody. I tried to call Xanthia and . . ."

"Scott, I'm glad you called. There's been a fire. Xanthia's in the hospital."

"Is she all right?" Ralph evaporated, replaced by a more present terror.

"Smoke inhalation is what the doctor said. She was lucky; she got out in time. She's there mainly for observation. She'll be out by morning; then she's coming to stay with me."

"I'll be there by then," I said. "I'm coming home."

"She's all right, really."

"Tell her I'll be there by late morning."

"Okay."

I hung up and began throwing things in the bag. Better to be on the road with nighttime radio programs than be in bed with my fears and dreams. I didn't like this fire at Xanthia's. It was too much of a coincidence right after the death of her father.

I stopped by the office and got the middle-aged lady in curlers out of bed. I checked out, then piled my stuff into the car and headed east out of town, planning my route through the Columbia Gorge.

It was a long drive, and outside Ritzville I had to stop at a rest area and sleep. Ralph returned and plagued me through a bitter, three-hour nap. I woke in another universe and had to spend five or ten minutes reconstructing this one under the eerie mercury lamps of the rest stop. As dawn arrived I plowed through Spokane to Mill City. I arrived before nine and went for breakfast at the Big Dipper. I was halfway through my sausage and eggs when Billy Hart, the sports reporter for the *Sun,* walked into the café and saw me at the counter. He walked up and said quietly, "Hey, did you know that the cops are looking for you?"

I looked up, my jaw stuffed with half-masticated breakfast. "No."

"They want you for more questioning in connection with the Welch murder. I get the feeling they think you and Xanthia cooked up this conspiracy to do away with her dad and get his money."

"You're kidding me." I remembered the questioning by the chief, the feeling I'd gotten that he thought I was involved in the murder. I looked around the café. There was usually a cop on the premises, but fortunately none this morning. I wondered if my photograph had been circulated. "They want to arrest me?"

"Not so far, but the call's been out to bring you in for a couple of days. They were real disappointed to learn you weren't working for the paper anymore."

"Is there any new evidence?" I asked.

"The murder weapon," he said.

"What was it?"

"A hunting knife. They found it in the bushes. You see, that's one of the reasons they are looking at you again. There were no prints, but the knife was close enough that you might have thrown it before the officers arrived."

"Great."

"And then there were the marks on your body."

"Huh?"

"Don't you remember being photographed at the police station?"

"Sort of. That whole night is a fog."

"They have photos of scratch marks on your face and neck and arms. They think they were defensive wounds that Welch gave you when you killed him."

"I had a kind of scuffle with him, but that was because he was dying, kind of flailing in his last breath." How could you explain something like this unless you had been there.

"Still," said Billy, "it looks bad."

"Yeah, I can see that." I tossed a five-dollar bill on the counter and started out of the restaurant.

"You leaving?" he asked.

"Damn right. I know what a tenacious bastard Ryder is. If he gets me in that jail, he just might not let me go. I've got to figure out some things before I get in there and before I get the official word that they're looking for me. Would they have arrested Xanthia or taken her in for more questions yet?"

"I don't think so," he said, rising and following me as I left the restaurant with furtive backward glances. "Look, you can't tell anyone where you got this information. One of the officers told me in confidence that if I knew where you were I'd better tell you to come in—to save yourself some trouble and embarrassment. I don't think he's got around to Xanthia yet."

Billy looked troubled and a little confused about what I was doing. We got to my car and as I walked around to the driver's side, Billy said, "This yours?"

"Yeah. I bought it in Seattle. Hey, Billy, do me a favor, okay? Don't tell anyone you saw me. I just need a little lead time on this thing."

"Yeah, sure," he said, looking as though he had never expected his friend and fellow reporter to be a fugitive from the law.

I drove quickly to Ursula's house. Xanthia's Sirrocco was out front.

Ursula answered the door. She seemed a little scattered, but Ursula always seemed that way. She was a petite blonde with long hair and a cute butt. As she led me to the living room, I tried to keep my mind on the matter at hand.

Xanthia was in a robe, bundled up on a sleeper couch. She had orange juice, Morning Thunder, a box of Kleenex, and a bottle of some sort of throat medicine beside her on an end table. Sunlight streamed in through the windows. It was a pleasant, homey scene, and obviously she was being well taken care of. She pulled herself up on the bed as I entered and leaned against the back of the couch.

"Hi," she said cheerily.

"How are you? I hear you had a close call."

"God, I *guess* it was close," she said. "If my father hadn't been so safety conscious, I would have never made it out in time. There was a smoke alarm in my room and a rope ladder, so I managed to escape.

"And you'd be proud of me. I had on clean underwear." She paused for a moment and smiled impishly. Xanthia had an expression of awe and wonder at having survived that reminded me a little of the way Allison might have told the story. She seemed in amazingly good spirits, but that wasn't much of a surprise. Survivors are often manic about being alive.

"What about the house?"

Her expression saddened, like someone whose granola has

gone soggy. "Structurally it's okay, but there's so much fire and smoke damage that it'll be months restoring it. Ursula went over there with a fireman yesterday though and they got some of my personal stuff out of my room. Most of it is damaged, but it'll be okay after I get it cleaned." She indicated a stack of boxes in the corner, which contained clothes and shoes and toiletries. A stuffed elephant peered out of one of the containers.

I sat on the edge of the bed and resisted the urge to light a cigarette. "Do you know how it started?"

"No one is sure. It's weird." She gave me a big smile. She was manic almost to the point of hysteria. I wondered if they had given her some uppers at the hospital.

"Are you covered by insurance?"

"Oh, I haven't even checked into that," she said casually. "I'm not worried about it." As a sudden afterthought, she said, "Did you find out anything about my father?"

"Nothing clear-cut. I'd like to tell you about it later. I wanted to talk to you about something else. I'm planning to go back to Seattle to continue my research and I think you should go with me."

"Why?" Her expression became one of puzzlement.

"I think you might be of some help to me," I said, starting off with the positive. "And I'm also a little concerned about you. I think you may be in some kind of danger."

"Because of the fire?"

"This fire seems suspicious, and I just don't want to take any chances. I want us to know what we're dealing with before we relax and just chalk this up to fate or accident."

"I don't know," she said, biting a fingernail. "I'd have to find someone to run the shop."

"How about your assistant? Or couldn't you close the shop?"

"I could. I don't want to. When do you want to leave?"

"Right away."

"Why?"

"I have good reasons. I'd like to tell you about it on the way—if you think you're strong enough to travel now."

"Oh, I'm fine. They took me in just as a formality. I'm fine." She turned to Ursula, who had been leaning against the doorway listening to us. "Ursula, do you think you could help me?"

"I can try."

Ursula and Xanthia chatted about how to arrange things, hire people, etc., to have the shop cared for during her absence.

When they had discussed it all, I asked Xanthia, "Well, how about it? Can you go?"

"I'll go," she said smiling. "I need a vacation."

We packed one of Ursula's suitcases, since Xanthia's had been lost in the fire. A lot of her clothes would have to be cleaned before they could be used. Then she dressed and we carried it all to the car.

"Is this yours?" she asked.

"My old car blew up." I hoped she wouldn't think I had been too liberal with money I had not yet earned.

"Oh, I *like* it," she said, settling into the front seat. We stopped by the drive-in window of the bank and she picked up some cash, enough to have held me under normal conditions for three months. She must have had quite a substantial personal account in her own name even when her father was alive, quite apart from her new monetary system. I wondered where the forty thousand in fifties had gone. Did she have that in her purse, too?

We got in the car and I had to wait as Xanthia puttered with her seat belt for a moment getting it fastened. She'd always been the cautious type.

On the way out of town I stopped by Allison's day-care center and had a brief visit with her. She wasn't irritated with me the way she had been when I left and, in fact, seemed glad to see me.

While we were talking, as I held her in my arms, the lady who ran the place came up to me.

"Mr. Moody, did you know that someone from the police department wants to talk to you?"

"Why no, I didn't."

She nodded her head, affirming her own information. "They came out here the other day and wanted to know if I'd seen you."

"I'll take care of it, Mrs. Robitson," I said. This seemed the end of the matter to her and she left us.

Allison and I hugged and chatted as Xanthia waited in the car, and then I explained I would be gone for a while and Allison gave me a good-bye hug.

"Don't be gone too long," she told me as I walked out of the playground. And then she said, "See you later, when your legs are straighter." Something weird her mom had taught her.

Then Xanthia and I sailed over the bridge and out of town. As we were nearing the other end of the bridge, I noticed a cop car posted by the side of the highway. It was not unusual, but I noticed it this morning where I may not have noticed it before.

As we drove, I told Xanthia about the inconclusive results of my research. She didn't seem very surprised that her father's identity was false.

"But I do wonder what my real name is," she said. "Is there anything more?"

"No, that's about all, except for a few details."

"Don't most private eyes give their clients a written report or something?"

"Yeah."

"Well, I've never gotten a report from you."

"You mean I can't give it to you orally?"

Xanthia smiled and looked at me out of the corner of her eyes. "Is that a subtle reference to something else?"

"Not very subtle."

"I've always wondered about that word. Sometimes people talk about oral sex and I wonder if they mean 'oral' or 'aural.' " She tapped her ear with her finger.

"Uh, huh."

"It makes me wonder if they're going to listen or something."

"I get it." We looked at one another and chuckled.

"When they put me in the hospital I had a fantastic dream about you." Her preoccupation with the lighter side of life after all that had happened made me wonder again if she was on something.

She told me about a dream in which we had had sex in a variety of places and positions, and some of the activity was more athletic than I would have been capable of. I let her talk and pretended to be entertained. No use imposing your own lack of enthusiasm for a subject on someone else. Besides, at the end of telling me the dream she leaned over and kissed my neck and cheek and caressed my hair. We smiled and it was like we were on an idyllic vacation with no troubling mission at its center.

Ever vigilant to prevent such sweet moments from dominating my life, I asked, "How are you doing? About your dad's death? I know it's always going to be hard, but are you getting on your feet again at least?"

"I'm doing a lot better," she said. "I talked to my spiritual guide, and she made me feel better."

"Your spiritual guide?"

"Yes. She lives in Mill City. She's a psychic."

"Oh."

"She told me my father is doing well and loves me and that one of these days I will see him."

I was silent.

"You don't believe in this kind of thing, do you?"

"Not really."

"What do you believe in, Scott?"

"Not much."

"It troubles me that you are so lacking in any kind of faith. Sometimes it makes me think you're wrong for me."

I said nothing. Whenever someone doubts me, I don't want to be the one who goes on the defense. I have less faith in me than anyone else.

"Really, Scott. Don't you have any faith in anything? Don't you believe in God? Don't you believe in the afterlife?"

How could I change the subject? I didn't want to answer the question because the answer always upset people. And as part of the upset, I sometimes got banished from the land of their love. Still, I have the horrible tendency to believe that I ought to be able to express my opinion honestly in the land of the free. And after my experience with the afterlife, in which my spiritual guides had led me straight to hell, I had stronger convictions than ever. Quietly I said, "I don't depend on it."

"You should be more open to it," Xanthia said. "The universe is a wonderful place. It protects us and loves us. We will live to eternity."

I was silent.

"You don't believe in anything, do you?" she said, seeming suddenly to be angry with me. "You don't believe my father is still alive somewhere?"

I didn't say anything.

"Who are you to think that you are the one who knows the truth? You make me so mad sometimes. I don't know if I can be with someone who has no faith."

"I'm sorry."

"I know that we're different in some of our beliefs, Scott, but I hope that you'll make an effort to be more open-minded. I would like us to stay together, and I would like to be able to trust that you are right for me."

We drove in silence for a long while after that. The only incident of significance was an intrusion on our silence by a weird driver as we passed through Spokane. An old car shot onto the freeway from downtown. The driver was a big man with a ratty beard and long hair, equally untamed. He entered from the right-hand lane in an old Buick Riviera, shot onto the freeway bouncing on worn shocks, going eighty-five at least, crossed the three lanes from right to left without looking at anything but us, and the look he gave us was mean. The car was rusted, and a tail-light was broken. The right-hand signal was blinking as he was heading to the left. The gas-cap lid was open, and the gas cap was gone. He's a type out here—lost in the sixties, still on acid, compensating for being a loser by going Warp Five. It occurred to me to ask Xanthia what she thought of that guy's belief system, which must have included *some* faith in order to drive like that.

We arrived in Seattle late that afternoon, checked into a motel on Eastlake, and went out for dinner. Afterward, back at the motel, Xanthia had returned to being her affectionate self and nuzzled my ear, probably recalling various images from her dream, as I sifted through the records left by Andrew Welch.

"I think I've got an idea," I said after a while. By this time Xanthia had given up on my ear and was absentmindedly studying her father's phony birth certificate and military record.

"What?" she asked.

"I've got a name put together here," I said, "a name that may or may not be accurate, but it's something to begin with—Matthew Styles."

"How did you figure that out?"

"From the photographs. There are three boys here; one of them is set apart by the affectionate adjective 'little,' 'Little Matty,' and he bears a resemblance to your father. The other picture is of a man named John Styles. That could have been Little

Matty's father, or more likely grandfather. Therefore, Matthew Styles."

"That doesn't seem a very strong deduction," she said doubtfully. "Why couldn't he have been Graham or Bobby Greene?" she said, reading the other names on the photo.

I shrugged. "Could be. I just have a feeling."

"What if that *is* his name? What are you going to do about it? How can you trace that?"

"Go to the city records for 1930, 1931, 1932; look at the reports of births; and look under Styles. For that matter, while we're at it we can look for little Graham and Bobby Greene. Your father was from Seattle; it's possible he was born here. You are pretty sure of his age, aren't you?"

"Yes, of course. I know when he celebrated his birthday and how old he was. He wasn't the type to lie about something like that."

"Was it the same birthday as the one on his birth certificate?"

"Yes. Oh, I see what you mean."

"Then we have to just go with the age. He probably consciously chose someone who had been born close to his own year of birth. Problem is this could take a long time."

"It does seem like such a long shot." Xanthia pouted.

"It's not the only thing we have to go on," I said. "I do have a P.O. box your father rented. I suspect it's in the city here. With a little luck there will be letters and perhaps your father's name."

I reached behind her onto the nightstand and grabbed the phone book. I looked up post offices in the section for the U.S. government. Sure enough, there was a Wedgewood Station. "Hot damn," I said. "It *is* here. Pray there's a letter in it, and pray it's addressed to your father's real name."

"I can pray," she said. "No point in you doing anything."

I ignored the comment, pointlessly shuffling the paperwork.

"Do you want to do some dope?" Xanthia asked.

"You know I don't smoke," I said.

"You smoke those awful cigarettes."

"We've had this discussion," I told her. I didn't tell her that if she wanted me to become religious, she was going about it in the right way. Two hits of marijuana and I basically resided in heaven—usually as the supreme being. "I can't risk it. You go ahead. I have something to do."

She pouted again and began looking in her purse for a baggy of sensimilla. I grabbed the phone and dialed it. The phone was answered on the tenth ring. There was a pause and heavy breathing, combined with banging and shuffling. "Hello?" said the sleepy voice of Ira Sugarman. "You shoot 'em and I'll cover for you."

"Ira, this is Scott Moody. Remember me?"

"Remember you? Remember you? Of course I remember you. Who the hell are you?"

"The guy who bought the information about Andrew Welch—you checked him for a criminal record."

"Oh, you're the guy with the nose."

"Yeah, that's right." It's a good thing I'm not sensitive about my crooked proboscis. "I'm sorry if I caught you at a bad time." The time of my call and the TV blaring in the background confirmed my suspicions that Sugarman's office was in his home. Or vice versa.

"No sweat. I was just watching TV and dozed off. It was a class act though; I fell asleep watching the educational channel. What can I get for you this time?"

"I'm hoping you'll help me locate the military records for someone."

"Same guy?"

"Yeah, but under a different name."

"Slippery devil."

I explained the situation with Welch's identity, the fact that the small-time crook of the police records was not our guy and was dead to boot.

"That's a little unusual," said Sugarman.

"I think so."

"No," he retorted, "I mean it's a little unusual to take the name of someone who's as old as this Andrew Welch."

"What do you mean?"

"When you're looking for a candidate for a new identity, what you want is the name of someone who died fairly young— so they won't have a paper trail like this. Otherwise it's a little too easy to find out that you've assumed the new identity."

"I wonder why he'd have made a mistake like that. Welch, the Welch I knew, was pretty smart."

"In crime," said Sugarman, "competence is an on-again, off-again quality."

"Well, anyway, I have another name and I'm hoping for more promising results. All I have though are the names—no birth information or identifying numbers."

"That's pretty sticky. Do you have a middle name, too?"

"Nope."

"I can try. But unless we're lucky, this will take awhile. Your girlfriend will have to write a letter to a national archive requesting the information, and it will have to be a name she can show a relationship to."

"That's going to be tough."

"If he was associated with some local military organizations, I may be able to locate the information through my own sources. Cash deal?"

"I'll pay you for your time, plus a bonus if you turn up anything useful."

"Okay. Fire away."

I gave him the names and approximate ages. He said, "Shalom," and hung up.

I turned to Xanthia, who was by now thoroughly stoned. Her eyes shone with sensuality. She sat naked on the bed beside me, taking the last toke on her joint. I decided it wouldn't be too unpleasant to be in that dream of hers for a while.

# Seven

Xanthia and I were up early, had breakfast, and began our rounds. We started at Wedgewood Station with the P.O. box number and the combination Andrew Welch had left us.

We found the station out in the northeast quarter in a suburban area of pleasant wide streets and comfortable middle-class homes. I opened the little box and plucked out the one item it contained—a postcard. It was addressed simply to "Matt." I was more than a little disappointed that no full name was offered, but at least it was a partial confirmation of my earlier guess. Xanthia and I fought over the card a little, then settled for the compromise of holding it together between us, our respective finger and thumb firmly fixed on a side. The card read:

Dear Matty,

Hope life finds you well and, as usual, industrious. As you know, Bobby and I have taken more and more to a life of leisure. We are going on another trek to the Grand Canyon next month. We would like you to join us if you get a chance; old friends are rare these days. We all have to be careful, but we can get directions to you. Let us know.

Love,
Bobby and Phyllis.

" 'We all have to be careful,' " I quoted the text. "That means there are more like your father out there somewhere—hiding from something."

"Could we trace them?" asked Xanthia.

"Not without a return address. It's postmarked Denver, but that's a big place. I guess they figure he knows where to write, but we certainly don't. You didn't find an address book for your father?"

"I have one, but it's full of Mill City business addresses—and a few of the friends he had in Mill City."

"I'd still like to look at it. One thing though—at least part of my guess was right. His name is Matthew. Maybe I'm right about the second half, too."

Outside, Xanthia asked, "Well, what now?"

"We can keep checking the mail every few days," I said, "but for the moment we have a really miserable job ahead of us."

Xanthia turned out her lips in a sign of distaste. "You mean the birth records?"

"The birth records," I affirmed. "And we can hope that Ira Sugarman comes up with something."

"We're not going to spend all day down there, are we?"

"Do you want to find out who your father was or not?"

"I'd like to find out, but it's such a depressing way to spend a sunny day."

"C'mon, I'll buy coffee; then we'll get to it."

"Can we have ice cream later?" she asked as we started toward the car.

We spent the day looking for some record of birth for Matthew Styles, figuring there was at least a chance that he had been born in the Seattle area. We started with King County first. By the time we had done all that driving and dealing with bureaucracies we were pretty dejected. They helped us with a few searches with definite birth dates, but they balked at the wholesale search that would seem necessary without the exact birth date and without the certainty that the name would be found at all. We decided to try looking at the newspaper for birth announcements, went to the library and spent hours on the microfilm. When we gave it up late in the afternoon, we were pretty tired and dejected. I couldn't think of any other way to approach it but to try again the next day.

We brightened up a little after a nice dinner, and we discussed going out on the town to cheer us up further.

I called Ira Sugarman shortly after seven, and as usual he was in.

"Hi, Ira," I said, "this is Moody. You got anything for me?"

"Well, kinda. I have the police record you wanted for Andrew Welch. I also have something I found on Matthew Styles—a military record." Ira wasn't gloating and this seemed peculiar.

"That's exactly what I wanted," I said. "Is there something wrong with it?"

"Well, not exactly. I'll show you. I'll bring it over and show you. You still going to pay me?"

"Sure. I said I would and I will. Come on over to the motel. We'll be there by the time you arrive."

"Okeydokey," he said and hung up.

Ira was waiting when we got there. He was sitting in a little, red, 1968 Opel, looking bored and smoking cigarettes. He opened the door and climbed out. The little car's springs shot up to their normal height.

"Hello," he said, smiling his most ingratiating grin. He was looking at Xanthia, not me. He was still wearing his suit with the bowling ball tie, but his cap was different; it was a little black Depression-era cap. He looked quite dashing for Ira Sugarman.

I introduced them, but Xanthia's eyes didn't shine the way Sugarman's did. I managed to tear him away from her long enough to extract the military record he was carrying. He was, as the British say, "chatting her up" when I turned to him in disgust.

"Sugarman, did you look at the date on this record?"

"Well, you said to find Matthew Styles." I could tell from the sheepish look on his face that he had expected this. He was looking at his feet and nodding his head in a gesture of contriteness and cosmic impotence.

"This guy was born in 1889," I said. "He served in 'the Great War,' Ira. Do you know *when* the Great War was held?" I was standing not two feet away, about to grab him by the lapels.

"I got a rough idea—between 1910 and 1920—somewhere in there." He was smiling a little now and doing a soft-shoe. He wouldn't get around me that easily.

"The man we're looking for it is about forty-nine," I said. "Not"—I did the math—"eighty-eight. Where did you dig this thing up?"

"In the local historical archives. I figured I might find him because a lot of guys used to get shipped out with their units from their hometowns," said Sugarman. "Sure enough, his name turned up."

"His name turned up, but it's hardly likely it's the person we're looking for. Jesus, Ira, I thought you'd be more helpful than this."

"Hey, take it easy, Scott," Xanthia said. "Maybe he didn't un-derstand."

"Yeah, take it easy, Scott," said Sugarman. "Maybe I didn't understand." He smiled at Xanthia.

"Well, look," I said, beginning to control my irritation, "I can't use this. I mean what am I supposed to do with this?" I held up my hand as Ira was about to reply. "No, never mind. I can do without certain suggestions."

"I wasn't going to be rude," Ira protested. "I thought it might provide you a lead. After all, this Matthew Styles might be related to your Matthew Styles. Get it?"

I became thoughtful. "Yeah," I said slowly. "That could be. I just don't know how to use this."

"It's just a piece—possibly a piece. Perhaps it fits the puzzle, perhaps not," he said. "We have to gather more pieces. Maybe we could look for his son, relatives."

"All right. Let's do that. Pursue that. We'll continue our search for birth records. Maybe it'll help. I'll file it away. You couldn't find anything more timely, huh?"

"There was no record of such a man around or near the time of the Korean War or even World War Two."

"Well, I'll pay you for the day and we'll see if the older guy leads to our guy. By the way, Xanthia and I were going into town for a little entertainment."

Sugarman's face brightened and he looked at Xanthia once more. "Perhaps I should accompany you," he said. "I know the town. I'm a little financially embarrassed, however. Perhaps you could subsidize me?"

"Sugarman, you're hopeless," I said. "Sure, you may as well come along. Okay with you, Xanthia?"

She shrugged. "Yeah."

"Is this your car?" Sugarman asked as we approached my Saab. "I've never had the chance to drive a Saab."

"I wonder if you ever will," I told him, climbing into the driver's seat.

Two hours later we were at a table at some seedy Pioneer Square tavern Ira had coaxed us into. Xanthia was drinking beer and staring at the people. She seemed to enjoy slumming. I was pouting over a gin and tonic the bartender had garnished with an olive. The bars we had visited reminded me too much of my taxi-driving days in Spokane. The place was loaded with itinerant drunks in their soiled suits and laceless shoes, their bewhiskered faces animated by the fuel of alcohol.

Ira fit right in and was having a good time on our money, though at these prices the cost of the evening wasn't going to be exorbitant. Apparently in an effort to balance up the ratio of men to women, Ira had befriended a chubby female drunk who was giving us a blow-by-blow description of her life and hard times. She had a round, red face, was about Ira's age, and her body was an amorphous mass of flesh covered by a tight blouse and mammoth red polyester slacks. She held a beer and a cigarette, and as she talked, her lips became a blur of vibration.

"I've been reading about the theory of relativity," said the woman, who claimed her name was Penelope. "But you know the real problem with the theory of relativity is larceny."

"Larceny?" asked Ira, biting into the hook.

"Yeah, my daughter stole my book." Penelope and Ira laughed, and Xanthia and I joined them.

"She steals everything," said Penelope, "my clothes, my books, my food, my money. I have to hide everything. My whole house is a hiding place," she said. "Did you know I have three hundred and fifty dollars in my mattress?"

"I have to get you into bed," said Ira, and we all laughed again.

We eventually escaped the bar, but Penelope was still with us, following Xanthia and me and keeping pace with Ira Sugarman. Sugarman's original idea of using Penelope as a sort of ornament—only he would have chosen her for an ornament—had turned to a kind of fascination because she was intelligent, if flaky. Since Ira was intelligent and flaky, it was a pretty good match.

We were walking down a back street near the square in the semidarkness, silhouetted by the streetlights. Penelope and Ira were discussing logical positivism and Xanthia was reaching under my shirt.

We had just come out into the light of a main street when there was a deafening boom and a glass window shattered in the building beside us. A mannequin fell out of the window and rolled onto the sidewalk.

Penelope screamed and ran back toward the darkness. All of

us followed her, but Xanthia was yelling, "We can't leave them out there! Someone's been shot! They've been shot!"

"That was a mannequin!" I shouted in reply. Another shot rang out. I wasn't sure whether it ricocheted off the building to my right or if I imagined it, but I ran faster, dragging Xanthia by the arm. Penelope and Ira were falling behind.

We were a block away from the scene of the original shooting when we were able to turn the corner and hide behind a granite building.

"He's trying to kill me!" said Penelope, between her gasps. "I know he's trying to kill me!"

"*Who's* trying to kill you?" I asked.

"My ex-husband. I'm sure he was the one who shot at us. Who else would do such a thing?" Her eyes narrowed. "He's *such* a bastard."

I found myself hoping it *was* her husband, the bastard. Better him than someone after Xanthia or me.

"I think we have to be going, Penelope," Ira said. "We have to get up in the morning, and I have laundry to do, and my dog is having puppies . . ."

"Coward!" she said. "Chicken. Yellow belly. Snake in the grass." She took off running down the street.

"You can't let her run off," said Xanthia. "She might get hurt."

"What am I supposed to do," asked Ira, "*tackle* her?"

"Men aren't heroic anymore," said Xanthia petulantly.

"Let's get out of here," I said.

We walked nervously through lighted, well-traveled streets to the car, got in and drove away.

"Do you really think it was her ex-husband?" Xanthia asked when we were underway.

"I don't know," I said. "Who else could it have been?"

"Hey, this is Seattle," said Ira from the backseat. "It could have been anyone. It could have been for no reason. There are crazy people all over the place. Awhile back we had a guy shooting randomly at cars on the freeway. All the killers hang out in Seattle."

Under the pressure of such logic, I let the subject drop.

"Well, we're all right now," I said. "We're not in any danger, so maybe we should just forget it. Let's go have something to eat."

"In the safest part of town," said Xanthia, her voice still a little shaky.

"And not at the Doghouse," I told Sugarman.

"I wasn't even going to suggest it," he said.

We ate at a little restaurant on Eastlake where the cops were also taking a long coffee break, then returned to the motel. Ira Sugarman said good night and took off in his Opel. Xanthia and I were alone in the room again.

"You okay?" I asked Xanthia.

"Yeah, I think so," she replied. "But I don't think I'm ever coming back to Seattle again."

"It was a once-in-a-lifetime thing," I said. I recalled the last time I had been shot at and wondered how I could be such a liar. "Well, let's go to bed. It's all over now," I said.

"Okay." She started digging through her suitcase for her night things, and I went into the bathroom to brush my teeth and wash my face.

Not two minutes later she was at the open door looking upset.

"There's someone outside the motel," she said, agitated.

"Outside *our* door?"

"Yes. They . . ." But she didn't finish her thought. The thunder of a gunshot vibrated the room, and a piece of the front door exploded near the doorknob. "You are dead meat," said a deep voice outside.

There was another shot and the doorknob fell loose in the

flimsy mahogany door, slumped as if it had been mortally wounded.

I did the only thing I could think of—I grabbed Xanthia and pulled her into the bathroom. Then I locked the door with the handle latch and another pull latch near the top. I motioned her into the bathtub, and we crouched there as we heard the rending and cracking of wood as someone forced the front door. We hugged the wall and one another. A voice in the other room began a rapid-fire monologue, mumbling, "Where are you, you bitch? I *know* where you are. You ain't gonna hide in the toilet, you stupid bitch." Then there was another gunshot that ripped through the bathroom door near the lock. I held Xanthia's shaking body, then realized *she* wasn't shaking. *My arms* were shaking. Another shot went through the door and embedded itself in the far wall with a dull thump as the drywall surrendered.

I had never carried a gun, but I wished I had one now. I would have blasted the door with every round I had. It was funny that I chose this moment to remember the only day trip I had ever taken into town during my time in the mental hospital. They had let me go all by myself—a test to see if I was doing better. I walked around the small town near the hospital and made only one stop. I went into a sports shop and looked at guns—in particular a little Colt automatic. At the time I was a paranoid schizophrenic and thought that secret agents from the government or the army, or perhaps my old college, were going to kill me. But with my automatic pistol and my special powers to hit anything I pointed at, I would be safe. Now here I was, a couple of years later, wishing I had purchased the pistol. As it was there was nothing I could do for myself or for Xanthia.

Then something massive, like a person's weight, fell against the door. The door didn't give way.

Things were silent for a moment. Then the same voice had a different tone as it said quietly, "Now hold it, mister. I got a gun, too . . ." But before he finished there was an explosion that could have been a building blowing up. Something pushed forcefully against the door again and this time the lock gave way.

The door popped gently open a few inches. I waited for the last moments of our lives to be ones of terror and confusion.

But nothing happened.

Silence from the outer room. Eventually, I heard a soft moaning. Rage at the terror I was going through was taking over. I couldn't stay in the tub any longer. I climbed out and peered through the doorway.

A big, hairy man dressed in jeans, a vest, work shirt, and boots lay on the floor, his head toward the bathroom door. He bore a resemblance to the driver we had seen on the freeway in Spokane, but it was hard to tell for sure. His head and chest were a mess of blood and gaping wounds. The floor around him was covered with bits of human flesh, bone, and blood. He wasn't the one who was moaning. He was beyond that.

The one who was moaning was the motel manager. He sat at a chair in the corner with his face in his hands, a shotgun on the floor a few feet away.

We spent three hours with the police before we finally had them convinced that we didn't know the man, that we were tourists from out of town, and that we were plenty incensed about the kind of city this was. Through it all I just held my breath that they wouldn't run me for warrants because it was possible one was out on me in Mill City. If they did, nothing showed up. Xanthia handled it pretty well while we were at the police station, but afterward she couldn't stop sobbing.

When they finally released us, it was early morning. We checked out of the motel and into another one farther from the center of town. We slept till noon, then I called Ira Sugarman. He sounded sleepy.

"What's up with the goyim?" he said pleasantly.

"A lot," I said, "all bad." I told him about the shooting.

"What kind of company have you been keeping?"

"Only yours," I retorted. "We don't know what's happening, but I'm sure of one thing—I don't ever want to be in that situation again without a gun."

"What do you want from me?"

"I want you to buy one for me."

"My prices go up for such things," he said mildly. "I don't deal in guns, Kemo Sabe."

"It would be in your name, but I would pay for it—plus a little extra," I said. "Don't worry, I don't plan on a homicidal binge."

I could sense Sugarman nodding his head at the other end of the phone. Finally, he would shrug, then say, "It's your dime, Captain, where do you want to spend it?"

We agreed on a meeting place downtown near First Street, where Sugarman said there were a number of gun shops for the professional criminal or the youth on a weekend crime spree. I took Xanthia with me and we met Sugarman at the clock in the Pike Place Market. He was wearing a different suit jacket today, but the same old slacks and the bowling ball tie. We walked down the street toward the gun shops. Xanthia was quieter than usual, and I didn't know what to do about it. During the past couple of hours she had been talking a lot about going home. I didn't know what to say to her. It was probably the best idea, but the quiet streets of Mill City hadn't protected Andrew Welch and I told her so. She had agreed to stay with me, to continue our research, but grudgingly. She acted like someone who is doomed. Gone was the flashy walk and the easy smile. She followed somberly as Sugarman and I threaded our way through the midday crowd of derelicts, troublemakers, and tourists.

"You'll love this gun shop," said Sugarman, not in the least affected by our violent episode and a little irritating in his good cheer.

The shop wasn't a gun shop in that the sign didn't mention guns. It was a pawn shop. But inside it was a gun shop. Row after row of glass cases contained an alarming variety of firearms, from single-shot derringers to .357 magnums. The back room contained row upon row of rifles and shotguns in military-type racks.

The store was full of seedy types ready to bloom into weekend stick-up men and mass murderers. They were hunched over the various counters discussing in jubilant terms such things as "firepower" and "killing power." A threesome, two young ladies in street clothes and a young man in a khaki shirt, were studying a Japanese hari-kiri knife under the watchful eyes of a clerk. Apparently it was the only thing within their price range.

Ira led us down the aisle through the store to an open space at the counter. A man in his midthirties with a terrible scar down his cheek was dry firing a .357 magnum, a massive gun, blued with a red spot on the front sight. "Beautiful," he was saying over and over as he pulled the trigger. "That would stop some sonofabitch!"

I tried to get into the spirit of things, thinking about "blowing away," "wasting," and "pulling down," but my heart wasn't in it. I felt in the same league with the housewives who had been hearing noises in the yard and wanted some "protection."

"Can I help you folks?" asked a soft-spoken young clerk with wild eyes. You got the feeling looking at him that he could be unpredictable and dangerous, but his voice belied that impression. He was lean, black-haired, and red-eyed.

"We're looking for something for protection," said Ira quietly.

"I have just the thing," said the clerk. "Made by Charter Arms, a .38 special." He took the small revolver from the case and placed it in Ira's hands. Ira looked at it as though it might bite.

"Got anything by Smith and Wesson?" he asked.

"Yes. What's the price range you were looking at?"

Ira looked at me.

"I don't know," I said. "A couple of hundred dollars?"

"I have just the gun for you," said the clerk. "A nice little weapon, brand new, a hundred ninety-three dollars." He handed Ira a larger .357 magnum.

"Of course this will use the .38-special ammo," said the clerk, as Ira and I studied the gun.

"I don't know," said Ira. "I was looking for kind of a fun gun."

"Fun?" I said. "Fun? Jesus, this isn't for fun."

The clerk looked at us, like he hadn't seen quite our type before.

"Then I guess it will do," said Ira.

"It's a good little target-practice gun," said the clerk, expecting perhaps to inject humor into the conversation. "Though at twelve dollars a box of ammo it gets expensive."

Ira filled out the paperwork that was required, and the clerk's eyes stared wildly as I counted out the money. We had to leave the gun, but we got to take a box of ammo with us.

"You can pick up the gun in five days," said the clerk.

Five days without protection.

We left the shop and I considered what to do for those five days. I didn't want Xanthia out running around during that time—or at all, for that matter—though I knew I wouldn't be able to keep her cooped up all the time.

I suggested that she and Ira stay together at his place while I checked Andrew Welch's mailbox again. Neither of them seemed really happy about it, but they agreed.

We drove over to Ira's, an apartment in an older five-story building with a court. We took the stairs to the second floor. I noted that the security door wasn't locked during the day.

Ira's home office was about what I had expected. It was a

four-room affair with brown, stained carpets and the remains of the Tacoma landfill for furnishings. It looked like it had last been cleaned on V-J day. Xanthia looked around with distaste.

Ira was the perfect host, offering us our preference, Tokay or port, but we declined. We repaired to the cleaner of the rooms, a sitting room where the phone was. There were several stuffed chairs, and all we had to do was move the empty pizza boxes to sit down. Ira said he would try to find some coffee; he used to have some.

Xanthia and I sat at the couch by the window, facing each other. For a time we looked out the window, then occasionally at each other. I held her hand. It was obvious that she was very depressed.

"We'll get through this," I said.

"I don't think so," she told me.

"We will."

She looked down for a moment. "Do you ever think about getting married again?"

I was silent for a long time. This was not a really good subject for me.

"Do you?" she asked.

"Yes, but not with much optimism," I admitted.

"I'd like to marry before I die," she said.

Boy, she was depressed. "You're going to get out of this," I said.

"I don't know if I'm thinking about this because of what's happened, or if I'm thinking about it because of you. Your presence makes me think about it more. You're so strong and so spiritual. I know you don't think you're spiritual, but you are. And you've been there for me when I needed you. I've just always wanted to be with one person, ever since I was a little girl. And now, when it seemed like it would never happen, there was you."

What she was saying made me feel so good and at the same time filled me with foreboding.

"So what do you think?" she asked.

"About marriage?"

"Yes. And about us?"

"I don't know. Certainly, I like the idea. I long for that."

"But . . ."

"I haven't told you much about my history. I'm afraid of the pressure of marriage."

"Pressure? What pressure? It would be bliss—always being together, sharing everything."

I could see she hadn't been married. "That part would be wonderful, but there *is* pressure. It's a big commitment. And I'm not afraid of the commitment, but I've had mental problems . . ." I was thinking about my sexual insecurities. I was thinking about the mental weather that floated in and stayed for days. How would I be able to resist either of them once I was in a relationship—especially a relationship with a woman who expected perfect happiness?

"Mental problems! That's a new way of getting out of a relationship!"

"I didn't say I wanted out of the relationship. I'm only expressing my concerns about . . ."

"I never expected this of you, Scott. You told me you wanted to be with me forever."

"But I do . . ."

"I know what you're trying to do. I know you don't want to commit. You're just like all the other men. The only difference is that you're such a coward, you won't even admit it."

She walked out of the room, into the bathroom, and slammed the door.

She had never been angry with me before, and her words were like a whip across my face. A little boy, I pouted with the hurt stinging my heart.

What was going on? Here we were looking for her father's killer, her life was threatened, and she was talking about marriage. I felt a certain stubborn obstinancy rising in me. I had been faced by this scenario before. The dreams of all the young girls in the backyard playing house, filling coffee cups for their imaginary husbands, showing him off to their friends. They had waited all these years to be able to really play house with some likely candidate. There was nothing so terribly wrong about it, but it certainly wasn't flattering, being fitted into the scene like a job applicant satisfying the qualifications but knowing that this job could be filled by any number of candidates, so strong was the need to fill the position. My own desire was to be viewed, in some wonderful and quixotic way, as a unique and special love, irreplaceable.

And this is the dance between little girls and little boys. The little boys are looking to be loved unconditionally, as their mothers loved them. The little girls are looking for that too, but their love is tied to a much larger rule book than the one issued to little boys.

And now that I had begun to fall for Xanthia I was in that vulnerable spot. I fall in love by going to that place in my feelings where I first experienced love—where my mother first said, "I love you," wherein the awe of being loved by one's very creator is overpowering and completely unexamined. It's that same love that I bestow upon my intended, the love that is vulnerable and the love without which I feel I might die.

The love I might lose if I didn't go Xanthia's way.

And what of the requirements of this job she would have me fill? Did I really have anything to do with them? Were they merely the combined fantasy of Xanthia, her peers, and television? Was it merely a list that satisfied a series of romantic role plays that, when each was checked off as being satisfied, would mean that she was truly loved and happy? It made me think that perhaps women were not the romantics but merely the accountants of love.

I lit a cigarette and I got up from the couch. Sugarman came into the room with two cups of coffee.

"Where's Xanthia?" he asked.

"The bathroom," I replied. "Look, I think I'm going to check the P.O. box. You and Xanthia can hang around here. I'll be back shortly."

"We can watch some TV," suggested Ira as I walked toward the front door. He looked at his watch. "*The FBI* is on now."

I walked down the stairs to the car and headed for Wedgewood Station. Noon traffic was heavy and it took me half an hour to get there. The trip was a waste. Nothing was in the mailbox. I stopped at a phone booth down the street and called Ira's. Xanthia answered.

"How are you doing?" I asked. *The FBI* theme was blaring in the background.

"Uh, I'm okay, Scott. I was thinking maybe we should forget about all of this and just go home."

"Just going back home isn't going to change things. Someone can hurt you there just as well as here." I was wondering if she was more upset about the danger or our earlier conversation.

"I was thinking maybe you could go home," she said, "but that I might go for a little trip. You can keep what I've already paid you."

"Trip? Where?"

"Anywhere. I'd be safe then. They wouldn't know where to find me."

"Wait till I get back," I said. "We'll talk it over. Maybe you're right, just don't be impulsive. Can I talk to Ira?"

"He's out," she said. "He went to get a pizza. He'll be right back."

"Out! Goddamn it! Stay where you are and keep the door locked. I'll be there as soon as I can." I hung up before she could answer and jumped into my car.

I cursed Seattle traffic and its spider-web streets more than once on my way back to Ira's. It was half an hour before I located the right neighborhood, mostly by accident, then had to search for a parking space. When I got to the apartment it was locked, and naturally I didn't have a key. I knocked on the door half a dozen times with no answer. I was about to break it down when Ira arrived carrying a large pizza.

"Como esta, Kemo Sabe?" he said.

"Como esta, my ass," I replied. "Why the hell did you leave Xanthia?"

He hefted the pizza. "Sustenance," he said.

"C'mon, open the door," I commanded.

Ira handed me the pizza with what seemed an exasperated look. "She's probably not answering the door," he said. He opened up and I rushed in and began looking around for her.

"Hey, give me the pizza," he said, following. "It's getting cold."

"You could have sent out for pizza," I told him.

"Not this kind. I had to pick it up." He sat in a stuffed chair with the pizza resting on the arm and began opening it delicately as I called Xanthia's name and searched from one end of the apartment to the other.

"She's not here!" I told Sugarman. He was leaning back, holding up a piece of pizza, trying to keep the flowing cheese, olives, and sausage in his mouth and off his suit. He wasn't entirely succeeding.

"She probably went for a walk," he said, his mouth muffled by food.

"She wouldn't do that. I told her to stay put."

"Do people always do what you say?"

"Apparently not."

"Have some pizza, you'll feel better."

"To hell with your pizza."

"Blasphemy," he said, seeming genuinely shocked. "I'm sure

she just went out. I didn't think I was protecting a member of the mob. I doubt she's in any real danger."

"You evidently weren't *protecting* anyone," I said.

I called our motel and asked the manager to check the room. When he returned he reported no one present and nothing disturbed. I asked him to check again in an hour and to call me if anything had changed or if he saw Xanthia.

Then we waited.

It was three hours before I finally told Sugarman I thought he ought to report her disappearance.

"Why don't you do it?" he asked, still a little miffed over my irritation with him.

I explained that the police might be more interested in me than in her. That, I told him, was why the gun was purchased in his name, not mine.

"So, you're a fugitive. Is there a reward on your head?"

"Of course not. I'm not even sure I'm a fugitive. There was no warrant as of a couple of days ago. I'm just not taking any chances. Especially now that Xanthia is missing. If they pull me in, I won't ever get out."

"Too bad. Well, I'll do what I can. They aren't going to pay much attention to me, though, being she's been gone all of a few hours."

"Mention the attack of the other night. They have records of that and that would make them see the significance of it."

"Okay. By the way, I shouldn't know where you are," he said. "In case they ask. So get lost and if we should meet at Julia's 14-Carrot Café on Eastlake about seven-thirty that would be quite a coincidence."

"All right, I'll disappear. You don't know the motel I'm staying in either, do you?"

"No vay."

"See you later," I said and left the apartment.

# Eight

I was in the café with Sugarman. The table was full of food. Plates of pasta. Piles of pies. Ice-cream sodas. Eclairs. Maple bars. And we were eating as fast as we could. For my part I was still pissed at him. Every so often I would angrily pelt him with a pie or hit him in the side of the head with a baguette. He seemed unfazed. He caught the pies in his mouth and took bites out of the baguette. I was frustrated. I was furious with Sugarman. Xanthia was gone, but in the dream she would come back in ways that kept her just out of reach. She was outside the diner. I could see her at the window, or simply be vaguely aware that she was outside the door. But if I went to the door, she would not actually be there. And if I tried to catch her eye when I saw her through the window, she came up missing.

When I woke, Sugarman was not around. It was a good thing. I wanted to hit him with something harder than a pie.

I lit a cigarette as I woke from my nightmare to the real nightmare—my life. Sleeping had allowed my emotional guard to fall. It had brought home to me the full dilemma. Xanthia missing. Me under threat of a criminal charge in my hometown. My separation from my daughter. The shame I would reexperience with my ex-wife and my family. For the first time in a while I thought about my father. I had been angry with him when I got out of the hospital and he had shunned me. Now I was beginning to side with him. There was no reason to forgive someone who repeatedly screwed up his life. It would destroy any credibility I had built. I had a duty to achieve something, and I had been on my way to doing that at the newspaper. Now I had put it all in jeopardy.

If I stayed in Seattle I could not think of a thing to do to get Xanthia back. If I went home I was pretty sure that I would soon be defending myself from a charge of murder, or complicity in murder.

I finished the cigarette and crushed it in the glass ashtray on the Formica coffee table. I dressed in my usual cab-driver-quality attire and headed for the restaurant where Sugarman and I were to meet.

Julia's 14-Carrot Café was a kind of upscale granola restaurant on the east side of Lake Union. It featured homemade soups, heavy grain breads, and strong coffee you could sweeten with honey. Sugarman was sitting at a table by the front window, looking out at the traffic on Eastlake Way. He seemed a bit more somber than earlier. I think he realized it was no joke—Xanthia was really missing.

"I would like to apologize," he said, very serious, when I sat down. "I did not believe your girlfriend was really in danger, and then I did not believe she was really missing. I took the threat too lightly. I'm sorry."

"I'm glad you see the problem," I said, not too interested in letting him off the hook just yet. "What did the police say?"

"They said they are very interested in speaking to you."

"Why?"

"You are on record from the attack on her the other night. They think you might have the best leads to her whereabouts."

"I wish that were true." I lit a cigarette. One of the waitresses practically had a heart attack when she saw the smoke, and I quickly extinguished it. "Goddamned health nuts," I complained. Turning back to the matter at hand, I said, "What did you tell them?"

"I said that I would certainly advise you to make an appearance."

"I wish I could. I wish I could believe that I could trust them to figure this one out. I'd probably just end up in jail somewhere. And if I go to jail, I'd rather do it in a small town—not the King County jail."

"You don't appear to have much faith in the authorities."

"I have no reason to."

"You really don't believe that your girlfriend will return?"

"I hope like hell that she'll return. I hope this is a misunderstanding, or even a fight. I wish I could believe that she left because she was mad or scared. It just doesn't seem very likely. What I can't figure out is who is doing this. And that guy the other night is dead. I thought we were safer after that. I assumed he was the bad guy—for whatever reason. I thought he was the one who had killed her father. Now I have to wonder who he was. How did he get involved in this? And now that he's gone, who could have taken Xanthia?"

"If you have enough money," said Sugarman, "it's not hard to find someone who will do bad things on your behalf. I do have a few facts about your attacker. Would you be interested?"

"Would I?"

"Of course you would. The police have identified him as Jake Longfellow. He was a biker type. His home of record is a town by the name of Desert Hot Springs, Southern California. As the name implies, it's somewhere out in the desert. This type of person was probably a hireling; there are lots of bad people with time on their hands. The problem, of course, as in every business, is finding people who are competent to perform the deed."

"Don't I know it," I said bitterly.

Sugarman rose. "I thought we were over our little difficulty. I am truly remorseful over my lapse in competence, but I see no reason to rub salt in the wound. I'll be leaving now."

"Hold on, hold on," I said. I was pissed at him, but smart enough to see I didn't have too many friends at the moment. "I'll knock it off if you'll continue to help me. You have to understand I'm a little upset over this, and you might be considered to have been a little remiss."

Sugarman stood by the door, his porkpie hat already on his head. "Fair enough," he said, at length. "But no more cracks."

"Deal."

We sat there for a couple of hours talking about our options, then repaired to our respective domiciles. There wasn't much that I could think of to actively move our investigation forward. We had the post office box. I hoped something would show up there that would give us some leads. We had the police. Maybe they would turn up something on Xanthia. We still had the possibility that Xanthia would call, or return, that she was gone voluntarily. Sugarman could continue to look into Andrew Welch, whatever his real name might have been. As for me, I decided to move to another motel to hide my location from the police. I wanted to be responsible. I had been raised to be law-abiding and believe that the policeman was your friend, but I never wanted to be in a jail cell again and I could not make myself believe that they wouldn't put an innocent man behind bars. I was concerned about moving in case Xanthia tried to call, but I figured that she could always call Sugarman.

We got a bit of a break three days later when two pieces of new mail arrived in Welch's mailbox. One was a postcard from Pueblo, Colorado. It was from the couple we had heard from before: Bobby and Phyllis. But this time, in addition to their greetings and good wishes, they had included an address—a P.O. box. At least it was something.

The second piece of mail was more cryptic and businesslike,

but provocative in its own way. It was a letter from a place called the Longevity Institute of the Desert. It had an address near Palm Springs, California. The content was the cryptic part. It said, "Dear Mr. Welch, Here's the tracking number on that package that has come up missing," and was signed "Miss Salter." Welch, with his health-food habits and California lifestyle, would figure to have had contacts with something called the Longevity Institute. My suggestion to Sugarman was that each of us follow a lead.

"You can afford this kind of extravagance?" Sugarman asked me at our early morning meeting at the Doghouse, so that we could both smoke. He was burning up another Sher Bidi, those horrible little cigarettes that foreigners foist on unsuspecting Western fetishists.

"I can afford this kind of extravagance," I said. I did not follow up with the information that I had discovered that Xanthia's suitcase contained more than fifty thousand dollars. I was as paranoid as a tourist in Tangier—thrilled I had the money and terrified that someone would kill me for it. I had hidden it in the trunk of my car and had checked that it was locked four times before leaving it. "What we need is someone who knew Welch," I said. "We need to begin to find out some reason for his death, for Xanthia's disappearance. I didn't know him that well, but I can't figure out a motive that would originate in Mill City. At least, not a motive that would include Xanthia, or that would make sense in the context of the amount of money Welch seems to have had."

"You want me to wait at the P.O. box for Bobby or Phyllis— no matter how long it takes?"

"We'll stay in touch. I'll give you a thousand for expenses to begin. I'll tell you to give it up if it doesn't look promising."

"Done and done," he said. "Comparatively nice weather there this time of year." We had been having a bit of a heat wave in Seattle the last few days. The ninety-degree heat combined with the humidity was miserable. "And where will you go?"

"Palm Springs."

"Maybe you should delay your trip," he told me.

"Why?"

"You obviously haven't traveled to that part of the country at this time of year," he said, and left it at that.

"By the way," he said.

"Yes?"

"Desert Hot Springs is about five miles from Palm Springs."

I drove back to my motel, packed, and checked out. I called the airline and made arrangements for a flight to Palm Springs. I presumed that Sugarman would be soon making his arrangements to fly to Denver, then on to Pueblo.

I found a parking area near the airport where I could leave my car for a few weeks, then caught a shuttle to the airport. My flight was in a couple of hours, so I wandered through the terminal, nervously hugging the small pack that carried a few personal things and the small fortune in cash left behind by Xanthia. I spent my time wondering what had happened to Xanthia, whether Allison was okay, what Andrea thought about me, and whether or not there was a warrant out for my arrest in Mill City. Two hours of thinking about it didn't seem to help.

# Nine

I looked out the window of the small commuter airplane at the valley below. It was the biggest beach I had ever seen, but it had one other odd feature—there was no ocean. The miles of sand were only relieved by small patches of trees and bushes. True greenery was contained in rectangular enclaves—fancy housing developments and gated communities that looked tidy and toy-like from the air. The valley floor was the color of the sand that covered it, held in like an ocean by surrounding mountains that were dark brown or purple, depending on the light. The beauty of the blue sky, tinged with orange and pink at the horizon, contrasted with the starkness of the valley floor. Heaven and hell met in the desert.

The plane circled a little to get the right approach to the airport, then dove to the runway in the turbulence of the desert air. It felt a little like a toboggan coming down a bumpy hill and reminded me of the approach taken by jets coming into the airport in Saigon during the war. They came in the same way to avoid another kind of turbulence—gunfire.

We were bounced pretty good for the few minutes of the descent, climaxing in one good thud as the plane hit the tarmac, balanced on two wheels, then came down on its nose wheel. I took an involuntary breath. Even in my present depressed state I didn't want to end up squashed like a bug in the desert.

When I walked out the door of the plane, I knew for sure I wasn't on a vacation. The desert heat enveloped me. I found it difficult to breathe. Many years ago I had been surprised by the heat of Vietnam. This was worse.

I claimed my duffel bag and caught a cab. I directed the driver to find me a motel on a main street—nothing too expensive.

The place he took me to lived up to that request. It was a few blocks from the bus station, always a good sign if you're cheap and want to be on the cheesier side of town.

And though I wouldn't have expected it, Palm Springs had a cheesier side. In the area of my motel on the north side of town, the houses were uniformly flat and cheaply built one-story desert houses, covered by a thin skin of plaster and painted desert colors—tan or white.

The motel was a two-story, flat-topped building and, like the houses, had a sand-colored plaster exterior. It was L-shaped with a pool at the center that was guarded by a plaster wall and iron gates. The pool was surrounded by striped umbrellas and white plastic tables. Even the hundred feet between the cab and the motel was excruciatingly hot. When it gets hot where I live they say you can cook an egg on the sidewalk. Here they would have exploded like hand grenades.

I checked in at the front desk with the heavy-set, dyed red-headed clerk. She was wearing a massive green and white floral print dress and glasses that had the little cords attached so that she could let them hang around her neck and look even more like a dork.

"It's hot here," I said, as I approached the counter. I had proved it by sweating my clothes through during the cab ride.

"It's not too bad for this time of year. And it's a dry heat."

I decided not to argue with her, but I had heard this "dry

heat" comment several times and it was beginning to irritate me. After it gets to about 110 degrees, I think the dampness of the heat would have to be considered less of an important issue.

She directed me to my room on the second floor overlooking the pool. I trudged up the stairs and down the walkway guarded by the wrought-iron guard rail.

I opened the door, went inside, and nearly passed out. The room was at least ten degrees hotter than the outside. I threw my duffel bag in the corner, found the air conditioner, and turned it on full. Then I walked back down the stairs, straight to the pool area. I emptied my pockets onto a table, then I walked toward the deep end and fell into the pool.

God it felt good.

The clerk was a little upset at my having entered the pool in the wrong attire so I bought a swimming suit at the front desk. I returned to the pool and stayed in the water for the next two hours. By that time the room had cooled a little. I bought four cans of Sprite at the Coke machine, then sat in my room in my wet bathing suit looking down on the pool area. It's odd how something like your personal comfort can so affect your mood. Even the desperate nature of my current problems seemed minor when compared to staying cool in this little Hades.

The phone book happened to be nearby on a small table so I looked in the yellow pages under hospitals and found the number and address for the Longevity Institute of the Desert. I lit a cigarette, walked down to the office, and bought a *Map of the Desert Cities*, which included Palm Springs, Desert Hot Springs, Palm Desert, Rancho Mirage, and Indio. Surprisingly, they hadn't named any of these places Inferno, Hades, or Heat Stroke, although farther down the road there was a little town called Thermal. I would have to go there someday and meet the people. I would expect they might be unusually honest.

I returned to the room and looked at the map, comparing it

to the address. The institute was located between Palm Springs and Desert Hot Springs. I remembered as a boy being taken to a natural hot springs over in Montana. It was a pleasant memory, so the notion of hot springs brought pleasant things to mind. However, by the time a cab took me to the institute, my impressions had been corrected. There was a lot more hot than springs in Desert Hot Springs. It was the Sahara at midday. Even the date palms looked parched. The valley was full of date farms, though their ranks were thinning out as the condo developers chopped down the trees to put up cheap housing for snow-birds—the winter residents from snowy climates.

As the Longevity Institute grew in size with our approach, I heard the dark, opening score of some fifties horror film. I found that, at 110 degrees, I could still feel a chill. The building was a pyramid. It was made of glass, not stone, and it was tinted dark, almost black, shining like a jewel someone had tossed casually onto the desert floor.

But it was a pyramid.

I felt now that I had traveled not only to a different part of the country, but had entered a different realm, a world at the far side of the river Styx. I didn't black out, but I got a light-headed feeling and a fear that the images I saw might start swimming like a mirage on a hot day. I lit a cigarette and touched the door handle of the cab just to be sure I was not in a dream.

I told the cabby to pull up across the street so I could take a look.

"You sight-seeing, huh?" asked the cabby. He was a middle-aged Hispanic. He lit a cigarette and looked at me in the rearview mirror.

"I'm thinking about having some plastic surgery," I said. "People told me this place did good work. I have an appointment here later today."

"You get your nose worked on, eh?" he asked. He was grinning.

"Yeah, sure," I answered, but I was a little irritated. No one was going to touch my nose.

After a few minutes of watching the place, I said, "Let's go," and had him take me to a restaurant near the motel.

I got out and paid him. The heat, as usual, was unbearable. It was as if you were standing in front of a big space heater turned full up and you couldn't get away from it. I knew it was burning the hell out of my face.

Inside the restaurant, I ordered a hamburger and sat reading a newspaper at the counter. When my food came I reached for the ketchup bottle, but as I looked up I noticed an older man at the counter looking at me. He was white-haired and had a mustache. His black, horn-rimmed glasses made him look like a college professor who had retired to the desert, but his build was surprising for an old man; he looked like a bodybuilder. Maybe out here his type was normal, but where I came from you did the expected as you aged—you got fat from too little exercise and too much food, or you became wizened as your bones gradually deteriorated.

I tried to ignore the old man and eat while keeping an eye on my waitress. She kept dive-bombing my coffee cup. She would drift by, coffeepot casually dangling from her fingers, and strafe the counter with coffee. Since I like to doctor my coffee with the exact amount of sugar and cream, this airborne attack altered the relationship of the components. Despite my vigilance I was strafed one more time, even though I had encircled the cup with my arms, keeping it near my chest. The result was another messed up cup of coffee and some runoff dripping from my thumb. I looked up as I cleaned up the mess with my napkin and saw that the old bodybuilder had left.

After eating, I returned to the motel for a conference with myself about the best way to approach the institute and couldn't come up with anything but a direct approach. Maybe it was the heat that had caused the loss of creativity, or maybe I didn't have any in the first place. I called the institute and talked to the receptionist. I asked her for the name of the director.

"That would be Dr. Forster," she said.

"Could I make an appointment with him?"

"Normally we make appointments upon referral," she replied.

"This is a business appointment."

"Perhaps you should talk to our business manager."

"Not in this case. I need to talk to the doctor about one of his partners."

"Perhaps you should give me the pertinent information and leave your phone number. Then the doctor could give you a call."

It didn't sound too promising, but it looked to be the best I could get. I gave her the information, then hung up.

I sat at the table by the window and smoked cigarettes. I looked out the window. A number of people, mostly women, lay around the pool taking in the sun. I thought they must be nuts. It was like having radiation therapy. I dug into my duffel bag and came up with an old pair of binoculars I had brought with me to use for surveillance. I pointed them at the pool.

My interest in the scene was at its height when the phone rang. I jumped about a foot.

"Hello," I said.

"This is the receptionist at the Longevity Institute of the Desert. I passed the information you gave me to the doctor's wife, who is his assistant, and she just informed me that he won't be able to meet with you. He says he doesn't know you and is too busy for such a meeting. Perhaps you could write him a letter."

"It's very important. It's about a missing person." I was winging it again. I should have told her that in the first place, but I actually thought my odds were better if I approached this in a more routine business fashion.

"I'm sorry, but they said it isn't possible. I can give you the mailing address. Perhaps you should write a letter."

"I have the address," I told her and hung up.

I sat for a moment, thinking. Then I dressed in my best clothes, a pair of light slacks and a short-sleeved shirt, and headed out to see if I could do this in person. Another cab took me to the institute and this time I had him drop me off at the front entrance.

I entered and told the receptionist who I was.

"Sir, I told you the doctor wouldn't see you."

"I know, but it's important and I thought perhaps I could wait until he has a moment."

"I don't think he can see you."

"I'll just have a seat and wait," I told her, and went to the plush leather sofa in the waiting area. A middle-aged female patient looked up at me and smiled. I sat near her and picked up a copy of *Vogue*.

I waited more than an hour, thinking I would end up leaving without seeing Forster, but at about six o'clock a man who looked like a doctor burst into the waiting room. He was tall, white-haired, and imperious. He wore the long white coat that is often the badge of doctors. He scowled at the nurse through his horn-rimmed glasses.

"Who wanted to see me?" he asked. He had a handsome face that reminded me of the older scientists from the horror movies of the 1950s—the guys who looked good and had deep voices. The only odd thing about this handsome scientist was that his skin was blotchy with shiny reddish areas. He was very white otherwise, but he had blotches of very pink and red skin that almost looked like lesions. They covered his hands as well as his face. The blotches continued up onto the top of his head, and I could see them through his thinning white hair.

The nurse didn't answer the doctor; she just pointed timidly at me. I nodded when he looked my way.

"Yes?" he said, not moving any closer to me. It was clear he expected to give me about three words before he returned to his more important activities. "My nurse said you were looking for someone. Who is it you're looking for?" asked the doctor.

"I'm looking for information on Andrew Welch. I'm trying to locate his daughter, Xanthia Welch."

"Xanthia—odd name. Andrew Welch is a silent partner in the firm, but I don't know anyone named Xanthia. I don't know how you got the idea that she was here, but you've been misled." He motioned me toward the door. "Now I'm very busy. You've been lucky to get in to see me at all."

"But . . ." I stammered.

"Dorothy," he called. "Mr. Moody is leaving. Good-bye, Mr. Moody," he said, and guided me to the door, his hand on my elbow. He was an older man, but he was a couple of inches taller and very forceful. Not to mention that he was putting me off his own private property. I didn't struggle, allowing myself to be escorted. He shut the door. It was a glass door so I felt even stupider since we could still see each other. I turned and walked away.

I was still wearing clothes that were too hot for the climate. I was pissed off and I had no idea what I would do to continue my search for Xanthia. More than that, I had no transportation and there were no phones in the area. I was walking. What a hell of a climate for that. I thought about putting out a little pamphlet for their chamber of commerce: So, You've Moved to Hell . . .

I trudged down the road. About a quarter of a mile away I was sweating. I was as hot as I had ever been. Vietnam was an icebox compared to this place. Still, I could see a gas station a quarter of a mile away. There was hope.

Then a car came up from behind me and stopped. It was an older Mustang, a beat-up and dirty metallic blue. The driver rolled the window down on my side. It was the old guy I had seen at the restaurant earlier. The bodybuilder.

"You want a ride?" he asked.

I looked down the road at the gas station. I looked at the guy. I didn't like a total stranger showing up in my life more than once. I wanted the ride but said, "I like to walk." Drops of sweat were running over my face and clouding my eyes.

"You like to walk?" he asked, incredulous. "Bullshit!" he said and he drove away.

Wearily I trudged to the gas station and called a cab.

In my motel room I felt depressed, but too hot to focus on it. The fact that I could not go home without facing a serious legal problem was less immediate than the discomfort and torpidity caused by 110-degree heat.

I read the newspaper. It mostly contained full-page ads for air conditioners. Heat was also a news item. The hot spell had been causing a crime surge. The police had been busy keeping up with it. It had to be some desert kind of criminal. I wouldn't have been able to mug anyone in this heat.

A cloud of crickets had invaded a nearby city. Where the hell had I landed—the holy land?

It's cooling down, they say. Only 108 degrees today. Not so bad.

Jesus.

I casually looked down at the swimming pool from my second-floor motel room. A few sun worshipers were lying beside it as Mexican workers were carting in huge blocks of ice to put into the pool. It was interesting for a while, something I had never seen—the biggest cocktail in the world, ice cubes floating around in it. A few brave souls soon tried out the pool, cooler now, swimming in the cocktail.

I looked at the classifieds. I needed a car. I wondered what I should buy. I had plenty of money, but I didn't want to spend it carelessly. When I returned to Mill City I would have to account for the money I'd spent. I read an ad for an AMC Gremlin selling for $1,200, but I did not consider it. Even I am not that stupid.

I looked down at the pool again. A strange figure caught my attention. It was the old man who had offered me the ride. He headed across the pool area until he went out of view toward the motel building. Just my luck to have a weirdo staying at the motel.

I sat around for a couple of days before I decided to follow the doctor. I had no reason to follow the doctor. I didn't really figure that he would lead me anywhere important. I just had nothing else I could think of to do and the bastard had pissed me off. Even if it would do no good, I would follow him for that.

I bought a 1976 Plymouth Duster with air-conditioning, a twelve-pack of pop, and a cooler. Then I returned to the institute, parked on the road, luckily locating a shady spot. I waited. I waited all afternoon and into the evening. It was a miserable way to spend one's life. Why the hell anyone would want to be a detective was beyond me. I read a stack of newspapers over and over again as I waited.

The local news was kind of depressing—not that anything would have cheered me up. There was a murder-for-hire case about to go to trial. Some senior citizen had been burned when his bed caught on fire. Here was a good one, one I could identify with. A murder suspect in Los Angeles had killed his victims to get souls for Satan. Cool, dude.

Another story was about an impostor at the sheriff's department. He had fake ID and pretended to be a deputy. He managed to check some women prisoners out of jail and fondle them before being caught. What some guys won't do for a date.

Then one final item caught my eye. It was about a biker who had been hospitalized after being hit by a car. The story made reference to a couple of local gangs, as though this area was a biker hangout. I remembered the biker who had tried to kill us in Seattle. I could pursue that lead—find out if anyone in Desert Hot Springs knew him. But even in my depressed, hopeless state, the thought of going around and asking questions of a bunch of bikers gave me a little chill.

Darkness never came. It was summer, and in Palm Springs summer is about as summery as it is anywhere in the universe. It was after six before there was much movement of people in or out of the institute. During the day there had been a slow trickle of cars—people who looked rich enough and dressed in a manner to appear to be clients. A little before six some cheaper cars started arriving, Chevy Novas and Fords carrying people wearing white uniforms, nurses and orderlies I guessed. At a little after six there was a small flood of nurses and order-lies leaving the institute. It was a smaller staff in the evening, but there was an evening shift. The doctor, however, did not emerge until after nine, accompanied by a large, handsome, younger man. They got into an older Lincoln Continental. The big man drove as they sped out the driveway. I wanted to stay far behind so as not to be spotted, but he made that easier by driving like a maniac and I had trouble keeping up. Luckily, the traffic was light and the roads were long and open so you could see ahead of you. He headed into the north end of Palm Springs, the low-rent district. He wound through the streets until he stopped in front of some sort of medical institution. That's all I could tell at first. It was medical because there were people in white clothes inside. Also, I could see a wheelchair resting outside the front door. God forbid that anyone should grab hold of it; it had been in the sun and would probably have lit your cigarette.

The doctor got out of his car and went inside. I found a place to park and looked at the sign on the lawn: CONVALESCENT HOME OF THE DESERT.

What was the connection between the Longevity Institute of the Desert and this nursing home?

I sat and waited. Jesus, it was hot. I had read all the newspapers. I had drunk most of the pop. What I really needed now was to take a pee. I was sweaty and miserable. I decided to take a chance and go into the nursing home, to have a look and see if I could find a bathroom.

I walked up the path. The automatic door opened and I went inside, into the wonderful coolness of real air-conditioning. It made me jealous with the recognition of how bad the air-conditioning in my room and car were by comparison. After a few days in the desert, all you want is to be cool. You begin to lose all other priorities.

I forgot for the moment what it was I was there to do. I just stood by the door in my ragged shorts, letting my body become reassured that we would be staying in this environment for a moment.

"Could I help you, sir?" the woman at the counter asked. She was wearing a nurse's hat and a white uniform.

"I'm just waiting for someone," I told her, caught by surprise. I hoped that would get her to leave me alone.

"I see. Are you going to visit a patient?"

"Yes. With my friend. Her aunt." I was winging it, hoping these answers made some sense.

"Do you know her name?"

"My friend?"

"Her aunt."

"No, I'm afraid not."

"Well, have a seat." She evidently liked her waiting room kind of neat and didn't want any unsightly strangers standing around.

"Could you direct me to the rest room?" I asked.

"Down the hall on your right,"

I headed that way and ducked in the door just as Dr. Forster was coming out of an office farther down the hallway. He was accompanied by another man, a stocky doctor type, younger than Forster, probably in his fifties.

I was happy enough to have found a rest room, but by the time I got out, the doctor had left. I decided to wander around a bit.

It was a U-shaped building, fairly large. The grounds were nicely kept—green grass, which was probably expensive in this heat. And there were trees to provide a nice shade. The rooms were what you'd expect in a nursing home; they were nice, but medicinal smelling. The people were not retiring here; they were dying. The care was long-term, but terminal. Most of the rooms were full. There were signs of home in the rooms, personal comforts such as stuffed chairs and the occasional dresser. The beds, however, were strictly hospital, and there was the usual medical equipment, IVs, and testing equipment, cabinets full of medical supplies.

As I returned to the lobby the nurse at the counter said, "Did you locate your friend?"

"No," I told her. "Maybe we got our wires crossed. I must have misunderstood her."

"I see."

I turned and walked out the door into the oppressive heat. This time of the year it might not have been too bad to be aging and pampered in a nursing home. I would try it some time.

I followed the doctor for the next several days. His pattern was pretty simple. He lived in a nice house up in the hills over Palm

Springs. He would leave there early in the morning, always accompanied by the large young man, go to the institute and stay there the whole day, usually into the evening. Once a day, sometimes twice a day, he would also stop by the Convalescent Home of the Desert for a brief visit.

My days were spent driving around behind him in my air-conditioned car with my cooler full of pop.

About the third day of this, following him, driving in traffic, I became aware of the pattern of the drivers and types of cars. Most of the cars were expensive—Cadillacs and Oldsmobiles, with a heavy spicing of Mercedes, BMWs, and the occasional Rolls Royce or Bentley. They were painted garish colors: pinks, purples, and reds and greens, often with heavy chrome and whitewalls. The convertibles were flashy, red with white tops, plush leather interiors.

And then there were the drivers—old folks. They were in their seventies or eighties usually. The hair was white if it was a man, and if the man had hair. The hair was white or bluish gray if it was a woman. They wore horn-rimmed glasses and wing glasses. Some of the old folks drove slowly, some barely able to see over the steering wheel, straining to see a little of the landscape outside their cars. Some drove like a bat out of hell, but with no more apparent awareness of the dangers in their surroundings than the ones who drove slowly.

I was on the path to a kind of elephant graveyard. A rich, senior-citizen elephant graveyard. They all came here as they approached death. They would live for years, but the graveyard was their destination soon enough. In the meantime, they comforted themselves with expensive and tasteless clothes, garish cars, and garish jewelry. They had come from all over the country, but especially from the cities of the north and from Canada to spend the time that remained in the sun of the Southwest. They golfed and shopped and ate "earlybird" dinners. Their children visited, somewhat taken aback by the foreign place their parents had ended up in, not at all like the towns that provided their childhood memories. The old people were here, all together, elephants at the graveyard, here to spend their last days and die in a nice place like Palm Springs.

I was at a dead end. I hadn't seen Xanthia, and the only suspicious character I had noticed was the old guy who had tried to give me a ride the other day. He seemed to be everywhere. It was a small-enough town that it was probably a coincidence. But I kept seeing him and he kept giving me significant looks, like we had a connection of some kind.

I was about to give up and begin preparations for the trip to my hometown jail when I got a surprise during the night.

At my motel the walkway was right next to my front window. So when you were sleeping, anybody on the walkway passed by about two feet from your head. You could pull the curtain, but it was flimsy and almost transparent. There was a light outside the room to illuminate the passersby, just in case there might be a chance you would go to sleep.

I had returned to my room relatively early and somehow managed to get to sleep, partly due to a depressive madness that wanted to shut me down and make me live in dreams; but I hadn't slept for long when someone said, "Wake up!"

I thought Ralph had said it. When I woke, I was already sitting halfway upright in bed, half in the room, half in nightmare. I tried to figure out what was going on—who was threatening my life or my sanity now. I had just about concluded that it was my imagination, as usual, when I saw the shadow on the curtains. The shadow was only a couple of feet away so I jumped when I saw it and bolted for the far side of the bed. I was about to put more distance between me and it when I heard someone say, "Scott!" in a loud whisper.

Who the hell in Palm Springs would be calling my name?

"Scott!" the voice said again.

I looked for my courage, which had been checked into a safety deposit box several years earlier. I found some trace evidence of the substance and used it to move myself to the window. I pulled the curtain open at the edge and looked out. Staring right into my face was Xanthia Welch.

# Ten

I jumped back, startled, letting go of the curtain.

"Scott!" she said again.

I opened the curtain as she stood back from the window, more into the light of the pathway so I could see her face better. I closed the curtains, went to the door, and opened it.

I looked up and down the pathway to make sure that no one else was around. Then I pulled her into the room.

I hugged her. "Where have you been?" I asked. "I didn't know where the hell you were. I didn't know how to find you." Tears flooded my eyes.

She hugged me, kissed my face. "I'm so sorry," she told me. "I know you've been worried."

"Worried? I wasn't worried. I thought you were *dead*. God, where have you been?"

"I've been here," she said, as she nuzzled her cheek against my neck, kissing me again. I looked at her, kissed her. How beautiful she was. How much I had missed her beauty and her touch, the warmth of her brown skin.

But suddenly I was angry. "You left *voluntarily?*" I asked her, holding her away from me.

"Sort of," she said. She was clearly nervous about this part of the explanation.

"We have been worried to death about you!" I was shouting and I didn't care who heard me. "I have traveled halfway across the country because I thought you were kidnapped or dead!"

"You need to quiet down," she said, gesturing it with her hand.

"Quiet, hell! What happened?"

"Someone came to get me," she said. "I had to leave with them right away. My life was in danger, and they were protecting me."

"Who the hell was that? Who would you trust?"

"My aunt," she said quietly.

"I thought you didn't have any relatives."

"I mentioned my aunt to you. I hadn't seen her since I was a child. I didn't know where she was. Somehow she found me."

I thought about this as I looked for my pants. I found them and put them on. Then I lit a cigarette and sat at the table by the window.

"Tell me what happened," I said.

"I was waiting for you at Sugarman's," she said, "when this woman came to the door. I don't know why, but I just wasn't afraid because she was a woman. I didn't expect her to be dangerous because . . ."

"It's men who usually kill people."

"Something like that," she said, embarrassed to be caught in a moment of incorrect thinking. "Anyway, she introduced herself as Amy Welch—the same last name. She told me she was my aunt; she said my father was her brother. I found it impossible not to listen to her. She showed me some records and photographs of her and my father when he was younger. She wasn't able to explain much to me, but she said my life was in danger, and, you know, after what had happened that wasn't hard to believe."

"Yes. Because you were in danger, you were supposed to stay with me and Sugarman."

"Scott, I couldn't turn down the chance to be with my aunt. And besides, no offense, but I wasn't sure that you guys were going to be able to protect me. You didn't seem to be too good at it."

I didn't answer. I was tired of admitting incompetence.

"Why didn't you wait and tell me about it?" I asked, finally.

"My aunt didn't think it was a good idea to tell you because she said you wouldn't let me go with her. I didn't think you would have allowed that either."

That much was certainly true.

"Where have you been staying?"

"I've been staying with my aunt and uncle," she said.

"Who are they? Where do they live?"

"My aunt's married name is Forster. She and her husband own the Longevity Institute of the Desert."

"The Longevity Institute. Then Forster was lying to me when he said he didn't know you."

"To protect me, yes. Even now I'm taking a chance in coming to see you because someone may be watching you, and that can lead them to me. I'm hiding out because someone seems to be trying to kill me. And my aunt and uncle."

"I certainly don't want you to be in danger," I said. My cigarette was down to the last drag. I reached for another from the package of cigarettes, found my lighter, and lit it. "I just wish you had informed me some way."

"I'm really sorry about that."

"What now? You know I can't go home without you; they'll think I killed both you and your Father. I'll rot in jail." Much as I was worried about her, I wasn't very happy with her at this point. I felt that somehow I was living with borrowed trouble—hers.

"I couldn't go back, at least not now. If I talk to the police, it will come out that I own part of the institute. If they look into the institute, I'm afraid they'll find out what we really do. We need to keep it a secret. If it comes out, it will ruin people's lives."

"What do you mean, 'what we really do'? And what about *my* life?" I asked peevishly.

"You know, I have real faith that this will be over soon," she replied. "I had a really good session with my psychic reader yesterday, and she said the major problems in my life will be resolved soon in my favor."

At this moment it drove me nuts that she wasn't joking. "Well, I had a midnight meeting with *my* spiritual advisor, and he said I was in deep shit."

"This is the one thing I can't stand about you, Scott, your cynicism. You have no faith. You have no belief." She walked to the window, stood there looking out.

I felt I had earned my cynicism on this point, but I didn't want to lose her or alienate her after I finally had her back. With some effort, I finally said, "I'm sorry."

She turned back toward me. "Look, Scott, I know you've had a rough time of it and I apologize for that, but what we're doing here is important. I'll make a deal with you. If you come with me and let me show you and tell you about the institute, I'll consider going back to Mill City with you—if you still want me to. But I think you'll understand that it won't do any good because it will put us both in more danger than we're in now."

"You mean you want to go over there now—in the middle of the night?"

"Yes. My uncle is there, waiting for us. It's better for us to do it now because there's no one around and whoever is following us will be easier to spot if they show up."

I looked at her. I looked outside at the moonlit oven. I recognized the feeling that had come over me. At this moment I felt that I had walked directly into one of my nightmares, that I was living in the twilight world of strange behaviors and strange situations.

"I'll go with you," I said finally. "I'd at least like to know what the hell is going on."

"Remember, everything I'm telling you is a secret. You can't ever tell anyone."

"I won't—unless I have to."

"Let's go," she said.

"Give me a minute." I put on my shirt and shoes, then went to the sink to throw cold water on my face. I followed her out into the heat of a Palm Springs night.

She was being chauffeured in the doctor's big car, parked in the rear of the motel parking lot. It was being driven by the big guy I had seen accompanying the doctor around Palm Springs. He was a handsome, dark-haired man, who looked like an FBI agent—professional, well-dressed, indifferent. He opened the rear door and we climbed into the backseat. The big car pulled away and we were on our way through the nearly deserted streets.

At the Longevity Institute the bodyguard opened the door and we headed toward the entrance. I would normally have opened the door for Xanthia, but I was distracted and a little upset so I started to go through the door ahead of her. The bodyguard, to my surprise, grabbed my shoulder, gently but firmly. "Miss Welch will go first," he said.

Apologetic, I stepped out of her way. "Of course," I said, "I'm sorry."

"Thank you, Doug," Xanthia said, as he held the door for her.

The doctor greeted us in the lobby. I was entering the secret chambers of a pyramid at night, just like in my dreams of old.

Xanthia said, "Scott, this is my uncle, Wendell Forster."

The doctor offered his hand and I shook it.

He stared at me for a moment, then said, "You know, we could probably fix that for you," meaning my nose.

I ignored the comment and followed him as he turned and walked toward the elevator. We took it to the top floor and got out in a large pyramid-shaped room. The windows all around us looked out on the desert at night. It was a beautiful scene, but otherworldly under the circumstances. The doctor flipped on a light that didn't help to relieve the dreamlike quality of the scene; it provided lighting from the corners of the room, shining up, like the light in a horror film. And it was a very yellow light that gave everything an odd cast. It provided basic visibility, so we could see the cubicles and desks. But it also lit up the inside of the pyramid, making the shape obvious, and it blocked most visibility of the scene outside.

In the middle of the pyramid-shaped room was a big cube, ten feet tall and twenty feet on each side. It had a couple of doors and in a few places there were small windows. It was evidently a room for the storage of hospital records, and the room with windows might have contained an accounting computer. The doctor went to one of the doors in the cube, opened it, and went inside. We waited for a couple of minutes. The big guy, Doug, the bodyguard and chauffeur, stared at me the whole time.

Finally, the doctor emerged, carrying a stack of medical records and what looked like a large album, like a photo album but bigger. He spread them out on a desk.

"Xanthia, get a couple of chairs so you can both sit down here."

I located one chair as Xanthia went to one of the cubicles and retrieved another. We pulled them up to the desk where the doctor was already sitting, the records before him. I sat at the chair nearest Forster with Xanthia to my right.

Forster reached over to a flexible desk lamp and clicked it on. He adjusted the arm so that the light shone down on the stack of medical records in front of us. Then he looked at me with a certain intensity, a kind of pay-attention look.

"What I want to show you now is a program that we are trying to keep secret—for some very good reasons that will become clear. We want you to know about this so that you will understand how important it is. We want you to help us to keep it a secret. And we hope that you will allow Xanthia to stay with us, where she will be safe."

At this point, I was still intimidated by the doctor's presence, but I needed to know something. "Does this have anything to do with Andrew Welch's death?"

"I'm not sure, but I think it's likely," said the doctor. "He was a participant in and a representative of the program I'm going to tell you about. On the other hand, I'm not at all sure that his murder was related. Unless your police department develops some specific evidence as to the killer's identity, we can't be sure there wasn't some other reason."

"How could this 'program' have been a motivation for killing Welch?"

"I'll explain, if it doesn't merely become clear in the telling," he said.

"Okay."

"This regimen is referred to simply as Program Nine. We started working on it forty years ago, in 1940."

"Why nine?" I asked him as he prepared a space to spread out the book and other documents."

He gave me a withering look. "There were eight other less successful programs before we arrived at nine," he said.

The doctor touched the cover of the photo album–type book as though caressing a precious object, then pulled open the large cover and carefully laid it flat. He turned the first large page, which was blank. The next page had a small amount of cover text, the largest of which said: "Patients of Program Nine." He turned to another blank page, then to the first set of records. The records were laid out on the two-page spread, a page about 14 × 16 inches. There were several photographs of the patient, a woman, apparently at different ages. These were before and after photographs. On the left she looked a little more worn, a little more wrinkled. On the right, her face was smoother, less wrinkled, and perhaps a bit more tanned. An envelope had been stapled on the right-hand side of the page. The doctor opened the envelope and retrieved additional documents. The doctor took the set of folded records, opened them, and spread them out for me to see. The top one was a copy of a birth certificate. The year of birth was 1901.

"This woman," the doctor said, "is one of my patients. She is seventy-eight years old."

"These aren't current photographs," I said.

"These photographs were taken six months ago."

"That can't be. She looks too young for seventy-eight."

"That's what we do around here—make people look too young."

"I've heard of plastic surgery, but I've never seen anything this good."

"It's more than plastic surgery, Scott," Xanthia volunteered. "Dr. Forster uses plastic surgery, but this is a program of real life extension—diet, yoga, exercise, medical treatments, special medications. It's a wonderful opportunity for people to live longer, better lives."

"When you say 'life extension,' what do you mean?"

"Xanthia has jumped the gun a little," the doctor said. "Let's look at a few more patients. We'll try to explain as we go." He returned the records to the page and turned to a new patient. It was another woman who looked to be about forty-five. He pulled the records, opened them, and handed me the birth certificate. The year of birth was 1910, making her sixty-nine. She was very pretty for sixty-nine. One of the photos was of her playing tennis. If she was really sixty-nine, then the law of aging had been repealed.

He let me look through her documents. They were the typical paper trail left at the end of a person's life—birth records, a marriage license from the 1930s, various driver's licenses from various states and times. They all appeared to be authentic and in sync with the birth certificate as far as her age was concerned.

He turned the page and we looked at another set of records—a woman again. I realized as he turned this page that I was probably looking at a sales document. This had been put together for the time when a prospect was really ready to accept the notion of joining the program. As a sales document it was pretty effective. It was convincing me.

We continued to look through the records, stopping from time to time as the doctor commented on this or that about the person. He volunteered that I would be able to meet some of them if I wanted—to verify for myself. Others I would not be able to meet as they lived too far away.

We talked and he turned the pages until, as he brought one new page into view, I was stopped dead in my tracks. The photo on the page was of Xanthia's father, Andrew Welch. I sat staring at it. Xanthia turned and walked away. By her demeanor she might have been crying.

The doctor took no apparent notice of the reaction. He simply removed the records as he had the others and unfolded them. He handed me the copy of the birth certificate. The date of birth was 1891, making Andrew Welch nearly ninety at the time of his death.

"I find it very hard to believe that Andrew Welch was eighty-eight," I said, looking at the birth certificate.

"First," the doctor said, "his name was Matthew. We called him Matt. He was a friend of mine and a partner. The name you knew him by was a necessary alias."

"Why did he need an alias?"

"I'll explain more about that, but for now let's just say it would have been difficult for him to continue as Matthew Styles if he was going to appear to be thirty years younger than his true age.

"Second, he was every day of his eighty-eight years. I knew him for fifty of those years. We met in 1929."

"I don't see how that could be. I don't believe he was in his eighties. I knew him. He was in his forties, fifty at the most. No one could make someone in his eighties appear to be in their forties."

"To set the record straight, *we* are not the ones who do most of the work. The patient's ancestries do most of the work. We just help them along."

"I still don't believe it, but now I don't even understand what you're saying."

"The cornerstone of our program is simple genetics. If members of your family have lived a long time, perhaps you will live a long time. How about you, Mr. Moody? Perhaps you're a candidate for our program."

I wondered if there was just the slightest hint of a bribe coming, the biggest bribe of all—a long life. If I believed, if I went along, if I didn't cause a problem with this murder case, perhaps I would qualify for some kind of scholarship.

"I don't know," I said. "My family dies pretty young." It wasn't true, but I wanted to see what he would say.

"You still might qualify," he said. "Your family members in the past might have been victims of some bad lifestyle habits—most likely smoking, or chewing tobacco, or perhaps eating a high-cholesterol diet. It might not have been the genes.

"And genes are our most powerful ally, Mr. Moody. We never select people for this program without carefully screening their family histories. We do a chart of the family as to the diseases that are common and the age of death of each of the family ancestors." The doctor searched through the records on Welch. He pulled out a piece of paper, which unfolded to 11 × 17. It was a family tree—a series of circles and squares, connected by lines, with hand-written names and familial relationships listed below each of the circles and squares.

"Matthew was one of very few of my personal acquaintances who was qualified for the program. Almost all of his ancestors lived to very ripe old ages—into their nineties, and a few even over one hundred. That's the first qualification for anyone in our program; they have to have a terrific genetic background. Then we can help them."

"I don't see how you help them if they're already going to live to be ninety years old." I was getting a little testy. Andrew Welch was dead. I was out of a job and estranged from my daughter. The police in two cities wanted to talk to me and probably both wanted to lock me up. With all that going on, I was being persuaded to enter a science fiction story.

"You know what morbidity is, Mr. Moody?"

"Not unless it's the kind of attitude you develop when you get really depressed . . ."

"As amusing as that is, it's not quite what I mean. You see the real problem of aging isn't just making it to the finish line—dying old. It's how you live on your way there.

"Most people begin suffering various serious problems of aging sometime during their fifties and most certainly by their sixties. Now these complaints may not be too bad at first; they are more of an inconvenience. Still, people begin to look older. Sometimes the health problems slow them down, complaints of joint problems, you know the kind of thing. Hip replacements, knee problems, osteoporosis. There may be problems with the prostate gland in men. Both men and women commonly have problems with normal urination. And, of course, some people suffer very serious health problems—heart disease, kidney failure, et cetera."

"I'm getting depressed," I said.

The doctor laughed, the first time I had made him laugh. I wanted to entertain my audience even when I didn't like them. "You get the idea. The older you get, of course, the worse the problems get. One day you realize that while you may still be alive, you can't really enjoy your life. Certainly, you can't pretend that you are young anymore. And you don't look so young anymore."

"And you can do something about that?"

"Damn right I can," he said, sounding more like a proud auto mechanic than the head of a medical clinic. "And I have. I can significantly slow the effects of aging—if I have a patient with good genetics, a cooperative patient, a patient who has a lot of money and a willingness to work. Oddly enough, it's harder to find the 'willingness to work' quality than the 'lots of money.' "

"How much money?"

"A lot. It's very expensive. In order for people to follow my program, they are required to have a lot of monitoring and a lot of treatment. The program is based largely on diet, exercise, and the practice of certain disciplines, such as yoga. But as people age, we don't rely entirely upon these methods. We have to resort to a certain amount of plastic surgery, perhaps a lot of plastic surgery. Normal surgery is also required if we think failure in internal systems may be threatened. We do a fair amount of vein reconstruction, for instance. We also have expensive drug treatments and chelation. We provide special drugs that help with brain blood circulation; it's no good getting old in good health and not being able to think clearly. And we also help the patients psychologically. The program is not easy to follow; it requires a lot of discipline on the part of the patients themselves. And growing old, regardless of your good health, means that you are losing a lot—old friends and family, for instance. And a lot of the people choose to move away from their friends and family so there will be fewer questions about how well preserved they are."

"How much does all this cost?"

"I can't give you exact figures, but I'll give you an average annual cost—three million dollars."

"You're kidding."

"That's one of the reasons it's a secret. We don't think that it would do any good to advertise that there are wealthy people who can afford to live that much longer and better than people without money. There's enough hostility between the rich and the poor without that. And that resentment was worse when we started this program in 1940."

"I don't see what treatment you could have given in the forties that would have been effective. There was little plastic surgery. A lot of medical treatments were unavailable. It seems so unlikely to me that Andrew Welch could have been in his eighties when he died. It would help if you could just begin at the beginning. How did you start this thing? Why did you start this thing?"

"I was twelve years old when I watched my father die. That was in 1917, near the end of the First World War. I never accepted his death, you see. My mother died eight years later, and I was left alone. Both of them died of what was then considered old age, though they were both only in their sixties—worn out, used up. My father was an invalid when he died; my mother had been bedridden for two years.

"I went to medical school and became a surgeon, but I read and did research in the field of gerontology. At that time there was little encouraging information; people didn't know much about aging. But in the thirties I began to learn things that were happening in other cultures. I realized that we weren't the best teachers in this area. Our entire medical model is based on fixing things when they've broken. Even my own work as a surgeon is only the ability of a good mechanic or body-and-fender man. What I wanted were ways to improve overall health. I studied the diets and personal habits of other cultures—including the Hunza peoples in Pakistan and the primitive people of South America. I learned a lot from studying their diets as to why there are so many people in those cultures who live long lives. People in our culture are not used to thinking of living long lives. Why do you think that is, Mr. Moody?"

"We like bacon and eggs?"

"You're not so far off. Diet and stress and a lot of stupid attitudes. You know, Mr. Moody, many people in the world take long life for granted. There are parts of the world where people live routinely to one hundred—and many to one hundred and twenty and thirty."

"Where is that?"

"Have you ever heard of the Hunza people? The Hunza people of the Kashmir region of Pakistan?"

"No, I haven't."

"Many of them live over one hundred years. Some have lived to the incredible age of one hundred and forty. The combination of genetics, altitude, diet, climate—it's routine there.

"Naturally, I studied all that I could learn from Western medicine—any development that seemed to point to triggers for old age or to reasons for early morbidity.

"But, naturally, the most important factor I've discovered is the one that the individual may or may not have—good ancestors. I knew of this fact through reading about studies that have been done in families with septuagenarian parents and grandparents—that the children in such families will live twenty or more years beyond the typical life expectancy."

The doctor removed his glasses, leaned back in the chair. "I started this program with exactly five patients. All of them had enough money to help pay for the cost of the treatments we knew about at that time. Our institute was in a run-down medical center in the suburbs of Chicago. It wasn't much of an institute. We experimented with treatments and diet. A staple of our program was exercise. And, of course, the patients were chosen very carefully. However, until Andrew's recent death, he was the only survivor of that original group. What I'm trying to say, Mr. Moody, is that this program has had its failures as well as its successes, and we didn't learn what we know today without suffering some defeats. And, like I said earlier, genetics is still our strongest ally. We just try to help it along."

Dr. Forster scratched one of the pink areas on his forehead. "Now, I'm going to give you a painful example of the limits of our program—the people we can't do much for." He lowered his hand again, rested it on the desk. "It can't help me." He gestured with both hands to indicate himself. "I look pretty much my actual age—which is seventy-nine."

I was going to say I didn't think he looked a day over seventy-five, but I didn't think hc would laugh.

"I'm years younger than Andrew was, but I look older. I'm pretty healthy. I still expect to live to a hundred, maybe more. But I'm not going to look as young as some people.

"My wife. She's another good example. She was Andrew's younger sister, but she always looked older than he did and she had more health problems.

"We've been able to improve and lengthen my life and my wife's life, but we haven't been able to measurably slow the appearance changes that are caused by aging. In my case it's partly this skin condition—an allergy to sunlight—and because I abhor the notion of plastic surgery even though it's my craft. Even if I'd had some surgery, it wouldn't have done the good that it did Andrew.

"Some people just do better than others. Andrew was one of our best patients. We've had many failures. Some are not able to stay with the regimen. It's difficult and sometimes unpleasant. Some people like to eat too much. Our program requires a spartan diet and occasional fasting.

"Of course, we are able to make the discipline a little easier by offering people various mood-adjusting drugs, from something as simple as amphetamines in very controlled doses to the new antidepressant drugs. It takes very small amounts of these drugs in our relatively disciplined group to help keep our clients within the parameters of the program.

"We've had a few people leave, of course. They just couldn't take it, or they couldn't afford it, or they didn't think they were getting the right results."

At this point I was only half-listening. I was remembering Andrew Welch's fussy eating habits, his mania for regular exercise. And I was remembering my conversation with Frosty Shields. He had commented on Andrew Welch's unexpected knowledge of World War I. Could Andrew Welch, aka Matthew Styles, really have been a veteran of World War One?

"What if I made this all public?" I said, just to see how he would react.

"I doubt people would believe you. Over the years we've been *exposed* a number of times, but without consequence because the media and the public would not accept such things. The only fear we have is that one of our number should become really famous—so that the entire world could witness the lack of aging. I think even then it would be seen as an anomaly, and it would be quite a while before any realization would set in."

"If nobody will believe it, why the secrecy?"

"Well, it's no better to be thought a quack than to be thought of as someone who is giving an extraordinary privilege to the rich. Either way, it's preferable to remain very private. As a matter of fact, right now we believe that someone who was connected to the program is trying to hurt us, perhaps kill us. And we think it may be because they were rejected when they wanted to join our program. Of course, we're not sure who they are; they haven't come to talk to us. They've made anonymous threats and . . ."

". . . killed Andrew Welch?"

"Perhaps. If so, it's a kind of jealous revenge—a sort of 'if I can't be part of the group that gets to live longer, then I'll make sure you don't live so long.' "

"Do you know the name of this person? Do you have any idea where he, or she, lives?"

"We wish we did," the doctor said, closing the book on Program Nine. "But the only person who likely knew the identity of the murderer was Andrew Welch. We don't always know everyone that Andrew contacted. As I said earlier, he was a representative of the program and made the early choice on whether people would be invited to participate. We only knew the most likely prospects and the ones who actually joined the program."

"Then Welch *was* a salesman." I pulled the book toward me and opened it again to the page on Andrew Welch. I thumbed through some of the copies of his more recent life records—things like his voter registration and driver's license.

"I think salesman is a very poor term for what he did. He was a recruiter, an advocate for the program, a supporter of what we did."

Once again, I was half-listening to Forster. I had found what I was looking for in Welch's records—an address other than his house in Mill City, an address that could have been the headquarters for his secret life as a representative of the Longevity Institute. The address I found was a building in downtown Seattle that I was familiar with, a fancy residence for people of money. I was at the moment not so interested in Dr. Forster and his Program Nine. I wanted out of here, and I wanted a cigarette. I would have said so, but thought the doctor just might not approve. I settled for taking out my lighter and playing with it. By the look on his face he didn't seem to like this activity much more than smoking.

This situation was pretty ironic. We were sitting in the Longevity Institute discussing ways to prolong people's happy lives, yet I was the least likely prospect for such a future. I would probably be put to death by lethal injection or hanging for something I did not do. The doctor and Xanthia were under death threat by a prospective client who didn't want to be denied an extended life span. It was pretty laughable, but I didn't think I would mention it to the doctor; he didn't seem to have much of a sense of humor.

I thought the interview with Forster was over, that now I would return to my motel room to have my cigarette and contemplate, but instead he said, "Come this way."

We got up from the desk and Xanthia followed as we walked toward a door in the cube and he ushered me into a room. It was a surprise to see that the room was full of people, about eight in all, sitting in stuffed chairs and small love seats. The room setting looked like it might have been used for group therapy. Weirdest of all, some of the faces were already familiar. They were faces from the book of patients I had just been studying.

I stood there a moment, not quite sure what to do. Dr. Forster said, "Well, why don't we start by briefly introducing ourselves to our guest, Mr. Moody."

No one stood, but the woman nearest me, a gray-haired, attractive woman of perhaps fifty-five, spoke. "Hello, Mr. Moody. My name is Helen." She had a high-pitched, slightly gravelly voice, the voice of a pleasant aunt. She sounded older than she looked. She was dressed in casual desert elegance, a white silk blouse, plum-colored slacks. "I'm originally from Brooklyn, New York. I've been in the desert now for five years. I was a housewife until my husband passed away ten years ago. As you know, since you've been looking at the program book, I'm a member in good standing"—she smiled at her joke—"of Program Nine. I was born in 1904, making me seventy-five years old this year." I was not sure how to react to what she was saying. Her presence, the impression she gave of being someone's sincere and well-intentioned auntie, or youngish grandmother, added to her credibility. She looked around at everyone, as if to see if she had done all right, then settled back in her chair.

Now a graying but still young-looking man spoke up. He wore the desert golfing attire: a green and white polo shirt, tan slacks, white shoes. "My name is Daniel Butler. I was born and raised in Detroit. I owned a manufacturing plant there until about ten years ago. I've been in the desert for eight years. I don't leave much anymore even in the summer. I spend most of my time golfing these days. I've been in Program Nine for twenty years now, since I retired at the age of fifty-six."

That would make him seventy-six now. He looked closer to fifty.

One by one, each of the remaining members of this unique little club introduced themselves, giving his or her age. All were over seventy by their testimonies. One man claimed to be over eighty. He did look a little older, nearer sixty perhaps, but nowhere near eighty. Of the four women, all had been house-wives—with wealthy husbands, I supposed—and one had been a fashion designer in the Midwest. The men were all wheeler-dealers, the type I had been taught to hate on my father's behalf in the view that anyone who was successful had to be a crook. One was a manufacturer, two were realtors and developers, and the fourth was the owner of a large fleet of cabs—him I was pre-pared to hate on a more personal level.

All of them seemed pleasant enough, authentic, and nowhere near their stated ages.

It occurred to me how odd this all was. I was in the desert. I was in a building that was shaped like a pyramid. I was sitting here with this group of well-dressed suburbanites. This situation was sort of bizarre. I had, after all, lost my sense of the bizarre versus the normal, but even for me this situation seemed bizarre. Yet it seemed familiar, too. Years before I had attended a late-night session with the members of a church that used a Ouija board to contact the dead. In comparison with that, I guessed this wasn't that weird.

"I need a cigarette," I said out of the blue. I swear it must have been Ralph who made me do it. I wouldn't have had the courage.

"We have a room where you can do that," Forster said, obviously irritated, but willing to accommodate me for some unknown reason. "It's a place for our more recalcitrant patients."

I nodded my good-byes to the patients of Program Nine. The lady in the plum-colored slacks responded, "It was very nice to meet you, Mr. Moody."

Forster led me through a couple of doors into a room with a view of the valley. Xanthia followed and the two of them sat a couple of chairs away as I lit a cigarette. I reached across the marble end table and pulled a glass ashtray nearer to me.

"So, I need to understand. What do you expect of me? Why did you bring me here and show me this stuff about Program Nine?"

"Scott," Xanthia began.

"Let me explain," said the doctor. "For one thing, Xanthia cares about you. She felt that by being so obvious in following me you were putting yourself into unnecessary danger. You need to be very careful because there's someone out there who wants to harm us. They may harm you as well. At least I have a bodyguard. You don't."

"The driver?"

"Douglas. He watches over us. I imagine we'll have a bodyguard from now on—even when this thing gets resolved. After this, I'll never feel quite safe again.

"In addition to the danger you're causing for yourself, you are drawing more attention to us. And we don't want you to go to your local police department. That not only would further endanger us, it would endanger our program. And it wouldn't do any good. We don't know anything that would help the police find Andrew's killer. Our best bet, in fact, is if they are able to track his killer down through evidence unconnected to us."

I responded, "If the killer's motive had something to do with your program and the police catch him, he's going to tell them about your program."

"A person could tell a story about us that could be considered a motive, but not necessarily a sane motive." Dr. Forster paused. He looked at me with the same intensity applied by my high school principal when I had skipped a day of class to drink beer. "We need to know whether you're going to keep our secret," he said.

"I don't know." I lit another cigarette. "My life expectancy doesn't seem that good right now, so I'm a little peevish."

"We'll do everything we can to help to clear you of these charges. I'm not sure what we'll do. I'll have to give it some thought. Certainly we can provide money for the best possible defense."

"The greatest help would be for law enforcement to know that someone else had a reason to kill Andrew Welch."

"Scott, we can't reveal anything right now," Xanthia said. "You should talk to my aunt. Maybe that will help you understand. You can meet her tomorrow. She can talk to you about my father. I'm sure she doesn't know who killed him, but she can explain who he was. That will help you understand that he was not a criminal."

"I'd be happy to meet her," I said. Even if she didn't provide much information, I wanted them to jump through as many hoops as possible. It made me feel more included in the situation that was threatening my life.

"We'll call you at your motel in the morning," Xanthia said.

I stood. "All right. I have to think about this, about what I'm going to do. If I can't get help finding Andrew Welch's killer, I'll have to decide whether I'm going back to Mill City to face the charges there—since, I guess, Xanthia won't be going back with me." I looked at her. She shook her head no.

"Do you mind taking a taxi?" asked the doctor.

"No, that's fine."

"Xanthia, why don't you go downstairs with Scott and wait

until the taxi arrives." He picked up a phone and dialed a number.

The two of us walked out into the hallway, took the elevator, and meandered back to the entrance. I wondered what had happened to the people who had been there to convince me about Program Nine. Had they left to their desert homes? Were they still in the building?

We waited in the lobby for ten minutes before I saw the cab pull up in the parking lot.

"Are you going to be all right?" I asked Xanthia. I was not really thinking of her so much as I was wondering if *I* was going to be all right. *They* were abandoning *me*, not the other way around.

"Sure. I'm safe here," she said. "I hope you understand about this. It has to be a secret. There's too much at stake."

I walked out the door into the sweltering midnight heat and got into the waiting cab.

At the motel I sat in the dark room and lit a cigarette. I stared out the window at the mountains. I thought about what I had seen and heard. The Longevity Institute. Maybe it would prosper and proliferate. Dozens of pyramids on the desert floor. It would be easy to imagine pyramids here, competing with the mountains for attention, providing additional options for the well-funded nearly dead. It seemed appropriate somehow, in this place where people came to live out the end of their lives and to die, that there would be some sort of scheme to delay mortality. And that it should take place in a pyramid. No one had yet come up with a grander or more fanciful scheme than the Egyptians.

And, as I daydreamed in the way only a psychotic can daydream, I saw another figure bloom in the desert—a black sphinx, shiny like the Longevity Institute pyramid, as though made of obsidian. But it was not the Egyptian Sphinx. This one's nose was broken, not missing. This Sphinx had matted and unkempt black hair and a mustache. Moody the Sphinx. Moody for the millennia. Moody impervious to the blowing sand or the punishing heat. Moody with a heart of stone. Moody become eternal. Moody forever.

But, of course, I was not the stone Moody. I was a very sad and weepy Moody. In a way, I was heartbroken. I realized that I loved Xanthia. I had not allowed myself to think in those terms before because they frightened me—to love anyone, much less to love someone with whom I so disagreed about the nature of reality, the interpretation of how to live one's life. But there it was. I could feel it. Both in the pain of the loss of her if she were to stay here in the desert, and in the pain of betrayal of understanding that she would allow me to return to Mill City to face the guilt and the punishment related to her father's death. Even if they were willing to try to help, that's what it came down to.

I finished the cigarette and lit another one, then dialed the telephone.

"Speak," said Sugarman, when he came on the line. I heard the theme music to *The Late Late Movie* in the background.

"Sugarman, this is Scott Moody."

"I see," he said.

"I found Xanthia." It wasn't quite how it had happened, but it sounded better, like I had accomplished something more than merely having occupied my motel until she came to me. I explained how I had followed the doctor between the Longevity Institute and the Convalescent Home of the Desert, how after a few days Xanthia had turned up one night at my motel.

"I'm very glad," Sugarman said, sounding relieved. "I had about come to the end of the proverbial rope in searching for her here. I've regularly checked the hospitals for days.

"By the way," he continued, "you have some minor police problems here in Seattle."

"How so?"

"How easily we forget. The young lady was missing and I reported it. They still want to speak to you. In your stead they might be willing to speak to the young lady."

"I'll have her give them a call."

"At this point a call might not be enough, but I'll speak to them and get back to you."

"I'll stay in touch. You can reach me at this motel. I'll let you know if I'm going to leave. I may come to Seattle before returning to Mill City. I may use it for a base while I try to figure out some legal strategy for dealing with the suspicions of the local police in Mill City."

"I'll be leaving for Colorado in a day or so," Sugarman said. "I take it you still want me to pursue this thin lead."

"Yes, please." I was actually a little irritated he had not already done so. "I could use any kind of link to Welch that would make the cops suspect someone else. If these people in Colorado knew him, perhaps they know someone who would want to kill him."

"I'll be happy to continue to be of service," said Sugarman. "I've never seen Colorado." I could hear the flick of his lighter as he ignited another Sher Bidi. "I'll speak to you in a few days."

"Take care," I said, and hung up the phone.

I slept until nearly noon. I woke to a phone ringing. I managed to get to it, but I wasn't awake when I spoke. "Mom?" I said.

"I'm a mom," said the voice, "but I don't think I'm yours."

I entered the current dimension. "I'm sorry. I'm just waking up."

"Is this Scott Moody?"

"Yes." Unfortunately.

"My name is Amy Forster. My niece asked me to call you. I think she was hoping that I could put your mind at ease about my husband's medical practice and business dealings. And she said you wanted to know about her father."

I was sitting up, wide awake now. The voice over the phone

was very pleasant and sane and decent sounding. "Yes. I would like to know about Andrew Welch especially."

"That was a name he used. I never got used to it. He was always Matt to me."

"So I understand."

"Could we have lunch?"

"That would be fine." I grabbed the ballpoint pen from the nightstand and wrote the name and address of the restaurant she suggested.

"It's a quiet place, and kind of out of the way. I'll see you there at one."

"How will we recognize each other?"

"I'll know you," she said and hung up.

But she didn't have to identify me. I knew her when I saw her sitting in the air-conditioned area of the restaurant. She had been in the lobby at the Longevity Institute the day I had initially tried to visit her husband.

She was gray-haired, but other than that she didn't look anywhere near the seventy-five years of her age. And she was very pretty, youthful and bright, like an actress only a few years in retirement from a glamorous career. I was getting used to this. No one looked their age. I had entered *The Twilight Zone*.

She stood and held out her tanned arm as I neared the table.

"I'm so happy to meet you, Mr. Moody," she said. "You're as handsome as my niece said you would be."

I felt myself unaccountably blushing. I had not expected to be nonplused and attracted to a woman of seventy-five.

"Glad to meet you," I mumbled. I sat down.

"I understand that you're not quite convinced about the need to keep secret the institute's special programs."

"I don't necessarily want to reveal it. It's just that I'm in a bit of a bind. If I can't find a way to redirect the police investigation into Andrew Welch's death, they'll be putting me away."

Mrs. Forster stopped smiling. "His name was Matthew," she said. "I always called him Matty. I never liked the name Andrew. He chose to take the name to keep a low profile, but I never liked it."

"Why did he do that anyway?" I asked, happy to have a chance to cross-examine a new witness.

"As much as anything it was because he continued to live part-time in Seattle. That's where he was raised after our family moved out from Chicago in 1901. His friends in Seattle were all old men. Matty, for all practical purposes, was still a young man. He didn't want to run into someone he knew while under his real name. Of course, I suppose he could have pretended to be his own son."

"Just exactly how old was your brother?"

"He was eighty-eight. I suppose that's why it's a little easier to accept his death. Even though it was a tragic way for anyone to die."

"How do I know that's the truth?" I asked.

"I'm not sure I can provide absolute proof. You've already seen a birth certificate, lots of other documents. First, let me show you how old *I* am. I know that's unusual coming from a woman, but I think it's necessary." She reached into her purse, took out her wallet, and presented her driver's license. She was born in 1904, according to the document, making her seventy-five. She was Mrs. Amy Forster. By her looks she couldn't possibly have been a day older than sixty and could easily have been taken far younger.

"You look wonderful," I said, without planning it. Her appearance for her age turned me into a TV talk show host.

"Thank you," she said, taking her wallet back. She pulled something else from her purse. It was a photograph of a young girl and a young man. The man could have been Andrew Welch, aka Matthew Styles. The girl could have been Mrs. Forster.

"This is a rare picture of my brother and me. It was taken in

1915." She smiled, and we both looked at the photograph. "Matty was always so handsome, always so wise. He was a wonderful older brother."

"I find it so hard to believe that he could have been in his eighties," I muttered.

"I know this is confusing," she told me. "Me being seventy-five and looking, well, somewhat younger. And Matthew, at age eighty-eight, looking, well, I would say never more than fifty."

"Younger," I said, adding my own testimony.

"But Matty always looked younger. He took after our father's side of the family. And when Wendell, that's my husband's first name, started this program, this regimen, Matty took to it with great enthusiasm. He was as disciplined as anyone I've ever seen. He did the exercises, he kept to the diet, he took the skin treatments, he took the supplements, and he came to the institute at least four times a year for checkups and treatments. If everyone put as much effort into themselves as Matthew did, at least some of them could look as good."

I remembered some of the traits she talked about. The man I knew as Andrew Welch was incredibly fastidious about what he ate. He had an exercise room at his house and used it often. He was a fanatic about his diet and saw to every detail at the restaurant he ran. The story wasn't completely implausible.

I stayed with Mrs. Forster for another half an hour as she told me other stories about her brother, explained why she wanted me to help them to keep the program a secret. "So we can continue it, for one thing. And so we can be safe from this person, whoever it is, until he is put away."

Then we said our good-byes, and I got into my car and drove back to the motel.

I sat at the table in my motel room. This chair and this spot had become my old friends, my new home in this journey to a strange land and a stranger experience. I sat looking out the window at the women by the pool. I looked at each of them and wondered about their ages.

I didn't plan on taking a nap, but as I leaned back in my chair a nap took me. By the clock on the nightstand it must have been about a three-hour nap. When I woke I had sweat on my forehead and drool on my shirt. I also had the fresh memory of a dream about having been lost in the pyramids. It seemed at least as real as my actual memory of the visit to the glass pyramid the night before.

I called the airport and booked a flight out that evening to Seattle. I packed my few belongings, checked out, and looked for a place to park my car. I stopped at a little store and bought a car key box; then I found a street that looked like it was used to vehicles hanging around for more than a week. I opened the trunk and checked the contents. The satchel of money was there. I added a few items that I wouldn't need again, then closed the trunk. I hid the key box. In a while I could call Xanthia and tell her where the car was. She could have it and the remaining money.

I walked to a local store and called a cab. Forty-five minutes later it took me to the airport, where I waited two hours for my flight. It was more comfortable in the airport than anywhere else in this particular heat, and the airport allowed me to believe I was on some tourist junket, or new adventure, not going home to meet my fate at the hands of the local police. Well, what the hell. I would hire a lawyer, and I would certainly tell them where to find Xanthia. I had seen *The Maltese Falcon* and I wasn't going to take the fall for a woman.

During the last hour of my wait for the plane, I became bored enough to look through my paperwork again. I looked at the photos. I reviewed the documents. It was while I was reviewing the documents that I noticed something very very weird, something that seemed to support the story I had been told. The documents were the autopsy records for Andrew Welch and the military records for one Matthew Styles. As I casually reviewed the military records, half-asleep, looking at the information disinterestedly, it occurred to me that the basic physical descriptions for the two men were very similar. They were the same height and about the same weight. The hair color was indeterminate because Welch's was gray. Eye color for both was blue. But what knocked me out was an area that described physical scars. Styles had evidently been wounded during his service in the war Frosty had referred to as the Great War. He had several scars on his right thigh and left shin. The way they were described they could easily have been the result of shrapnel or bullets. He further had a scar on his cheek, an inch-long scar that could have been the result of a childhood accident or any of a hundred other things. It was that scar that made me review Welch's autopsy report because I remembered that Andrew Welch had had a scar in the same area.

The autopsy report focused mainly on the injuries that had caused Welch's death, but there were the routine autopsy descriptions of the physical marks on the victim's body. Among those scars was the one on his right cheek—an irony considering the wounds on his face. But, weirder than that, he had scars on his right thigh and left shin—the same as those of Matthew Styles, born in 1891.

He had been murdered, but perhaps his life hadn't been cut quite so short as it first seemed.

The plane landed in a dark and cold Seattle at a little after eight. I got my Saab out of the parking lot and headed toward town. I thought about calling Sugarman, but what I would have to tell him was too depressing for me to say right now. Besides, he might remind me that the cops wanted to talk to me.

As I was heading up I-5, nearing Seattle, it came to me that I knew an address that would be fascinating to visit if I could get in—the home of Andrew Welch. I doubted it would help my case, but while I was still free and curious it was something I really wanted to see—how this guy had lived when he was not in Mill City. Who was he when he was out of town and living whatever life he had lived on behalf of Forster and the institute?

I turned off at an exit downtown and searched for the building. It was a tall, beautiful, granite, art-deco building just up the hill from town, east of the freeway, toward an area called "Pill Hill" because of all the medical buildings. I parked, got out of the car, and walked to the polished granite entrance, noting the brass on the frame of the revolving door and the shine and polish of the lobby. The place had a concierge, making it more difficult than I liked to gain entrance.

Then, remembering my old career, I barged through the door and walked up to the concierge. She was a blonde woman of thirty, overqualified for this job, and bucking for brigadier general.

"Taxi," I said.

"We didn't order a taxi."

"One of your tenants, a Mr. Walsh."

"I don't recall a Walsh. Let me look." She turned to consult her records. I crossed the short lobby and pressed the elevator button, then hovered between the elevator and the front desk.

"I'll just go on up. He said he needed help with some bags. He's on the top floor."

I got lucky at that moment because the phone rang, causing a further diffraction of her attention.

"All right," she said, waving her hand at me, preferring to trust me rather than deal with it anymore. "But I think the name is Welch."

It gave me goosebumps to hear his name uttered by a stranger's voice in this place far removed from Mill City or the desert. I stepped onto the elevator when it arrived and pushed the button for floor twenty-one.

The elevator had dark wood paneling inside and brass buttons to select the floors. There were a couple of mirrors inset into the paneling, and I stared dolefully at myself as I soared skyward.

"Still here, I see," I said to myself.

I stepped off at twenty-one and looked for the apartment number I had committed to memory. I arrived at the door, then dug in my pocket for my key ring. I looked for the key I had put on the ring some weeks ago when Xanthia and I were still in Mill City, still together, still safe. I put it in the lock and turned it to the right. The deadbolt moved and I pushed the door slowly open.

I was startled that the door opened. I'd assumed my luck wouldn't run this far. Now that I was inside the apartment, even with a key, I felt like a burglar. I shut the door and turned on the entryway light.

It was a gorgeous place. Not that I had expected otherwise. The entryway featured an English highboy decorated with ivory Chinese figures. More Chinese art hung from the walls.

I walked into the living room. The view was staggering. Welch was dead and creating havoc in my life, but I was still impressed by the things he had owned and the places he had lived. I stood in the darkness for a minute, looking out at the cityscape and the Sound beyond. Then I turned on a small lamp on an end table. The living room featured a marble fireplace, more gorgeous furniture, an Oriental carpet, several large cabinets, and an armoire. Nearby was a dining area, equally elegant.

I quickly searched the apartment. There were two bedrooms, both beautifully appointed, but containing no clues. There were items that could have been considered personal, a few clothes, a couple of watches, toiletries, and the like. But there were no records that identified the occupant. I didn't locate any sort of study, and the drawers in the small kitchen contained only cooking utensils.

I looked around the kitchen until I found an ashtray. I lit a cigarette and moved into the living room. I enjoyed befouling his air this way, even though he wasn't here to appreciate it. I looked out the window and smoked, halfway satisfied just to be using this beautiful apartment. It wasn't much compensation for my troubles, but it was better than nothing. I wondered if I should spend the night here. Probably not. Sooner or later the concierge would want the cabby out of the building.

A small leather chest sitting near the fireplace caught my eye. It was probably just for decorative purposes, but I picked it up and took it to the sofa. I opened it. It was a treasure chest of memorabilia. I took out the items and put them on the coffee table. They included a straight razor, some old marbles, a small case containing perfume dated 1912, a railroad timetable from Chicago's South Shore Line sometime in the thirties, ruby cufflinks inset with diamonds, a map of Los Angeles in the 1920s, various French coins and notes, a leather-bound copy of *The Complete Works of Shakespeare* published in Philadelphia in 1879, a World War I naval cap, an old penknife, a box of Dr. Morse's Indian Root Pills, and a deck of Southern Lines playing cards. Then I found something I'd rather not have found. It was a military identification dated 1918. The name on the card was Matthew A. Styles. I experienced that involuntary rippling of the flesh that people refer to as your hair standing on end.

I put the card on the table and lit another cigarette. I turned out the light and stared out the window. World War I didn't seem so long ago at the moment. All of recorded history seemed to have collapsed for me so that two thousand years didn't seem such a long time ago. The Romans, working and eating and building, and the moments going by so subtly and quickly that they couldn't have predicted that before they knew it two thousand years would have passed and it would be all over for them.

I had a history of this kind of thinking, of course, so I stopped it soon enough. I went to the liquor cabinet I had found and poured myself a glass of scotch. I had just taken a sip of it and turned the lamp back on when I turned toward the door and was confronted by the old man with the white hair, mustache, and horn-rimmed glasses who had offered me a ride in the desert a few days earlier. He was a little odder than usual because he was now in Seattle, where I wouldn't have expected to see him, and he was still wearing a Hawaiian shirt and Bermuda shorts.

I was plenty startled, but I couldn't think of a reasonable response. I put the drink down on an end table.

"How about offering me one?" he asked. I had left my cigarettes on the coffee table. He went to the table, took one, lit it, and stood in the middle of the room. He carried a beat-up briefcase, which he tossed onto a chair.

"Who the hell are you?" I said acidly.

"I'm Wallace Billings," he told me. "Who the hell are you?"

"How did you get in here?"

"Like an idiot you left the door open. I said, who are you?"

"I'm Scott Moody. What do you want?"

"I want to know what your connection is to the Longevity Institute."

"I don't have a connection. What's your interest?"

"If you don't have a connection, what the hell were you doing following Dr. Forster all over the place?"

"I don't know who you are or what you want."

Billings pushed his glasses up on his nose. "Look, Moody, I'm not fooling around. I'm looking for my daughter. I've been actively looking for my daughter for four years now. I don't have much patience, especially with scumbags like you." The old man, whom I saw as a candidate for a rest home, had a lot more vigor than I was prepared for. He was fit, like a man who did weight lifting; and further, as he showed me by lifting his loud Hawaiian shirt, he was armed with a .38 revolver in a small leather holster attached to the belt of his Bermuda shorts. "Do you get my drift?" he asked.

"I don't have a connection to the Longevity Institute." I looked toward the doorway of the apartment, wondering if I could run faster than a bullet.

"That's bullshit and we both know it." He moved forward and jabbed his finger into my sternum.

"Oww!" I said. "Hey, c'mon."

"Sorry," he said, backing off, "but I'm pissed. I've been following you for two weeks. I had to follow you all the way up here—without benefit of a change of clothes. Half the time I followed you, you've been outside the Longevity Institute. Want to look at some photographs of yourself over there?"

"Maybe," I said, unable to resist sarcasm. I was calculating how to approach this. "I have been watching the Longevity Institute. I don't consider that much of a connection. I'm looking for a girlfriend who's missing, and the word I had is that *she* had some connection to the place. I haven't had any luck at finding her, however, and I'm about to give up and leave for other parts."

"Where are you from?"

"Spokane."

"Washington?"

"I didn't know there was another Spokane."

"Wiseass," he said. "Who's the girlfriend?"

"Allison Brady," I told him, coming up with a name that combined my daughter's name with the Brady Bunch.

"More bullshit. I've got to tell you again that I'm not kidding. I may be an old fucker by your reckoning, but I box, I'm armed, and I don't give a damn about you. I'd guess that your girlfriend is Xanthia Welch. Her father was Andrew Welch, now deceased."

"How do you know that? What's *your* connection to the Longevity Institute?" I reached for a cigarette and sat on the sofa. Billings sat in a chair. We were silently agreeing to have a conversation.

Billings took a cigarette out of my pack and lit it. He was

kind of casual about being a health nut—weight lifter and smoker was a weird combination. "As I told you, I'm looking for my daughter. She got involved with this institute and they defrauded her. She lost a lot of money—family money—almost all she had. I haven't seen her in the last four years. The few times we talked it was over the phone. When we talked, she talked about revenge against that place. I'm trying to find her before she acts and gets herself into more trouble than she needs."

If I could only get her name. If I could only get this guy to talk to the police in Mill City. "It may be a little late. Don't you think she might have been involved in the death of Andrew Welch?"

"I don't know. I'm hoping not. I'm concerned. If she was, she'll have to face that music and I'll help her."

"Are you a private detective? Carrying a gun and all, doing surveillance. You seem to know what you're doing."

"I'm a gerontologist," he said.

I had no reply to that. I took a drag on my cigarette. Looked out the window.

"Really," he said.

"I'm pretty confused," I told him earnestly. "I'm involved in something that is not really my business, and I'm trying to find enough answers to get clear of the problem. Tell you what I'll do. I'll tell you my story if you tell me your story. Maybe we'll be able to help each other."

"That works for me," said Billings. "You first."

"I'll tell you part of my story. I'll be honest about that—it's partial. When I hear your story, I'll decide whether to tell you the rest."

"I can live with that," said Billings.

I told him about the death of Andrew Welch, about my connection to Xanthia. I told him most of the things that had happened. I left out Program Nine and Xanthia's whereabouts. I explained that I was involved for one reason only—that I was suspected of a murder I had not committed and was trying to get clear of it. Other than that I didn't want anyone to hurt Xanthia, but I realized I couldn't protect everyone everywhere.

When I had finished, Billings said, "You didn't say anything about Program Nine. Does that mean you don't know anything about it?"

"Program Nine?" I hoped I sounded baffled.

"You know—this life-extension bullshit."

"I haven't heard of it," I said.

"Well, I'll permit you the little *faux pas* of lying to me about this; the bastard probably swore you to some kind of secrecy. But I'm pretty sure you know what I mean because I know you were over there last night talking to that asshole. And the girl you are looking for was there too."

"You were watching."

"Sure I was watching. You think I came all the fucking way from Chicago to sit around my motel room?"

"I don't know what you're doing," I said. "You haven't told me your story."

"Well, then, goddamnit, I'll tell you my story. I'm looking for my daughter. Do you have any kids, Moody?"

"Yeah. A daughter."

"Okay, maybe you'll understand then. My daughter, Cynthia, isn't a kid anymore, she's almost forty years old, but she's as precious to me as she was when she was three. She's always been and will always be my little girl. We've been out of contact for four years, but really she's been gone a lot longer—it's almost fifteen years since she came out west.

"Ironically, a lot of her troubles were caused by money—the family has too much of it. We've had money since the Civil War when my grandfather made a fortune provisioning the North.

My generation, I was born in 1905, was still part of the old school—you work no matter how much money you have. But my daughter was spoiled by my late wife. She was treated almost like a child's doll. I love her, but she's self-absorbed, selfish. When she graduated with a degree in English, I thought she might become an editor or a writer, but instead, when she came into her trust money in 1955, she started traveling and spending money. And she had a lot of money. Her trust provided more than four million dollars a year."

I whistled involuntarily.

"I told you the family had more money than it knew what to do with," Billings said. "You want to see some pictures of her?"

"Okay."

He retrieved the battered briefcase, reached into one of the pockets, and pulled out a tattered manilla envelope. He brought out half a dozen photographs. Some were school photos, others were snapshots of family. The pictures were of a teenage girl, a young woman in her twenties, a pretty woman in her thirties. They were all the same person. And I recognized her. She was not Cynthia Billings to me; she was Mrs. Allbright. She wasn't as pretty as she had been in her youth, and she had a terrible scar on one side of her face. She was Welch's neighbor.

"I've met your daughter," I told him.

"Where? When?"

I explained the circumstances.

"I'm not surprised she was near Welch. I don't think it means she killed him." The way he said it, though, sounded like he was skating on thin ice.

I spread the photos out on the coffee table. She had been a pretty girl, a pretty young woman. None of the photos indicated any kind of scar. She was perfect.

I pulled out my wallet and took out a picture of Allison. "This is my daughter," I said. I don't know what made me do it. Seeing his daughter just brought out the reflex. And I missed her so.

Billings smiled, chuckled. "She's a cutie," he said. "She looks like a little imp."

"She can be."

He handed the photo back.

"So what happened to your daughter?" I asked. "She could have been an editor, but she didn't want a career?"

"No. She did the worst thing people with money can do—she lived off the money. She became a kind of child philanthropist, helping out all kinds of nutty people. In the sixties it got worse. She moved to San Francisco, where she got involved in the hippie movement and wacko religions.

"Of course we stopped having civil conversations because I was so damned mad at her.

"Around 1970 she met Andrew Welch. Welch convinced her that she could live to a hundred and twenty and still be a young woman. 'You'll never reach fifty in biological years,' he told her." Billings paused long enough to grab another of my cigarettes. "I don't know what the hell was supposed to kill her at a hundred and twenty if she never reached fifty," he said disgustedly.

"So what next?" I asked. I was hooked, listening like a child at bedtime.

Billings exhaled a cloud of cigarette smoke. He fiddled with my lighter. He looked tired. Old, even. "I find that telling this story is wearing me down a little. You hungry?"

I thought about it. I had not eaten all day except for a snack on the plane. "I could eat." It struck me odd that we were going to treat each other like ordinary social acquaintances, considering the circumstances.

"Well, let's go then," he said, standing and putting his brief-case in order, tucking in his gun, and poking the cigarette into his mouth.

I remembered where we were. "You know, I think it's going to be a problem leaving. I might want to get back in here. I haven't finished looking around yet."

"Isn't this your place?"

"Does this look like my place?"

"Hey, I can afford this place and I don't look like so much."

"Well, it's not my place. I'm surprised you don't know. This is Andrew Welch's apartment."

"Well, I'll be damned. I've been trying to locate his hideouts. You've already looked around?"

"Some." I pointed to the assortment of items that I'd located in the little leather chest.

He put his briefcase down and studied them. "So you think this means Welch was somehow actually an old guy named Matthew Styles and these are mementos of the old days."

"So you know about Styles."

"I've been following Welch for a long time."

"So what do you think? Don't you believe Welch was Styles?"

"Not if Styles was supposed to be in his eighties."

"I don't see any other explanation," I said. "You know I have records that would strongly indicate that Styles and Welch were the same person. And they aren't records that anyone manufactured because I got them independently. One of them is Welch's autopsy report that shows scars and other features that are exactly the same as the military record for Matthew Styles, who served in World War I. Not to mention that Welch had other belongings and identification that belonged to Matthew Styles, or that his sister, who claims to be younger than him, says that his real name was Styles."

I was pretty sure that I had some pretty convincing evidence that would require some explaining, but Billings merely looked irritated.

"You're the most naive bastard I've ever met. Let's assume I'm right and that this is a scam. Let's say that I want to establish my identity as someone older than my true age. To begin with I could start by searching for records of people of the right age—people already dead—who have my general traits—height, weight, eye color. It might take a while, but you agree that that is possible, right?"

"Sure."

"Then what could I do? What could I do as the final step in the process—enough of a step to be convincing, at least to the gullible?"

"I don't know." My mind was blank in a way only an ex-mental patient's mind can be blank.

"I'll give you a hint," he said, with an emphasis that indicated he was giving the hint to an idiot. "His coconspirator is a plastic surgeon."

A little light went on. A dim little idiot light that illuminated a brain occupied by a half-wit.

"They gave him the scars he needed in order to appear to be Matthew Styles," I said. I was the star pupil in a Special Education classroom.

"Bingo."

"So exactly how do you think this worked? How would Welch use this secret identity? Why go to such lengths? Welch was wealthy. He didn't need the money."

"If Welch was wealthy, it was from stealing the money; but I think a lot of the wealth is phony—to make it appear he has money. Rich people trust you if you're rich.

"As to how Welch did things, I think it was like this: he would seek to meet women who had money, middle-aged women worried about getting older. At first it would be a pleasant romantic interlude with an attractive, wealthy bachelor. Then, I think, he would accidentally on purpose begin to reveal this supposedly *secret* identity—Matthew Styles. He would appear to try to keep it from them, which would make it seem all the more plausible and interesting. Eventually he would trot out all the records and all the mementos and the stories of the old days, and they would see him as this almost immortal figure. Then is when the real work began. He would introduce them to the other members of the club. They would begin to see the possibilities for their own lives. After that, getting their money and agreement was the easiest thing in the world."

"You don't think that they would be skeptical?" I was remembering my time with the members of Program Nine.

"Not if they aren't any brighter than you. Besides, if they aren't interested, you say Sayonara and go on to the next one— like any other kind of sales. But I think he had a knack for finding people who wanted to believe in the Age of Aquarius."

Billings walked into the kitchen and began rummaging around. "Let's get something to eat," he said.

I took a seat on the bar that looked in on the kitchen and watched as he rounded up TV dinners, frozen vegetables, and wine. I was enjoying his company, this camaradarie. Whoever the hell he was, it was better than being alone.

As he was working, I asked, "So what happened to your daughter after Welch, aka Matthew Styles, convinced her to enter Program Nine."

"Oh so now you've heard of Program Nine," he said sarcastically.

"Yeah. So what was it? What happened?"

"Program Nine is a hodgepodge of religion, medicine, homeopathy, diet, and bad plastic surgery," said Billings. "My daughter used to call me, excited, and tell me that she was studying yoga. She told me about her diet, which sounded horrible to me but not harmful—lots of brown rice and kale and so forth, all that horrible shit they sell in health food stores. She told me about a lot of medical monititoring—visits to the institute for batteries of tests." Billings poured two glasses of wine and handed me one. He tasted his and nodded his approval. "Some of the treatments worried me—like chelation. But the most dangerous aspect of the program was the amount of plastic surgery; she must have gone for two or three operations a year. Eventually that's what got her."

"Got her? What do you mean?"

"She was scarred in her last operation. There was an infection. I never saw it, but I heard about it."

I remembered her face, the scar. It wasn't as bad as she probably thought it was, but it was a far distance from her earlier perfection.

"And they couldn't fix it?"

"Apparently not. But by that time they had pretty much raided her trust. She wasn't broke, but she didn't have enough to interest them anymore. That's when Welch broke up with her." Billings gave me a look that conveyed his hatred and contempt for Andrew Welch. Welch had defrauded her, then had the gall to reject her when she needed him most. They had stolen most of her money. It was a hell of a thing.

"C'mon," he said, "let's eat."

Billings served the dinners at the dining table. For TV dinners they weren't bad and the extra vegetables and canned salads added a nice touch—a picnic in Andrew Welch's penthouse.

"I don't care much for Seattle," said Billings, as he began to eat, "but I'm sure glad to be out of that heat."

"What with all the old folks there, I would have thought you'd feel at home in Palm Springs," I said.

"You have a real mean streak, don't you?" Billings retorted.

"Sometimes. I'm just cranky. And, frankly, you're not what I would have expected a gerontologist to look like. I guess I just thought a gerontologist would have been younger."

"Pretty funny. I just took care of old folks long enough that I became one."

"So after your daughter's face was scarred and she ran out of money, did you see her again?"

"No. She wouldn't come home—too ashamed, I think. She wasn't entirely out of money, either; she had enough to live on, just no fortune. You'll like this part—what she did after that. You have a mean streak, so you'll think this is funny."

"What happened?"

"She moved out to the desert, to Desert Hot Springs, and took up with a biker. I think she's got her own Harley."

I didn't say anything. There were a lot of mean jokes that I might have made, but this was his daughter and I didn't think this was the way he had wanted her life to turn out. Besides, I was thinking about the Harley in Cynthia Billings's driveway when she was posing as Mrs. Allbright.

"So what do you want from me?" I asked, tired, ready to get out of this conversation and back to my journey to Mill City and jail.

"All I wanted to begin with was to find out how you fit into all of this. Now I know. You're a patsy."

"Thanks."

"But as it happens, now that I know you're not party to the scheme, I could use some help surveilling the institute—watching the activities of the doctor. For instance, if someone dies at the Convalescent Home of the Desert, I want to know if Dr. Forster was present."

"Why would you want to know that? In a nursing home people die all the time."

"True. But I think some of them are getting a helpful little push."

"C'mon, why would they kill people?"

"I think the nursing home is a dumping ground for problem clients of Program Nine."

"I don't quite get what you mean?"

"As early clients of Program Nine get older, they may notice that they aren't being helped enough to justify the amount of money they are giving. Some of them have probably been in the program for as many as ten years now. If it looks like they are going to go to the authorities, or cause any serious problems, they may be moved to the nursing home, where they take a turn for the worse."

"They couldn't get away with that."

"Oh, they could. Nursing homes aren't that well regulated. I know, I own some. All the members of Program Nine are loners. The nursing home doctor is like a god to the staff. If that doctor wants to do something to a patient, he can get it done."

"One thing is inconsistent with your theory about Program Nine."

"What's that?"

"Your daughter isn't alone. She has family. She has you."

"True. But when she came out west she was pissed off at the family and pretended she didn't have any relatives. By the time Welch and the others found out, it was too late. They were probably dependent on her money at that time. Besides, they were pretty sloppy about everything." Billings retrieved his briefcase and took a document from it. He handed it to me. "Here's some proof of that."

I studied the piece of paper. It was a death certificate for Matthew Styles. He had died in 1969.

"Still think Welch is Matthew Styles?" he asked.

"I guess not."

"What are you going to do? Are you going to help me?"

"I don't know. I was figuring on going back to Mill City, turning myself in. I'm tired. Dog tired."

"Don't be in such a hurry to give up. And hey, we've got to finish our work here before we do anything."

"I've looked around. I didn't find anything."

"Well, let's give it another shot, eh?" said Billings, with a wink. "What say we just leave our dishes on the table and don't clean up?" He got up and took another of my cigarettes. Welch would have hated both of us for what we were doing to his apartment.

"Let's have a look around," he said, flicking his ash on the rug.

He led the way down the hallway and began searching through the bedrooms. I watched him. I had been over this ground. After he had looked through the two bedrooms and the bathrooms, we were standing in the larger of the two bedrooms, a corner room with a king-sized bed, a marble fireplace, and a small love seat. This room, like all the others, had several windows and a beautiful view of the Sound and downtown.

"I wonder about that door." Billings said, indicating the white door in the corner of the room.

"We both tried it. It's locked, and I think it's closed off— probably leads to some part of another apartment."

"I don't think so. It doesn't look right to me. I think it's either another closet or some smaller room."

Billings walked out of the bedroom and I could hear him rummaging around in the kitchen. He returned with several large knives and a screwdriver. He set to work on the door. A few minutes of crunching wood and rending metal resulted in the opening of the door. He reached inside the opening and flicked a switch. An overhead light came on and illuminated a small study with a desk and a few bookshelves.

"There was a small suitcase in the hall closet," said Billings. "Get it."

I did as instructed and returned with the case. Billings was sitting at the desk, pulling papers out of the file drawer. I opened the suitcase and he started loading them in.

"What are you doing?"

"Collecting evidence," he said. "I've found letters written to Welch, and I found a journal he kept."

He unloaded the file drawer into the suitcase; then we looked around for anything else.

"Here's some interesting reading," Billings said, pulling something off the shelf. He handed it to me. It was a blue volume titled, *How to Live at the Front,* subtitled *Tips for American Soldiers.* I took it out into the bedroom and looked at it. It was written by a British soldier who had already served in World War I. It was intended to be a primer for American soldiers, an account of every-

day life in the war zone—the problems soldiers would encounter, anecdotes of the experiences of the writer and his acquaintances. It was good research material for a dirty
sonofabitch who wanted to pretend to be a veteran of that war,
who wanted to build up a set of stories he could tell that would
convince people not only of his age but of his heroism. Between
reading this and talking to Frosty Shields and others, Welch
would have had a pretty good story to tell.

There were other books that served a similar function in
other areas, books of biography and autobiography set earlier in
the century, books on daily life before World War I. The little
study Billings had discovered was the Welch research library for
his con and also was a record of some of his exploits.

When we had emptied the closet of the documents that
Billings felt were important, we took them to the living room and
sat there for a while, reading through stuff. The most compelling
documents were several letters from Cynthia Billings to Welch.
These pleaded with him to pay more attention to her. They
didn't make any direct appeal for help in getting some of her
money back, but that help was implied by the way she begged for
the return of his friendship. Billings read and reread these letters, muttering, "That dirty sonofabitch!" from time to time.

I spent most of my time looking at Welch's journal. It was a
leather-bound volume of dated pages in which he kept his calendar of future events and notes on how the previously scheduled events had gone. In it were the names of a number of ladies,
including notes on their value as prospective clients. Some featured stars by their names, indicating that they met the important requirements—interested in the program, had money, and
had very little or no family to interfere. Even under the circumstances I found some of Welch's journal funny. In margin notes
he sometimes wrote complaints, such as, "Too damn many
cruises!" and he had a point. According to his calendar for the
previous year he had been scheduled to go on four seven-day

cruises within a two-month period. But cruises were probably one of the great ways to meet wealthy widows interested in being young.

After about an hour of reading the documents, Billings and I simultaneously tossed the paperwork onto the coffee table or into the open suitcase. I had a sense that we had both reached our limit with living in Welch's mind and life.

"What now?"

"Back to Palm Springs," he said. "I'm going to put this stuff with the other evidence I've collected. Then I have another little business trip for research. After that, I think I'll be ready to call in the authorities."

"So you want me to follow this guy again?"

"It would help. I can hire someone else, but that will just take more time. I'd probably want to hire someone from out of the area—someone living in Palm Springs might know the doc."

"I suppose I could do that, but I'm not sure what that will do for me. Sooner or later I've got to decide whether or not I should go home and face the music. I don't know if staying around here will help me; and the longer I'm gone, the worse it looks from a law-enforcement perspective. And I can't see my daughter while I'm down there."

"I hope you'll consider helping me," said Billings. "The research I'm doing right now should help resolve this pretty soon. If I can get some definite proof of wrongdoing on Forster's part, I'll go to the authorities—in the medical-regulation field and in traditional law enforcement. When I do that, and it could be as soon as a couple of weeks, you could go home with some leads to offer your police department. And frankly, no matter what you think of the girl, you have to tell them where she is. You can't be such a fool that you would let yourself be prosecuted for murder while protecting her. You don't know that she didn't do it." Billings smiled impishly. "Besides," he said, "if you still believe in this life-extension crap, you don't know but what she's not too old for you. She might be forty-five or fifty, you know."

I didn't think it was funny, and Billings stopped laughing after about five minutes. He straightened up and pulled his .38 and holster off his belt. "Fucking thing hurts my side," he said. "I need to get a new holster."

"Why do you carry that thing?"

"I think these people are dangerous," he said. "Besides, I'm as wealthy as Midas. I've carried a gun for thirty years."

I offered him a cigarette and took one myself. I lit his, then mine. We were getting to be colleagues, me and this old fart who had turned up a couple of hours ago. It was very peculiar.

"I'm inclined to go along with you, but I'm a little concerned that I don't really know who you are. I'm taking everybody at their word, then finding out that they are conning me."

"I can understand that. Let me see if I can get you some references. You can call them. Then, if that's satisfactory, we can work together a little. Maybe we can get some results that will get you out of your jam."

"Maybe." But would it get Xanthia into a jam while I was at it?

"How'd you happen to have the key to this place anyway?" asked Billings.

I told him.

"Hot damn. That means we were legal all the way here. You have the key as the agent of the current owner. And we can get back in whenever we want."

"I can," I said, feeling petulant.

"You can," he allowed. "Now let's check on flights to Palm Springs." He reached for Welch's phone.

The next flight out was not until morning, so we gathered up our evidence, locked the door, and left. In the lobby the concierge barely took notice of us, figuring, I guess, that I had found Mr. Welch.

We booked a couple of motel rooms near the airport. I slept, but that night I was back at Giza, never outside, only inside the pyramid, buried in a horrific ceremony, then sealed in the tomb. From time to time I woke myself, got up, and walked around, looked outside; but the moment I lay down again, the pyramids returned. It was that way all night long.

In the morning I got up, brushed off the dirt from my imagined grave, and flew to Palm Springs.

When we got in, Billings said he'd loan me his car to use for surveillance so they wouldn't be as likely to spot me. He suggested I follow the doctor's car from at least a block away, since I could always pick him up again at one of his institutions in the unlikely event that I lost him. He said that all he needed was to make sure that the doctor didn't leave the area, and that if he did, he would like to know where he went. He wanted a log kept. When was the doctor in his office? When was he at the nursing home? Was the bodyguard always with him?

"What are you going to be doing?" I asked when he had finished his instructions.

"I'll be doing some research out of town for a few days. I'll fill you in later. I'm just looking into Forster's background. I'm hoping it will be a break that will put him in the kind of hot water we need to get law enforcement to go after all of his records."

"Why can't you tell me?"

"Don't worry, I will."

"Where will you be?"

"Just leave messages for me at my motel. I'll be checking every few days."

"Okay."

Then we left the restaurant and exchanged cars.

I stood there a moment, stifled by the heat, but used to being stifled now. I got into Billings's car, started it, turned up the air conditioner to full, and drove to a parking spot near, but not too near, the Longevity Institute of the Desert.

I followed Dr. Forster for the next few days. I did my best to be discreet, not to be spotted. I did it partly because I wanted to be able to complete the job, but also because I wanted for once to be an effective private investigator. I didn't want Billings to come back and have failure as the only result of my surveillance. So, when in doubt, I stayed even farther away from Dr. Forster's Lincoln Continental than I probably needed to, and parked farther away from the institute. Sometimes I left the car an extra block away, parked among others, so it would not be noticed, then kept an eye out from beneath a tree. When I saw the doctor and his bodyguard emerge, I would hotfoot it to the car, start it, and come around the corner just as they were pulling out of their parking lot.

The doctor was pretty cooperative in keeping to a routine that was easy to follow. He spent a lot of time at the institute or the Convalescent Home of the Desert. Usually he went to the convalescent home two times a day and stayed for about half an hour.

I kept a log so that I could document exactly where he had been each day.

11:35: Dr. Forster and his bodyguard leave the Institute of the Desert in doctor's Lincoln Continental.

11:40: Dr. Forster and his bodyguard arrive at the Convalescent Home of the Desert.

12:05: Dr. Forster and his bodyguard leave the Convalescent Home of the Desert.

12:15: Dr. Forster and his bodyguard arrive in downtown Palm Springs. Go inside Nate's Delicatessen for lunch.

They are joined by two other middle-aged men,
unidentified.

Sometimes the doctor's wife joined them. On a few occa-
sions another fat, older man wearing a Hawaiian shirt came with
them when they left the Convalescent Home of the Desert, joining them for lunch. The older man appeared, by his manner
and the fact that he came from the convalescent home, to be a
doctor.

I didn't see Xanthia. She was apparently still hiding out,
probably in the big house on the hill to which the doctor, his
wife, and the big bruiser of a bodyguard returned nightly.

Each night, after the group had returned to the big house,
I would wait a respectable distance from the house, waiting to
see if anyone went wandering. I wondered if Xanthia would try
to come and see me again, or if she expected that I had dutifully
left town to return to my fate in Mill City. I was quietly resentful
that that might be her expectation, and as the nights wore on,
I bore a small grudge, feeling I was probably being used, again,
by a woman who expected me to be the guy who took the heat
for her.

My nights ended at about midnight when I decided that
there was no further reason to tail them since I was working
alone and couldn't be around every minute. I would return to
the motel for the comfort of a bowl of cereal in my room before
bedding down to my pyramid dreams. They had been pretty con-
sistent every night until the fourth night, when I had a new
dream.

It began sometime during the middle of the night because
I felt deep in my sleep, deep in the throes of nightmarish consciousness—when it feels like you are awake, but you have some
knowledge that the tunnel vision, the inability to move or save
yourself, the muffled sound, or no sound, means that you are not
really conscious but dwelling in dreamland again.

In this dream I was in my motel room, face down, dead to the world, when three strange men, perhaps Egyptians, came in stealthily and held me down. My panic and my screams went unheard, silent even to me as they held me down, the one man pressing his bare knee into my back while another prepared a long syringe, which he stabbed into the flesh at the top of my buttocks. I began to cry in my dream, as I had cried when, in the mental hospital, a similar scene had occurred as three orderlies and a nurse had cornered me, in a manic rage in the cafeteria, held me up against a cafeteria table, and subdued me with an injection of Thorazine.

The result this time was exactly the same as that time in the hospital as my consciousness plunged into a deep pool, fell forward, and swirled down to the center of the earth, toward darkness.

# Eleven

When I woke the next morning, if you could call it waking, I was sure that I was still in a dream. One thing was certain; I was having a tough time waking up. I was, of course, not myself, in the same way that I was not myself every morning of my life. I went through the usual process of trying to discover my identity, my location, and my current life circumstance.

Identity wasn't too difficult, though, as usual, it was a little disappointing to discover that I was still Scott Moody, loser, man with a bad attitude, man in a jam that was ruining his life. I remembered that I was in Palm Springs somewhere and that I had been following Dr. Forster, partly on my own behalf and partly on behalf of an old gerontologist named Billings.

What I was having a real problem with was my location and my physical circumstance. I wasn't sure where I should have been waking up, but the hallway of some unfamiliar building didn't seem right. It was a kind of unpleasant pastel green and the lighting was twilight, partly from the low-powered fluorescent lights scattered along the hallways, and partly from light that came from the hallway intersection that I could see about ten feet ahead of me.

I was sitting, I soon discovered, in a wheelchair. What was even worse—the revelation that sent me into a panic—was the fact that I couldn't move. And I didn't feel well. Not well at all.

My stomach was upset, and I had some vague pains and discomfort. I was drooling a little from my lower lip, but I couldn't feel it in a normal way; it was kind of like your mouth when it is numb from Novocain and you're drooling over your half-dead lip. I wanted to yell, to call someone, but I didn't seem to be able to do that either. I was heavy everywhere. I could feel my muscles' intention to move, but couldn't get them to follow through—the weight, the paralysis, was too great. I could move my mouth just the slightest amount, a movement like opening it to speak. But as I moved it, I felt all of the muscles of my mouth and throat freeze. And whenever I tried this action, tried to speak, I also found that a gag reflex nearly caused me to vomit rather than speak. This reflex discouraged me from trying very often.

Was I still dreaming? Where was I? What had happened to me?

I could still hear, but initially there was nothing to hear. The hallway was silent, cool, twilight—a passage in that pyramid I had feared all those years in all those dreams.

I was not cold. I was wearing hospital pajamas—not a gown, but pajamas with slippers—and I had a light flannel blanket wrapped around me, covering my arms so that when I looked down—without moving my head because I could not move—all I could see of my body were my lower legs and my slippered feet on the wheelchair footrest.

I was pretty panicky, but there was nothing I could do to respond to my panic that would not elevate my blood pressure and further upset my stomach. I waited for some revelation. I even considered going back to sleep, thinking that the next time I woke was bound to be better than this. But I couldn't sleep. I sat and waited.

After some period of time—I had no idea how long; I had lost all touch with reality—I heard voices around the corner ahead of me. They were female voices, chatty, laughing occasionally.

"Well, we'd better get him settled in," said one voice, and shortly after that, two women dressed as nurses came around the corner and walked toward me. One of them was older, in her fifties, with a pleasant dumpling face that women of that age often get. She had a dumpling body to go with it, covered by the white uniform. Her companion was younger, in her late twenties perhaps, and dressed in a uniform that in some way said she was not quite the same rank as her companion. Perhaps one was a registered nurse and the other a practical nurse.

I tried to speak to them, to express my panic and fear, but nothing emerged and once again I nearly vomited just from trying to speak. My eyes were watery and I could feel junk that had gathered around the corners during the night, but couldn't reach them to clear the stuff away.

"He's so young," said the pretty nurse. "What happened that he ended up here?" I thanked her for the question, but wondered why she acted like I was an object rather than a human being who could hear her every word.

"Stroke, I guess," said the older woman. "He came in early this morning from L.A. He'd been in a hospital there for about two weeks, according to the paperwork. I guess he's a transient. Dr. Walden takes about one charity patient every six months. They found him in this condition in a mission or something, and they couldn't identify him. He didn't improve, so they needed to move him to a long-term care facility. They're trying to figure out who he is, I guess, so they can notify his family— that's what the driver said who brought him in. The only thing they've got so far are his fingerprints and his description, so it may be difficult to do."

"Is he going to stay like this?" the young woman asked, then, "Oh, he's drooled on his chin." She was standing over me now, a pretty brunette with shiny black eyes and curly black hair. She took the flannel blanket, shaped part of it into a napkin, and wiped the drool from my lips and chin. My skin felt just like it felt when the dentist medicated me. I was in full panic now, terrified, electric with panic, but you couldn't tell it, even from looking at my eyes. I just sat there. Only a tear from one of my eyes would have given someone a clue. The young nurse saw it and wiped it away, then wiped my eyes generally, clearing away the gunk from the night. I didn't understand my present condition, or if it would improve, but I wanted her to stay around. At least she noticed me.

"We don't know if he's going to get better," said the other nurse, going around behind me and grabbing the handles of the wheelchair with the assurance of a truck driver at the controls of an 18-wheeler. She released the brake and pushed me away while the young nurse was still wiping my eyes.

They wheeled me down the hallway, around the corner, and down the other hallway to a room with two beds in it. The bed nearest the door was already occupied by an old man lying on his side. He coughed for a couple of minutes as we entered as if to remind them that he also existed. His coughs were phlegmy and liquid, like an emphysema cough. What the hell had happened to me that I ended up like this? How had I ended up in L.A. for two weeks? How *could* it have been two weeks? I didn't remember anything before this morning.

It took them a little doing to get me into the bed. They had to call an orderly to help, a big, blond, young guy, six-foot-six at least, with one lazy eye and a pleasant manner, who kept saying things like, "You doing okay, Mr. Doe?" each time he did something designed to make me comfortable. It was that sort of thing that really rattled me—the everyday normalcy of it from their point of view, the fact that none of them was saying, "What the hell is he doing here? Why can't he walk? Why can't he talk? What do you mean no one knows who he is? He's not John Doe; he's Scott Moody. He has a family. Where is his family? Call a team of doctors; we've got to fix this."

But nobody said anything remotely like that. They said

things like, "There, that's better, isn't it? You're all settled in now," and, "Sally, you'll have to get a couple of IVs set up. He needs to be hydrated and there's a prescription for heparin to help prevent further stroke damage. Later, you're to start feeding him soft solids. His swallow reflex still works they say."

And they left.

I remained at my post, lying half upright in the hospital bed. I had one IV attached to my limp left arm and the television was on to *Good Morning America*. If I had died and this was life after death, then there *was* a hell and I was in it.

I kept thinking that sooner or later I would wake up from this nightmare, but during the next two hours that didn't happen. I tried to move, I tried to speak, but that didn't work. I was paralyzed and I was tired, out of it, like I was on painkillers. I was stuck watching *Good Morning America*. I tried not to watch because I was so upset about my condition that I thought I had to do something to change it—and thinking was all I could do. I couldn't move or call my family or even talk to a doctor. But *Good Morning America* continued to be the only stimulation, so I began to watch it.

And as naturally as that I began to fall into a routine. It wasn't that I didn't return to thinking about my condition and wondering what had happened and trying to remember what had happened, it's just that no thinking I did helped me to remember or understand. Soon, while I hoped for a change in circumstances or for someone to rescue me, I concerned myself with waiting for the next bit of comfort or entertainment. At other times I thought about my life. I thought about my daughter and ex-wife. I wondered if they would ever know where I was. I cried, of course, at such times. At other times I thought about my life nostalgically, reliving it and enjoying it. I also mourned its loss, but it wasn't so much a sad time as a recreation, a way of passing time.

I got to know the nurses. Some of the nurses were nice; some of them were kind of mean.

And then there was Sally.

I had met Sally on the first day. She was the dark-haired, cute nurse who had helped settle me in. She was just over five feet tall. The second time she came into the room she was with another older nurse. "He's so young!" she said about me to the other nurse. "He shouldn't be here like this. He's so young. And he's kind of cute, don't you think?"

"I just try to take care of them," said the other nurse. "I try not to think about whether they're cute or not." She smiled at Sally. "Of course that's not much of an issue with most of them in this place."

And the older nurse started giving Sally instructions on what she was to do when she cared for me. After the other woman left, Sally told me her name as she was giving me a sponge bath. She said she was adopting me. She wasn't joking; she meant it.

And I needed adopting. Humiliating as it was, I was glad to have the attention from one person in the hospital who cared about me in a personal way. Especially since I had lost the ability to do anything for myself, even go to the bathroom. That part was hard, accepting being taken care of in that way, having simply to witness the processes of my body, which continued without my controlling them, then having to witness other people cleaning them up. For that, I preferred the people taking care of me be the ones I didn't like, the older nurse or the others who were more indifferent. I preferred that Sally take care of me in the more acceptable routines—feeding, massaging, and bathing me.

I took to her as if I were her husband and she were my wife, caring for me after my unfortunate accident, whatever it had been. She came most days, except for weekends, and spent at least a couple of hours with me—usually not continuous time, but interspersed during the day. The longest time would be the time of my bath or my massage. The bath was performed regularly to keep me clean and prevent bedsores. I felt sorry for myself, but I was probably better off than most other patients because I had been adopted. Not all were so lucky.

The mornings when Sally came to bathe and massage me were the happiest of my life now. The movement of my limbs under her manipulation and the massaging of them with a warm cloth or sponge were the nearest I came to the sensation of having a body or remembering that I had been a man, rather than a dead weight in a hospital bed. I was bathed in her presence too, alive with her pleasant company, as she prattled on about daily events in her life and observations about how I appeared to be doing. She behaved like a wife whose husband has become disabled, but she didn't mind so much because it allowed her to care for someone and to have that someone be unable to resist the caring or to have expectations of her—almost the same as the joy of having a doll that you could dress up.

And later on, I also had Russell to entertain me.

Russell was an old man who wheeled his chair into my room sometime during the second week, after I had begun to make my adjustment to a silent infirmity.

He simply pulled his wheelchair up to my bed and started talking. "My name's Russell," he said. "I used to be a reporter. I never got a degree; I wasn't one of those college boys. That was after the war though. Before the war I was an apprentice pressman at the newspaper. That's where I got the idea I wanted to be a reporter. I went to school after the war, but I dropped out after two years. I got a job and I figured why would I want to keep going to college when I had a job. During the war I was a radioman in the Pacific—on destroyers. I was quite a man then. I used to weigh one hundred and ninety pounds." He looked down at himself. "Now I'm three pounds lighter than a straw hat."

He continued relating his life to me—a silent stranger. As I listened to him I realized he was in a time warp. He was a time traveler. I was living among time travelers. They were trying to relate their lives all the time. They didn't write it down; they were oral historians. They related their histories constantly, but most people ignored them, too interested in their own brief interlude on the planet. I was a time traveler, too. I could remember the fifties, and Jackie Gleason, and *Leave It to Beaver.* I could remember Vietnam. I remembered the sixties. But I couldn't tell my tale, and if I could, nobody would have listened. Nobody was asking me to tell them about my time on the planet either. They were just waiting for me to die, or to provide a regular income from Social Security and Welfare, to be quiet and be a good patient. To be patient and die.

That became my life. Sally in the morning, Russell in the afternoon. Television. Meals—which were wonderful even though they were mashed. I became ravenous for those meals, for that sensation of life that I felt when I could taste; one of the few things I could do with the same strength as before, something that therefore became that much more important. There were a few things I *could* do—see, hear, smell, taste. That was it. Everything else was done for me. Except the heart beating and the breathing and the thinking, but they seemed almost superfluous to me. I wondered if being able to see, hear, smell, and taste were enough reasons to go on.

Some days the nurses would decide that I had been in bed too long and they would call the orderly, help me into pajamas and a robe, put me in a wheelchair, wheel me out into the dayroom or a hallway, where I had a view of the outside, and they would let me sit there.

While I was sitting there, I remembered a place I had forgotten. It was a place a lot like this, a rest home, a convalescent center, an extended-care center—they all have such nicely euphemistic names. An elderly aunt had spent two years in a place just like this, then died.

I had visited her just once.

Since I was tired all the time, drifting in and out of sleeping and waking, I didn't require as much entertainment as I had in my former life. I would watch the other residents or look out at the lawn and the trees and be pretty content.

Some days, when I was preoccupied remembering my life, I would ignore Sally, which didn't seem right, considering she was the only one who paid me attention. But some days I was too lost in the past. Sometimes, I was lost in joyous moments, remembering my daughter's birth, or remembering sweet times with her as a child. Sometimes I was lost in regret—bad treatment of friends, transgressions in my life, my madness. One day I spent remembering a long-forgotten dog. She had been my first dog, given to me by my parents when I was a toddler. The incident I remembered with regret happened when I was about twelve. My dog, Bootsy, was an old dog by then, mangy, and slow moving. She had tried to follow my sister and I to the movies. We told her to go back, but she continued to follow, looking pathetic and forlorn when we scolded her. Finally, I yelled at her and she stayed, and I never saw her again. Later, my father said she probably went off somewhere to die. And instead of comforting her, I had yelled at her. I could never forgive myself for that. I could feel the tears forming at the corners of my eyes, then begin to run down my cheeks, little streams of tears.

"John," Sally said to me, noticing the tears, "why are you crying? What's wrong?" She wiped my tears and held my hand. "You're so sad. Don't be sad."

Gradually the tears subsided. What a way to end, I thought, crying over my dead dog while this nurse, Sally, held my hand and comforted the man she knew only as John Doe.

. . .

I didn't get a lot of medical treatment as a part of my routine and I had come not to expect it. At first I had thought this was surely some temporary condition and it would improve, or the doctors would find some way to make it improve. But other than the visits by nurses checking my IV, I didn't see much of a medical staff. I woke sometimes in the middle of the night when some older man and the orderly came into my room and gave me a shot in my lower back and then I would go out again. Whatever medication was offered, orally or by injection or IV, I took it. I didn't exactly have a choice.

Then one day my experience changed and I began to have more visits than just the one in the night. And I was a little surprised by the person who made the visits.

It was an afternoon. I was watching soap operas. This was not the best time of day for me. I was usually awake about two hours at a time, then I might be asleep for a couple of hours. During the two hours I was awake, I was trying to make it through the soap operas. These were soap operas I had become addicted to simply by the accident that the television was on to these channels during the day. It had taken awhile, but finally I was beginning to wonder if Nick was going to cheat on Samantha and whether or not the secret of Dr. Masterson was going to be revealed at the big banquet.

Just about the time the banquet was starting, a man entered the room. I didn't pay attention at first, but couldn't avoid him as he came around to my bed. I wanted to yell that I knew him when I recognized his face, but of course I couldn't yell. I couldn't remember where I had seen him either, but gradually it came to me.

He was a chubby man in his late fifties. He wore horn-rimmed glasses, had graying black hair kept short and combed with Vitalis or Brylcreem. He was tanned and had lots of little liver spots on his face and arms and hands. He wore a loud

Hawaiian shirt, but the white name tag on his pocket identified him as Dr. Walden, Medical Director.

I knew he was a doctor. Or, at least, I had suspected it because he was the man who had accompanied Dr. Forster when I was tailing him. I had seen him from some distance, but knew it was the same man.

What did that mean? It meant that I was in that very nursing home—the nursing home out in the desert, the Convalescent Home of the Desert. How had I ended up here?

But the doctor didn't tell me anything. He simply looked at me, lifted my eyelids to look at my eyes, turned my head to look at my face and neck, lifted my arm and studied it, then let it drop. Then he left the room for a minute or two and returned with two syringes. He pulled the sheet down, pushed me part way onto my side, and jabbed the needles of the syringes into my lower back. It hurt. I could still feel there even if I couldn't move.

After that, I began to live on another planet. I heard the angels sing, the world began spinning, my eyes shut, and I went to live in the pyramid again.

After that day, I began seeing the doctor a lot. He came pretty much every afternoon and gave me another shot. I didn't look forward to that part of the day—the shot put me out and it put me into my nightmares, when it didn't put me into total darkness.

He always came in alone. He always brought the syringes. There was no banter or pleasantry. Just the shots, then I went to heaven or hell, whichever had been scheduled by my mind for that day.

Then, one day, there was variation.

I was out in the hallway again, parked, like half a dozen others, mostly older patients. We sat out there for hours as people walked by us as if we didn't exist. We weren't complaining so how could anything be wrong?

I was about to take up my usual activity—thinking about my past life in preparation for exiting this one—when the doctor came storming down the hallway. This always frightened me a little because I thought it might be time for my shots.

But I needn't have worried. He entered a room just two doors away from where I had been parked. He was in there ministering to a patient for several minutes. I heard Russell, my old visitor from across the hall, begin yelling. It was common for him to yell once in a while. Sometimes it was because his bedding needed changing. Sometimes he yelled as a complaint about the food. I had heard the nurses take care of him, then talk about him afterward. The doctor usually wasn't around when he had a fit, but this time he was. After a few minutes of this yelling, the doctor emerged from the other room. A nurse was approaching up the hallway.

"That's Mr. Perkins," she said.

"I know who it is," the doctor snapped. "I'll take care of that goddamned bellowing," and he headed toward the room, shouting something about morphine to the nurse.

"Doctor, that's a very large dosage for him. He usually gets . . ."

"I said get it, and I mean *get* it, or I'll get it myself!" shouted the doctor. His face was the color of sunburn and his eyes were exploding out of their sockets. He looked like a good candidate for a heart attack, and even in my lethargy I was hoping for it.

But no heart attack came. Instead, the nurse returned with the requested syringe and handed it to him. He told the nurse to accompany him and they entered the room where Mr. Perkins was yelling. There was a little more yelling; then Mr. Perkins was quiet. After a moment or two the doctor and the nurse came out of the room.

"He'll be fine," the doctor assured the nurse as he returned to his other duties, dropping the spent syringe into her hand.

But Mr. Perkins was not fine. I happened to be parked in the hallway the next day when they took him out on a gurney. What the hell. It was better for him anyway. It wasn't like he was going to get any better. It was the same for me. I wasn't going to recover from whatever had happened to me. I wasn't going to be able to walk or talk normally again. What was the point of going on? I wished I could yell or do something obnoxious so that the doctor would come and relieve me of the burden of living.

After that, I didn't have any more visits from Russell. I didn't expect there to be anything more that I could count as a loss, but Russell was a loss. I missed the recounting of his life—like a very long book that someone was reading to me, that the author was reading to me, based on his own life.

I had another shock to endure, one that gave me a clue as to the circumstances that had put me in this place and that guided me toward the destiny that awaited me in the succeeding days.

It was an afternoon again. It was sunny and warm in the room. The soap opera blared its unrelentingly banal and slow-motion emotional ballet. My eyes were fixed on the television when, with a bit of a commotion, several men entered my room.

When they came into my line of vision—I couldn't turn my head to see what was going on—I recognized Dr. Walden. Then I saw the giant blond orderly. Lars was his name. I had learned by experience that Lars was not up to normal intelligence. He came into the room fairly often to perform menial tasks, to clean things, straighten things, and to do some of the duties with the patients that the nurses didn't want to do. He argued with them about small details and was given to sudden outbursts, tantrums really, when he didn't get his way about something as small as the location of a wastebasket or the placement of items on the stands and tables. He was very ritualistic. He always wanted things done in exactly the same way, usually the way he had been taught by Dr. Walden, who appeared to be his god. He didn't seem to really be a bad guy, but like a lot of people who have limited intelligence, he was literal in his interpretation of life. He complied obsessively with the rules and hated anyone who didn't.

Finally, I saw the man I least expected to see, Dr. Forster. Forster looked right at me as Dr. Walden came around to my left side, manhandling my head and arm to examine my condition. I could smell the wet, heavy odor of his breath and the unmistakable signs of alcohol, probably whisky. When he was done, he turned to Dr. Forster. By this time Lars had performed a few minor duties in the room, mainly to do with my roommate, the old man with emphysema, and had left.

Walden said, "I don't know for sure, but I'd say about another week. I'll up the IV a bit—that should increase the reaction."

"As soon as possible," said Forster. "Just as soon as possible."

Dr. Walden nodded, took a cigarette from the pocket of his shirt, and stuck it into his mouth. He didn't light it; there was a no-smoking rule. I wanted Lars to return because smoking was one thing he really couldn't stand and he might even have struck his little god, Walden, for that infraction.

For my part, I wanted to ask Walden for a smoke, even if he *was* a rotten no-good murdering bastard. But, of course, I couldn't.

Dr. Walden was taking an old-fashioned Zippo lighter out of his pocket as Dr. Forster headed out of the room and I heard the soft pop as he twirled the lighter's wheel and the flame took.

"That's a disgusting habit," I heard Forster say.

And they were gone.


And now I knew what my fate would be and why. It wasn't clear whether I had had a stroke or not. Perhaps I *had* had a stroke. But it looked to me that, in some fashion, I was a man marked for a fairly quick death. "As soon as possible." Somehow Dr. Forster had seen me as a threat, and Dr. Walden and this hospital were his instruments of death.

I wanted to be angry and to do something about it, but by now I had decided that I could do nothing more. Whatever had happened to me, whatever they were doing to me, it was effective. I had no physical ability whatsoever, and psychologically I was broken. I had begun developing bedsores. I had pretty much covered a nostalgic review of my life to the point that thinking about it made me so morose I could barely stand it. No matter what I thought, the overwhelming realization was simply that I had lost my life—that I would never see my daughter, or my ex-wife, or my father, or my friends. They were as far gone as my old dog. No matter what love I wanted to express, or apologies for wrongs done, I would not have the chance to see them or do that. Nothing could be resolved but my life, and that would be resolved by its end.

And now that I knew that I was a helpless man marked for death, I was ready for them to get it over with.

Sometimes, as I went through my occasional roller coaster of emotion, I tried to find my muscles again, to see if there was some way I could make myself move, suddenly recover, miraculously be able to run from the institution, run as far as I could to anywhere—even if I couldn't see my daughter or loved ones again—just live in hiding somewhere, some quiet life.

The capper, though, was yet to come, and made for a kind of change in attitude. It happened on a day when I was being pushed out into the hallway for a period in the dayroom. I was being moved by Lars, whom I now suspected of being in on this little conspiracy, though he was, no doubt, too slow to realize its moral consequence. I sat in the chair and was pushed to the dayroom, where I would stay until they remembered to come and get me, and then I would be put back in the bed and later on I would get some shots. I was thinking about how good it was to at least move around now and then.

As we rolled past the door, I noticed an old man in the room across the hall from mine—the room Russell used to live in. I didn't get a good look at him because I couldn't swivel my head for a better look, but under the circumstances I was sure I recognized him. And I was pretty sure he was headed for the same fate that I was. The guy I was sure I saw was Billings. Billings had been rounded up as I had been rounded up, and it was the last roundup.

What the hell were they giving us? How were we paralyzed, disabled? It had to be in the injections, the IV somehow. What a humiliating, stupid, pathetic way to be treated. What a way to lose a contest of wills. I was incensed and sad and upset.

But it didn't stop me from watching the soap opera in the dayroom the moment Lars had locked my chair in place in front of it.

Life, though you would call it that only as a cruel joke, continued. I waited in the hallways or waited in the room for death to come. Occasionally I tried to get my muscles to work, tried to see if I could possibly imagine getting enough of them functioning to crawl away. And occasionally, I had visitors, strangers, but friendly strangers.

On one afternoon, after a long struggle, I had managed to get one leg to move just a little, to work well enough, long enough to move my foot off the support so that it rested on the floor. It was pretty useless, my leg being rather limp, but I thought perhaps my feeling would come back if I continued to try.

I was about to exercise it further when I saw some children and a dog who were visiting their relatives down the hallway. The dog was a special visitor, allowed in sometimes to cheer up the residents. It was a big, friendly, yellow lab that came immediately over to me, jumped up on me, and licked my face. "Jasper!" said the girl, laughing and running over to get him. But the big dog continued to lick my face for a minute or two before she and the boy could get him under control. The blonde girl and the brown-haired boy were about to lead the dog away when the girl noticed that my foot was off the support.

For my part, I had enjoyed the visit from the dog, a part of life I had forgotten, but now I was trying to say something, struggling to say something. The girl was looking at me, seeing the struggle going on on my face. I finally managed my first words since entering the nursing home.

"Help me," I whispered.

She looked at me a moment, puzzled, then she seemed to understand.

"I'll help you," she said, and came to my side. She put her hands under my foot and lifted with all her might until she managed to lift it and return it to the support. "There," she said with satisfaction, "you're back in the chair the way you're supposed to be." And she turned and ran into the room where the young woman and boy had gone.

I rested in the wheelchair. My arms were strapped to the rests. My legs lay heavily, outstretched, ending in slipper-clad feet on the aluminum footrests. Visitors walked past me without acknowledging my presence, except for the occasional embarrassed glance that said, "Thank God I'm not you." I had reached a somewhat predictably pathetic state. If I had died at that moment it would have been a kind of sweet, poignant death, at least for me, with my last thoughts focusing on my daughter, my ex-wife, and, for a fleeting moment, even on my father.

But that was not to be. Instead, as I sat there, my head lolling a little to the left as I tried to keep it from falling backward, I saw a large figure approaching me. He seemed an apparition at first, a figure from some dreamy past. And then he was right in front of me, looking into my face. It was Ira Sugarman, still in a suit, and wearing his little porkpie hat. He was sweating profusely.

Sugarman walked behind me, and I could feel his hands on

the handles of the wheelchair. He started moving me down the hallway. An orderly was walking toward us. He gave Sugarman a questioning glance.

"My brother. We're just going for a little walk," Sugarman said to him by way of explanation.

# Twelve

Sugarman took me down the sidewalk to the left of the nursing home. The heat of the outside enveloped me as though I had been wheeled into a sauna. While it was awful, there was something wonderful about it—just the fact that I could feel it. Somehow, all the time in the nursing home I had felt a little too cold. Now I wasn't cold at all. I was aware of insufferable heat.

But I did wonder what would happen now. I was glad to be with Sugarman no matter what, but I would have had to admit that I thought my chances of survival with him were probably about the same as if I had stayed under the care of the murdering nursing home doctor. Maybe whatever was wrong with me was now irreversible. I was free and I was a vegetable.

Sugarman did some explaining as the chair rolled down the sidewalk toward the corner.

"I don't know what happened to you," he said, "and I don't know if I can do anything to help, but I just had a bad feeling about you when I discovered you were in that place."

At his car, a big Oldsmobile rental, he quickly unloaded me from the chair to the passenger's seat. He almost dropped me once, and I was surprised he didn't. Sugarman hadn't shown that much competence up to now.

He looked at the wheelchair, seeming to be deciding what to

do with it. "What the hell, we may need it. I hope we won't, but we might," and he put it into the trunk.

Then he jumped behind the wheel, did a U-turn, and took me away from the Convalescent Home of the Desert. I was grateful, whatever had happened to me, to be back with someone who could identify me, could put the right name on the tombstone. Still, I wondered about Sally. I would miss her and I worried that she would be upset that I had disappeared.

The drive to Sugarman's motel took twenty minutes. Sugarman continued his explanations.

"I went to Colorado," he said, as he wheeled the big car through the traffic of Palm Springs. "I located the P.O. box from the postcard and waited two weeks for the people to show up. They never did, but I learned their identities from one of the clerks. When I went to look them up, it turned out that the two of them had been shot through the head in their living room about the same time that your friend Welch got sliced and diced. I didn't see any good reason for staying around, so I caught the next flight out of Denver for here. I went to your motel, but they said you had checked out. I asked did you come to check out in person, and the manager said no, some other guy had done the actual check out. That sounded pretty strange to me so I looked around the places you had told me about—the Longevity Institute and the Convalescent Home of the Desert. I saw you in the hallway yesterday. I talked to the nurse about you. She said you were a John Doe, paralyzed, couldn't talk. I don't know what they did to you, but I don't figure you got this way naturally, and I sure know you had ID and wouldn't be there as a John Doe. Anyway, I'm telling you this, hoping that you understand me and that you understand I'm trying to help you. If I'm wrong, I guess I'd rather that you die on your own out here rather than be stuck in there."

Sugarman continued explaining what he knew, what had happened in the time I had been incarcerated. I was shocked to learn that only about three weeks had passed since I had been taken prisoner. It felt like a lifetime since I had made the transition from neurotic ex-mental patient to nursing home resident waiting to die. I couldn't respond to Sugarman's speech, but I was grateful to him. I guessed that I would rather be with Sugarman with a chance to return to normal, even if it was possible that he would only be a witness to my demise. At least he could call my ex-wife; I hoped he would be able to do that. I assumed he was a good-enough detective to do that if I checked out again—out of the big motel, the third motel from the sun.

Sugarman was staying in a less well-heeled part of Palm Springs, at a small, inexpensive little place. It was the kind of place where people didn't pay attention to their neighbors, especially in this heat, and they didn't pay attention to Sugarman and me as he helped me from the car and practically dragged me into the motel room. Inside, he sat me on one of two double beds, lowered my body, then lifted me by the feet and rotated me until I was lying on the bed. Then he put some pillows under my neck and back and covered my feet with part of the bedcover. He was a lot better nurse than I had expected him to be, but I was wondering, *What next?* He had me out of there, but I was an invalid. I needed a lot of care—food, bathing, and . . . Well, I would not think about that now.

The next few days were as long as any of the days of my life. Sugarman became my nurse. He wasn't very good at it.

After a while he figured that I would need something to eat and drink. He brought me an assortment of baby food and juices. He fed me by spoon and used a baby bottle to allow me to drink. He evidently didn't think about the problems I would have with bodily functions until late the first night, while we were watching television. He was watching television. I was panicking because I could feel that I was about to have a bowel movement in the bed. I was sick, beyond the sickness of being paralyzed, of having lost my ability to care for myself. Within hours of leaving the nursing home I had begun to feel queasy and to feel a certain tingling in my arms and legs. I was sweating slightly, which Sugarman had noticed, and he'd begun wiping my face and neck. Occasionally, I had involuntary spasms and then stomach convulsions. At some point on the first evening with Sugarman, I had thrown up baby food just as he was lighting up a Sher Bidi in preparation to watch one of his favorite programs, *Three's Company*. He had to jump up and run to my aid. That was when I began to panic about being in Sugarman's care.

What, after all, did he expect to do? Just wait to see what happened? I had probably had a stroke, as they had said. Perhaps they were giving me medications to prevent any further problems, and now that I was denied the medication I would be experiencing difficulty—as appeared to be the case. Additionally, I had at least been guaranteed that nurses who knew what they were doing would be caring for my bodily needs. Humiliating as it was, I had become used to it, and the people who did it. Sugarman was not my choice for a caretaker, brave though he might be for taking it on.

And what about tomorrow? A maid would come in. Assuming I was still alive and had not died some horrible death aspirating my own vomit or something, she would be wondering who the hell I was. What then?

Worst of all, I could not ask Sugarman any of these questions. I could only lie on the bed, feeling the tingling in my arms and the occasional convulsions, and watch whatever program Sugarman chose to watch.

So that's what I did.

The various crises of the evening—when I needed to eat, when I threw up, when I had a bowel movement—had all been dealt with, not well, but well enough. I was wrapped up in blankets and midnight was approaching. I did not feel in the least bit sleepy; I had always been sleepy at the nursing home. I was still feeling feverish, the spasms were occurring occasionally, and a tingling was continuing over my entire body. My body felt as if it had had a shot of Novocain and the effects were wearing off, with the same attendant pain, a kind of burning, as feeling returned to my limbs. I wasn't sure if I was dying or getting better, but I couldn't do anything about it in either case so I lay there and waited for something to happen.

It was just after midnight, while Sugarman was watching *The Dating Game,* that I first spoke.

"Christ, Sugarman!" I said, without thinking about the fact that I was speaking out loud. "Your taste sucks!"

"This is a good show," he said defensively. Then he looked at me. I found I could actually move my neck a little, though it hurt, and look back. "You can talk," Sugarman observed.

"Yes, a little," I whispered. It was harder to speak now that I wasn't commenting on his bad taste. My voice sounded like it had one time when I was recovering from laryngitis. It hurt too. That was new. I hurt in a lot of places and for weeks I had felt little or no pain.

"Try to move your hands."

I did so. I could move my fingers a little. The hands moved a little, too, but painfully. Still, I was moving.

"You're going to come out of this," he said. "I don't know what they gave you, but they gave you something, and you're going to recover now."

And Sugarman was right.

But the recovery was not quick and it was not without pain.

By the second day I was able to eat on my own, and with Sugarman's help, I managed to get to the bathroom. My muscles were still painful—all of them—and they were weak. I could chew and swallow. I could move my arms and hands. But I did all these things as though I were recovering from some deadly disease, as though I had been near death and was now, slowly, gaining strength where none at all had recently existed.

I stayed with Sugarman for a week, getting gradually stronger and getting to know the Mexican maid, who probably wondered what was wrong with me that I stayed in the room all the time, sitting in bed, watching inane television, and occasionally eating soft foods.

My favorite things during this period were cigarettes and coffee—vices that had been denied a paralyzed stroke victim.

But as I recovered, I gradually noticed that one area didn't seem to be recovering completely. My entire left side still felt kind of numb—not entirely without feeling, but with less than the usual feeling. My left hand was functional, but cold, and without the usual sensitivity. The left side of my face was also cold and numb. It was a sobering possibility that I would not return to normal.

But compared to where I had recently been, that was a small thing. I mainly felt great joy.

On the fourth day I made a call home to Andrea. I caught her at the house early in the morning before she had left for work.

"Scott! Oh, my god! Where are you?"

"I can't tell you," I said. "I just wanted you to know I was all right."

"Allison's been asking about you. I'll tell her I've talked to you. And you must know the police here are looking for you. I don't know what's going on, Scott. I hope you can clear yourself."

"It'll be okay," I said. Compared to what I had just been through, being suspected of a crime was a smaller kind of trouble. "I'll be returning home pretty soon," I told her, "one way or another."

Sugarman, who was sitting across the table from me at the motel, looked at me with a that's-news-to-me look.

I said, "Say hello to Allison for me."

"I will," she replied. "Wherever you are, be careful."

"I will."

But first, I was intent on a little revenge.

# Thirteen

Dr. Forster was in the phone book. I had not expected that, but it made it a little easier on me when I decided that my first move would be to contact Xanthia. I thought about going to the house in the middle of the night, but that seemed more dramatic and risker than necessary. Instead, I would merely call the number from a pay phone and hang up if Xanthia didn't answer. I was hoping that they weren't being so careful that they wouldn't allow her to do so.

The first couple of calls were a bust. I called at about nine-thirty in the morning and the first voice I heard was clearly Mrs. Forster's. I quietly pressed down the lever on the pay phone to end the call. I waited a couple of hours until I thought that perhaps Mrs. Forster would have gone to work at her part-time job at the Longevity Institute, or would perhaps be out shopping or visiting friends. This time, however, the person who answered was a man, an unknown voice, possibly the bodyguard. Or, I thought, it might be a boyfriend that I didn't know about. I was insecure and damaged enough without that.

The third time, as they say, was the charm.

"Hi, Xanthia," I said, as soon as she came on the line.

"Scott? Is that you? I'm glad to hear from you. Where are you? Are you back in Mill City?"

"No," I said, choking back tears, "I'm not back in Mill City."

It hurt that she could have been so ignorant of my actual fate.

"Where are you? Are you still here? Are you still in Palm Springs?"

"I'm nearby," I said. Even though I was at a pay phone, and clearly safe, I was paranoid should anyone connected with that nursing home ever know where I was again.

"I thought you had gone home. Frankly, though I'd love to see you, I had hoped you'd gone home. I think it's best for everyone." She paused. "I don't think it's a very good idea for us to talk long. I'm not supposed to be on the phone much—just in case."

"I'd like to meet," I told her.

"I can't."

"It's really important. I really need to talk to you."

She paused for a long time. "Okay. If you think it's really necessary. But if we're going to meet, I want to make sure that we're not going to be followed. And we may as well make it pleasant. There's a place that's kind of pretty, an oasis outside of town. It's a tourist attraction—one of the reasons for the name Palm Springs."

"Just tell me where to go," I said.

She gave me the name. "Just tell that to the cab driver; I think taking a cab would be best for both of us. I'll sneak out of the house and go to another area to call a cab. But, Scott . . ."

"Yes?"

"This will have to be the last time we meet."

"I'll see you in about an hour," I said.

When my Orange Cab arrived at the gift shop at the top of the rocky mountain, there was already a Yellow Cab in the dirt parking lot. I told my cab to wait, hoping that he would still be alive when I got back—the temperature was well over a hundred. What a job to have in the desert. At least my cabby was Middle Eastern, so he had a head start on the surroundings.

Xanthia was inside the gift shop looking at the Indian trinkets for sale. She had a light misting of sweat on her forehead and upper lip. I was pouring fluid like a desalination plant.

I felt like hugging her, but it was so hot that we just touched cheeks.

"Let's walk down into the palm trees," she said.

The oasis was just that. It was a little ravine, down a trail from the gift shop. At the bottom of the trail were huge, old palm trees in small groves. Among them, a small stream flowed through the sand. You'd have expected caravans of camels to be arriving at any moment. And, blessedly, the temperature was ten to fifteen degrees cooler than it was at the top of the hill. I could see why travelers had looked forward to an oasis. We walked for a while in silence in this wonderful place. I could remember what I had to say, but I wished I did not have to say it. How could there be such a wonderful place in the same world with my recent experience and the problems I faced?

After a time Xanthia said, "What was it you wanted to tell me?" We were standing by the stream and she was holding the leaves she had picked from one of the plants by the stream. She looked up at me. She reached up with one hand and touched my face. She touched the side that was still partially numb.

"You look tired," she told me. "You've lost weight. Have you been taking care of yourself?"

I laughed, involuntarily. "Not really."

"Please tell me what's on your mind."

I thought for a moment about how to begin. "I didn't leave town," I said, "because I was kept a prisoner here."

She looked up at me with disbelief. "Prisoner?"

"Yes. I was given some kind of drug. I was held at the nursing home your uncle owns."

"I don't know of any nursing home my uncle owns. Why are you saying this?"

"I'm saying it because it's true." I was a little angry now that she was resisting the story.

"Go ahead and tell me the rest," she said.

I told her the story. I kept it as brief as I could. When I was done, the look on her face was not one of great concern or support. She was angry.

"What exactly do you want from me?" she asked. "Why did you tell me this?"

"I want your help with the police for one thing," I said. "I need your information. I also want your help in getting information on the Longevity Institute and on this nursing home."

She shook her head. "I just can't believe you would do this," she said. "You met my uncle and you know that we can't talk to the police. We told you that. We asked you to keep the secret. We are in danger. And now you come to me with this *story.*"

"It is the simple *truth,*" I said.

"I know you've had mental problems, Scott. But even that doesn't explain this. You know I believe in my uncle. You know I have to keep him safe, and my aunt, too. And you know I believe in the program. Are you so afraid that you'll do anything to keep yourself safe? Are you such a coward?"

I had nothing to say. I was speechless. I had not understood her capacity to disbelieve me, to lose faith in not only my sanity but my honesty.

"I'm leaving, Scott," she said, walking away. "I don't want you to contact me again. I don't want you to go to the police, but I can't stop you from that. I'm very disappointed."

I didn't try to stop her. I stayed at the oasis for a time and occasionally looked up as she made progress up the trail to the gift shop and her cab. About fifteen minutes later, after having soaked my face in the creek, I walked up the trail and took my cab back to Palm Springs.

At the motel, Sugarman was not all that surprised.

"I could have told you," he said.

"Shut up, Sugarman," I said. I was choking on tears, but I was angry. I wanted to strangle someone. And Sugarman was handy.

"Is that how you treat someone who saved your life?"

"I'm sorry," I said. "But if you're going to point out the cynical realities, try to be subtle and a little diplomatic."

"Fair enough," said Sugarman, lighting another Sher Bidi. He was at the table by the window. The curtains were pulled to prevent someone seeing us, but they were translucent and we could see out to the pool and the small crowd of radiation victims lying beside it.

Sugarman smoked awhile then said, "I have something to show you, by the way."

"What's that?"

Sugarman didn't answer, just walked to his bed and picked up his briefcase. He dug through it and pulled out two photographs. "Autopsy photos," he said.

I held the photos. They were ghastly. A man and a woman, shot through the head. I recognized them—Jack and Diane—Welch's companions on that wonderful night a thousand years ago when I had been in love and going to dinner with my darling Xanthia.

"You know them?" Sugarman asked.

"Welch's business associates. I guess this rules them out as suspects in his murder."

He nodded. "So what now?"

"Did you find my car?"

"Yes. It was parked about a block away from your former motel."

I had sent Sugarman on this errand before leaving to meet with Xanthia. I had hoped that Billings had returned it before his apparent capture.

"What about Billings's car?" I asked.

Sugarman shook his head. "No sign of it."

"That figures," I said. "When they took him captive they took the car. When they took me captive, my car had been with

Billings. We had some luck anyway. So now we should go and look at my car."

"Why?"

"The trunk is full of money."

"Oh."

We drove to the car, looking around for any sign of familiar, and therefore unfriendly, faces. At the car I located the spare key box that I had put under the rear bumper. The key was still in it. I opened the trunk and found the money still in the satchel. I checked it, then climbed into the car and started the engine. I turned on the air conditioner. Sugarman got in the other side and lit a cigarette.

"What now?" asked Sugarman.

"I want to go buy some guns." Then I wanted to go to the Longevity Institute of the Desert and shorten a couple of life spans—Dr. Forster's in particular, but also anyone else who looked vaguely guilty.

"Why do we want a bunch of guns? I already have one gun. It's a perfectly good gun. I went to the trouble of shipping it down here. Why not use it?"

"I want all the guns I can carry. I'm going to go over to the Convalescent Home of the Desert and I'm going to locate one Dr. Walden. I'm going to put a bullet through his fat head. I might shoot an orderly named Lars. Then I'm going to go to the Longevity Institute of the Desert and shoot Dr. Forster." I wasn't kidding. I wasn't considering the consequences.

"Let's see," said Sugarman coolly, "you're going to go and buy a bunch of guns, then you're going to track down some specific individuals against whom you believe you have a grievance, then you're going to kill them." He considered the situation. "I'd say that's murder one. Yes, that's good for the death penalty."

I took a deep breath, an involuntary one. I took a series of breaths.

Sugarman took out a Sher Bidi and handed it to me. I put it in my mouth and he lit it. It tasted awful.

"I tell you what," he said. "Let's save the murder one for later. Let's just start with a simple break-in, and we'll work up to the major felonies."

We devised a plan to get into the Convalescent Home of the Desert, where we would try to find Billings.

We shopped for orderly costumes at a local work clothes supplier. It took another hour to find a place where they would make the name tags—I knew roughly what they looked like after my time in the place.

The plan was simple. We would go to the nursing home after normal business hours, Sugarman would enter as an orderly, explaining, if he was stopped, that he was a temporary employee and new to his duties. He would let me in, dressed as an orderly also, and we would make our round of the rooms.

I considered shaving my mustache and cutting my hair, but then I decided against it. It was too much of a sacrifice for one thing. For another, if any of the villains in this place saw me, I wanted them to recognize me right before I smashed their faces in—except for Lars. I would have to shoot Lars. He was too big to fight with fists.

Getting in was not difficult. Sugarman went through the front door, right past the receptionist, at just after six P.M. He walked down the hallway to one of the side entrances and opened it. I walked to the door and we were both inside.

It was cool inside, but I was sweating and my hands were clammy. I was frightened and I was upset. I was in the place of my most frightening and most painful incarceration. My second worst had been while held in jail when I was mad. It was no honor to have an internal rating for the ultimate in such experiences.

The place was largely deserted. We collected some cleaning props from the utility closet. It was handy, in one sense, that I knew the place.

We started down the hallway with our cleaning fluids, our mops, and our rags. We looked into the rooms as we went.

I recognized a number of patients. There was the old lady who kept trying to escape because she couldn't remember why she was here. There was the old man who refused to eat broccoli; I remembered that he had made quite a fuss in the cafeteria on one occasion.

My roommate was still there when we looked into my old room. I was gasping for breath when I looked in there. I remembered Sally. I remembered the many sad memories I had experienced in that bed. It was still empty. I wondered what they had decided had happened when their patient had turned up missing. Sugarman had been listening to the local news and scouring the local newspaper, and there had been no mention of the incident.

"Looks like there's still a vacancy in case you want to come back," said Sugarman. I suppose he thought he was being pretty funny, and he was a little wounded when I stepped on his foot.

"Hey, you've lost your sense of humor," he said.

"Let's look across the hall," I told him.

The room across the hall was open. There was a stranger in the bed near the doorway, an older man with curly hair, sleeping with the oxygen tube apparatus attached to his nose. I walked around him in the darkened room and looked at the other patient.

"Smells like my old room at home," said Sugarman.

"I knew there was a reason you were such a slob," I observed.

"I am not a slob," Sugarman responded, truly hurt. "So, is it Billings or not?"

"It's Billings," I said. "I'm sure of it."

"What should we do?"

"Let's get a wheelchair."

I rolled the IV near the bed so that I could see what all was attached to the patient. I would have to take everything. If we could get him out of there, I would want to be sure the medication was maintained until he was under another doctor's care. I wondered where the hell we would take him. I decided that we would have to go to another hospital, another major hospital, and bring him to the emergency room.

Sugarman came back into the room with a wheelchair. The old man groaned a few times as we got him into the chair.

"Are you ready?" asked Sugarman. He was behind the chair.

I was still struggling with the IV, which was mounted on a rolling cart. It was top-heavy and awkward. Every time I tried to move it, it started to tip over. Finally I got the hang of moving it and said, "Yes."

Before we entered the hallway, I looked left and right. It was empty. Still I was nervous because I could hear female voices down toward the reception area.

"Let's go," I said, and we headed out into the hallway toward the right, toward one of the exits. We were about halfway there when the old man began grumbling.

"What are you doing?" he asked. "I'm sleepy. Can't you leave me alone?"

His voice didn't sound like Billings.

"Stop," I told Sugarman. He did so.

I walked around in front of the man, who looked up at me. He had Billings's hair, and he had features much like Billings's, and he had a mustache, but he wasn't Billings.

"It's not Billings," I said.

"Oh, fine," said Sugarman. "Who is it, I wonder?"

"I'm Charlie," said the old man. "I've always been Charlie."

Sugarman and I looked at each other. Without a word I went back to my station at the IV cart. We turned him around and pushed him back to his room. It took us five minutes to get him into his bed. He was still complaining when we left. We walked down the hallway to the next room just to get out of the open and away from the complaining.

"Bastards!" the old man shot at us as we went out of his sight.

"What do we do now, Kemo Sabe?" Sugarman whispered.

"Keep looking, I guess," I said. "I don't know what else to do. I'm less certain he's here now because that guy is the one I saw when I was an inmate here. What else can we do?"

"A very professional plan," Sugarman said dryly. "Why don't we go to the room where they keep the medical records?"

"I guess so. What will we look for?"

"Anything suspicious."

"I always admire a professional plan."

"We can look for your records. It would be good to have proof of your stay here."

"That's a good idea."

"Why thank you."

I stuck my head out the door to check that the hallway was empty. Then I led the way. We carried our cleaning props and tried to look as though we had a right to be there. The side of me that had not recovered from the stay in this place was cold and slightly painful, the way your nerves feel pain when they are just beginning to warm up from getting cold while playing in the snow. Perhaps it was partly in reaction merely to being in this place where I had been so tormented and threatened with an end to my life.

Near the nursing station we moved more cautiously, hoping not to encounter anyone. There was one nurse at the station, but her back was turned and she was doing paperwork. We passed quietly and walked down the hallway toward the business office. I had become aware that it was the business office during my many stays in the hallway, parked like an abandoned car on the freeway. At the door to the office I looked around, then tried the handle. It was open. We entered the dark room, and I closed the door behind me.

"I didn't think to bring a flashlight," said Sugarman, stating the obvious.

"We can probably turn on a light," I said. I don't think these rooms have any windows; they're in the interior of the building."

"Then by all means," said Sugarman, "let's turn on a light."

Without speaking, we began to look for a switch. I felt the wall to the left of the door. Sugarman was groping around to the right.

"I can't find a switch," I said after a bit.

"I, too, have been unsuccessful."

"Then I'll turn on the light," said another voice in the room, and a desk lamp was switched on. Sugarman and I were both in full cardiac arrest. We looked toward the desk, where a man sat looking at us. Weirdest thing of all was that it was Billings.

I could not think of a thing to say. It was like one of those moments in a dream when you realize that what is happening is so implausible that you must be dreaming. My mind was trying to process this situation, trying to decide whether to render me unconscious to put me out of my mental anguish or not, when Billings spoke.

"What in the hell are you doing here?" he asked. I noticed that paperwork was spread out on the desk in front of him, along with some pencils and pens. He was dressed in desert garb, light short-sleeved shirt and pants, but they were conservative compared to others he had worn in my earlier encounters. He looked like a man at work in his office.

"For one thing," I said, "we were looking for you."

"How did you know I was here? Maybe I've underestimated your powers as a detective."

"I thought you were being held against your will."

"Not quite," he said. "I'm a part-time accountant here."

"Does anyone mind if I smoke?" said Sugarman, pulling out a Sher Bidi.

We didn't answer him so he lit up.

"I thought you were investigating this place," I said. "How is it you are working for them?" I was very wary now. Billings seemed to have changed sides.

"Well," said Billings, "some of us like to do our investigating with a little more subtlety than others. I applied for the job so that I could get a chance to look at their records." He pointed to a door on the opposite side from our entry point. "That door leads to the room where the medical records are kept. I've been spending about an hour each night looking through them and making copies." He motioned to the copy machine on the other side of the room.

I sat at a chair next to Billings's desk. I pulled out a Camel and lit it. Billings looked at me as though he were waiting to be offered one, so I gave him one and lit it.

"Why were you sitting in the dark?"

"I wasn't until I heard you guys coming—like a herd of elephants."

"You're not an accountant, are you?" I asked. "How did you get hired?"

"I'm not an accountant, but I can keep a set of books. I gave them a phony résumé—told them I was in semiretirement, wanted a part-time job. I look like I'm in semiretirement, don't I? You see, unlike you, they don't know me by sight. Besides, the personnel director here probably doesn't know anything about the goings on of the Longevity Institute."

Billings took a drag on his cigarette. "What happened to you anyway? You look kind of peaked. I checked your motel when I got back into town and you weren't there."

I laughed. It wasn't a normal laugh at something funny. It was a deep, troubled, existential laugh. A joke-of-the-cosmos laugh. "It's a long story," I said. "I'd prefer to be somewhere else when I tell it."

Billings nodded his head, not understanding, but seeing that I wasn't kidding. He looked at his watch. "You know Elmer's, the steak house?"

I nodded.

"Let's meet there in about an hour. I need to finish up a couple of things here."

"Okay." I got up and Sugarman and I headed for the door.

"Moody," said Billings.

I stopped and looked at him.

"Be careful leaving here. I don't want to get fired."

"Okay."

And we left.

An hour later, at Elmer's, Sugarman and I were drinking coffee and smoking cigarettes. We had traded our orderly costumes for our crappy Palm Springs street clothes—for me, my cut-off jeans and a T-shirt, for Sugarman, a loud green and yellow flowered shirt with blue shorts and sandals. And, as usual, this fashion spectacular was capped by his porkpie hat. In Palm Springs he didn't look that unusual. We had found a booth toward the rear of the restaurant, just in case someone we didn't want to see came in, we would have a little warning.

We were on our second cup of coffee when Billings came to our table and sat down. He was comparatively well-dressed in his white short-sleeved shirt and tan slacks, looking every bit the accountant that he was impersonating. He was carrying an old leather catalog bag, six inches across at least, stuffed with paperwork. He borrowed a cigarette from me and I lit it. I wondered if he ever bought his own.

"What have you got there?" I asked.

"A few things you might find interesting." Billings pursed

his lips to grip his cigarette as he wrestled with the case and dug out selected documents. The cigarette smoke curled up and hung in the air around his eyes. He handed me a photocopy of a newspaper story. The name and location of the newspaper did not show on the copy. It appeared to be a pretty old issue, though, since the typesetting was old-fashioned, like it had been set when they were still using lead type. The photograph was dark and the dot pattern was big. It was the photo of a younger Dr. Forster, with a full head of dark hair and an unblemished face. He looked about twenty. The headline read: "Son Joins Local Auto-body Shop." I read the story. It identified the person in the picture as Clyde Hanson. Weirder, it identified him as the son and new partner of the proprietor of the shop. Dr. Forster's preparation for plastic surgery had been as a body-and-fender man.

"Where did you get this? Is this for real?"

"Kind of explains why he's not very good at plastic surgery, doesn't it?"

"I didn't know he wasn't any good at plastic surgery, but that would explain it." I handed the paper to Sugarman.

"As it happens, he's really fond of doing plastic surgery. But Forster is a fraud, posing as a surgeon. I got this picture on my last trip, a few days ago. I visited his hometown, Bakersfield, and got a tip from an old buddy of Forster's. He told me about the body shop, told me that Forster took it over when his father died and ran it for fifteen years. And then, he said, that Forster started acting kind of weird and became very interested in medicine. Instead of going back to school, he studied medicine on his own. That's when my informant got to know Forster. He was hired, along with a few others, to run the body shop, while Forster got a job at the local morgue as an assistant to the pathologist. He worked there two years; then he moved to a small town in the South and set up a practice using the credentials of his local pathologist."

This was Xanthia's hero—with feet of Bondo. "How long ago was this?"

"Just about forty years. He practiced medicine in the South for five years; then, during the war, he moved to the Chicago area—my backyard. After the war he moved out here. His old boss at the coroner's office in Bakersfield was dead by then and wouldn't protest the use of his background. Evidently no one has ever looked into his background. Maybe there were no complaints. Maybe all the complainants were dead."

I was hopeful now. This sonofabitch was going to be brought down. Andrew Welch, another sonofabitch, was going to be shown to have a connection. That would push the motive for his murder in this direction. Since there was no hard evidence against me, it would move the spotlight of the investigation to others, leaving me breathing easier and in the dark where I belonged. "What else have you got there?"

"Lots of things," said Billings, with some satisfaction. "I have copies of the educational background of Forster's old boss in Bakersfield. I have more information on the auto-body shop—proof that Forster is not Forster, but Hanson. I have copies of some medical records that are suspicious—records from the convalescent home."

"What records do you have from the convalescent home? Why are they suspicious?"

"I just looked through the records for anything odd. I looked for people who suddenly appeared at the convalescent home, then went downhill quickly. Most normal patients are on a waiting list because of the shortage of beds, and then their physical decline proceeds slowly.

"I looked for records of anyone who died in the nursing home. And I looked for the name of anyone who had been connected to the Longevity Institute as a patient. I still haven't been able to do much with most of them, haven't figured out their significance, if they have any."

"Can I look at some of them?"

He shrugged. "Okay."

He handed me a file. It contained half a dozen stapled documents. Evidently he had copied all the documents in individual files, then just stapled the copies relating to one person. I thumbed through them until I came to one John Doe. Under "Age" it said, "Undetermined. Probably midthirties." I turned the pages, reading the recorded notes of the nurses and Dr. Walden. I felt tears welling up out of my eyes and running down my cheeks.

"What the hell is with you?" asked Billings. Sugarman was looking away in embarrassment.

"These are my records," I said.

I explained my unfortunate adventure.

"Jesus, boy," said Billings, seeming genuinely affected, "I'm sorry you went through that." He placed his hand on my shoulder. "But there are a couple of good things out of this. You can testify against the sonofabitch. By now you must want the bastard as much as I do."

"Yes," I said, "I do. But there are others I want, too." I thought about Dr. Walden, thought about smashing my fist into his fat face. Or maybe I would give *him* a shot in the butt—with a .357 magnum.

"Well, I'm about to call in some agencies," Billings said. "I've been working with a local prosecutor, feeding him some of the documents I've been gathering. I've also been talking to medical regulation agencies and the IRS."

"When are you going to call them in?"

"Hopefully within a few days. But it could take some time for them to act against Forster. These are bureaucracies, after all. And I haven't located my daughter. I'd like to find her first."

"I don't want this to take a long time," I said, angrily. "I might have to do something on my own."

"What do you mean?"

I didn't answer. I was thinking about death again, but this time not my own.

Billings looked at Sugarman. "What's with him?"

"He wants to kill someone," said Sugarman.

"Well, he'll have to wait," Billings said, looking at me. "The best thing would be for you guys to just hang back for a few days. I'll give you my number and address. Just keep your eyes on the newspaper. When you read of the arrests, it's time for you to come in and add to the testimony."

And, very reluctantly, that's what we agreed to do.

I couldn't bring myself to sit and do nothing. So Sugarman and I went on surveillance.

But first we bought a bunch of guns. I insisted on it. When we went on surveillance, I was carrying two of them, one in a holster on my belt under my shirt, and a smaller one, a .32, in my pocket. I didn't know what I would do with them, but it felt good having them.

When we set up our surveillance, we were more serious about it than the first time I had watched the Longevity Institute. We did it around the clock, using two cars. When we needed sleep, we slept in the backseat of the big Oldsmobile that Sugarman had rented. Occasionally, one of us would take off to get food and bring it back to the car. Every so often we would change cars. We tried to stay out of sight of the Longevity Institute, but close enough that we could tell if anything unusual was going on.

After two days of this, Sugarman and I were both hot, sticky, and smelled like Sugarman's old room. We had noticed little of significance except that the activity at the institute had slowed down—there seemed to be fewer and fewer staff going in and fewer numbers of patients. This didn't seem so unusual that we were concerned about it. We were basically pretty happy. A situation like this gave us a chance to just hang around smoking cigarettes and talking about our lives and resting. Since we were both pretty lazy, we were content to be waiting for the cavalry to arrive.

I learned that, of all things, Sugarman had been a dairy farmer before becoming a private detective.

"You don't look like a dairy farmer," I said.

"I was quite a dairy farmer," he said. "Our farm was among the best producers."

"What happened?"

"My wife left me."

"So you gave up farming?"

"You have never been alone on a farm with three hundred cows, have you?" he said, as though the situation was obvious.

"How did you go from being a dairy farmer to being a private detective?"

"It wasn't a direct flight," he said. "First I drove taxicab for a long time."

I looked at him for a minute, wondering whether to tell him about my own path into the business. I decided not to deepen our discontent and kept silent.

We waited.

But it wasn't the cavalry that arrived first. It was a small fleet of moving trucks.

It was about nine o'clock on the evening of the third day of watching. They pulled up in front, backed up to the sidewalk, and put down their loading ramps. Then several cars arrived, including Dr. Forster's. Everyone went into the building. After that the activity was frenetic.

Then a flood of property was being loaded into the trucks. Much of it was contained in boxes, and I suspected that a lot of the contents would likely be medical and financial records—just the thing that would be needed for a case against them for fraud.

We stayed in the car, hoping that it wasn't too obvious in its location down the street from the institute.

"What the hell do we do?" I asked. "We never had enough discussion about what to do if someone started a wholesale move out of the place."

"I don't think we can call the police," said Sugarman. "This is private property and they have a right to move. No doubt they have a good cover story."

"Then what?" Looking toward the institute, we could see the figures streaming in and out of the front door. The figures were carrying boxes and furniture and loading them into the back of the three trucks.

"I don't know what," he said.

We continued to discuss our options. We were five minutes into the discussion when I noticed that Billings's car was among the others that had recently arrived.

"That's it," I said, "we're going in. I don't know what's going on here, but I'm not going to leave him in there alone and I'm ready to do something." I was going to use these muscles now that they were not paralyzed. I checked all my guns as Sugarman looked on, dispirited. He did not have my enthusiasm for this.

"Are you sure?" he asked.

"Shut up!" I said, starting the car. I drove into the parking lot, got out, and headed into the entrance of the pyramid.

This pyramid, a real one, sitting stoically in the twilight of the evening, was not going to be like the ones in my dreams all those years. It was not going to leave me locked in, running up and down the hallways looking for something I never found. It was not going to win.

When I entered the lobby, I found it full of muscular moving men. They were sitting around reading magazines and smoking—which was against the rules so I applauded them for it. Some of them glanced at us, but most didn't even notice. Still, I was taking no chances. I pulled out my two guns and said, "I want every one of you motherfuckers on the floor, right now!"

Sugarman, somewhat taken by surprise by my action, had reluctantly pulled his gun out of his belt and was waving it unenthusiastically so that they could all see it.

Most of them dove for the floor. One middle-aged balding bodybuilder type sat in his chair and continued to read a magazine. "You're not going to use that," he said.

I pulled the trigger on the automatic in my left hand. I shot up the chair to the right of the bodybuilder. He gave up his magazine and dove for the floor.

Sugarman and I used their packing tape to restrain the seven men. When we continued into the building, they were lying on the floor on their faces with their feet taped and their arms taped behind them. We didn't gag them so that they could pass their time with conversation.

In the hallways there was no staff. The lights in most of the rooms were off. Why had we not noticed this during the previous two days? They must have been shutting this place down for some time. That was why we had been seeing ambulances coming and going. They had been transferring their few resident patients elsewhere. And during the shift change this evening there had been fewer cars arriving. But the staff that had arrived had gone somewhere. And Forster was surely here. And Billings.

"Very odd situation," said Sugarman, as we headed down the hallway.

We came to a fork in the hallway, each way leading down a long row of offices and rooms.

"I think we should search the rooms on each floor," I said.

"Why not go to Forster's office?" Sugarman asked.

"I just want to be sure that we know who is here," I said. I didn't say that I was scared, being in the pyramid. I wanted to be very sure that each threat was eliminated so that I would be more secure. I had been in this pyramid so many times in my dreams, and yet I wasn't sure how I could prevent this real situation from turning into a nightmarish scenario.

"Okay. I'll go this way," he said. He looked at his watch. "We'll meet here in ten minutes."

"Fine. Be careful."

I headed down the hallway and began looking into the offices. I peered into each of the little windows in the doors first, then opened them and looked inside. Some of the rooms were patient rooms, others were laboratories or storage rooms. By the sixth or seventh office, I was feeling a little better. The hallway was quiet, the offices, examination, and patient rooms so far had been empty. It looked like the building was empty of threats, except for the known ones on the top floor, and I was looking forward to those, to bursting in on Forster and his bodyguard. I had not told Sugarman, but I fully intended to start firing at the first provocation. Between my hatred and my fear, I was a dangerous ex-mental patient.

But the eighth door was a surprise. I had peeked in and seen nothing. But when I opened the door and peered in, I felt large hands reach around from behind the door and jerk me into the room so violently that I dropped my guns. The big right arm, sleeved in white, encircled my neck. The other grabbed my left arm and brought it around behind me in a painfully forceful grip. And I was pressed up against my captor so that his hot, moist breath warmed my neck. How like the pyramid dreams this was.

But it was no Egyptian guard holding me. I heard a familiar voice. "Mr. Doe," said Lars, my former orderly, "you're supposed to be in your wheelchair."

"My name's not Doe. I don't belong in a wheelchair."

"You *are* Mr. Doe," he insisted. "You left. You weren't supposed to leave."

I was struggling against his grip, but I imagined myself as impotent as a child's doll that had come to life and was trying to get away from its owner.

"I'm going to get Dr. Walden," he told me, as though my

struggle meant nothing, as though I were still paralyzed in my wheelchair. I felt as I had in all my dreams—completely helpless, unable to overcome my opposition. He held me while he kicked my guns toward the door. He let go with one arm long enough to open the door. He kicked my guns into the hallway. I elbowed him in the side with my free arm. I began to feel that I might have a chance against him now. Maybe I could overcome this feeling of helplessness, this being-in-the-pyramid feeling.

But my elbowing him seemed merely to piss him off. He lifted me and shook me with one arm and hit me repeatedly on the back of the head with the other. When I was in the rest home I had not fully appreciated his size. I had been helpless to everyone. Now, when I thought I had my strength back and was fully in command and ready to wreak vengeance, I was helpless again against this six-foot-six half-wit. Lars finished up his work by throwing me across the room. I landed by a wastebasket, banging it with my head. Lars opened the door and said again, "I'm going to get Dr. Walden. He will want to see you."

Still stunned, I heard him locking the door. There were no windows except the little one in the door. I was imprisoned. As I stood up, I heard him still outside, picking up my guns.

"Lars!" I yelled. I pulled the lighter out of my pocket and reached into the wastebasket, retrieving a piece of wastepaper.

His slow-witted face appeared at the little window. "What?" he asked.

"I'm going to start a fire, Lars," I said. I held the piece of paper up and lit it. "And it will be your fault."

"You're not going to start fires," said Lars. "No one is allowed to start fires! We have to be careful of the oxygen tanks."

"I'm starting a fire!" I tossed the lighted paper into the wastebasket. The paper in the basket caught fire. This was going to have to work or I was going to be in a locked room full of smoke and flame.

I looked at Lars. He was glued to the window, very upset.

"Mr. Doe!" he said. He dug out his keys and unlocked the door. He opened it and came toward me, but he was more intent on the fire. I had been casing the countertops in the room looking for a heavy object and I had found one—a telephone, an older one, black, made out of Bakelite and very heavy. The wastebasket was in front of me, flaming and smoking, and in my right hand I was gripping the telephone.

Lars came toward the wastebasket, preparing to put it under control. After that, no doubt, he would be putting me under control.

But as he approached, I swung the telephone at his right temple, low enough for me to reach because he was bending over as he headed for the blazing wastebasket. It struck him hard on the right side, causing a considerable ringing in both our ears. His lazy eye was always out of focus and looking the wrong way. His other eye joined it. He crashed down onto the wastebasket with a huge clatter. The wastebasket contents emptied, scattering fire on the floor. I stomped the burning trash to put it out. When Lars started moving, I hit him, hard, with the phone a couple of times. I felt bad about it. I knew I had to do it and I did it with all my force, but I knew he wasn't an evil guy—he was just a kind of stupid guy who had been given really bad rules to follow. When the flames and Lars were both out, I dug through his pockets and got his keys. I gathered up my guns, walked out the door, and locked it. I took one last look inside to see that Lars was moving around a little bit. Not getting up, but just moving as an unconscious act.

I walked back down the hallway and encountered Sugarman at the intersection.

Sugarman looked relaxed, considering our situation. He was smoking a Sher Bidi. He had apparently been waiting for me.

"I didn't see anything down my way," he said, as I approached. "You see anything?"

"I ran into someone I used to know," I said.

Sugarman looked at me quizzically, but seeing I wasn't going to say anymore he said, "Are we going to search the other floors?"

I was thinking. Why would Lars be here and not at the nursing home? Maybe there was a patient here, a special patient. "I want to look down the hallway again," I said. "I want to check something out. Wait here."

"Okay."

I checked the rooms down the hallway from where Lars had appeared. In the fourth room, I found Cynthia Billings.

The moment she saw me, she began shaking, as if with fear. She was certainly not the confident, aloof woman I had met in Mill City.

"What are you going to do to me?" she asked. "Please, don't hurt me." She was wearing a hospital gown. She was thin and white. I would have expected her to be drugged, but she was not. She was strapped to the bed. Perhaps she had only recently been taken into captivity. Perhaps they had planned some other fate for her than the nursing home. They may even have believed that they had things under control now that they had her in custody. So far as they knew, she may have been the last active challenge to their continuing business as usual. After all, Jake Longfellow, her biker friend, was dead. But why then would they be moving out of the institute in such a wholesale fashion? Did they know that her father was stalking them and planning revenge?

And why was she afraid of me? Then I saw that the reason was obvious. I was carrying two guns. She probably didn't remember me at all from Mill City.

As I neared her I smelled urine from the soiled bedding. Lars hadn't been doing a very good job of caring for her, though her boss had probably emphasized keeping her restrained above all else.

I put the guns away. "I'm Scott Moody, Mill City, remember?" She looked at me, nodded, seeming to recall. "Here. I'm going to release you." I undid the restraints on her arms and her legs.

She tried to sit up, managing it after I helped her. She lowered her legs over the side of the bed, holding the gown, trying to cover herself. She was so white. "I need to get cleaned up," she whispered. "I couldn't . . . they wouldn't allow me to go often enough . . ."

"Don't worry about that for the moment," I said. "I'll get a wheelchair; you shouldn't walk. We'll get you to a hospital. Wait here just a moment."

"Don't leave me. Where's Lars? Lars will come back. He's really big, and he's not very bright. You won't be able to reason with him."

"I already reasoned with him," I said. "I'm just going into the hallway a moment." And I walked out the door. There was a wheelchair at a nurses' station. I brought it back to the room and helped Cynthia Billings into it. I found a clean blanket on a chair and put it over her, to give her a sense of security and to help her cover up. I was now more concerned with getting her to safety than I was with my revenge. I had been raised, as are most men, to be a hero. And for a change I was getting the opportunity to use that training.

I wheeled her down the hallway until we encountered Sugarman. He looked at me as though I had returned accompanied by a Martian.

"You remember Billings, don't you?" He nodded yes, but I could see he was about to say something like, *Yeah, I know Billings, but this isn't Billings.*

"This is his daughter, Cynthia."

Cynthia and Sugarman looked at each other, but without any greeting or acknowledgment, just with a look of slight shock and surprise.

"Keep an eye out," I told Sugarman, aware that pushing Cynthia in the wheelchair left me vulnerable if someone surprised us.

We wheeled her to the front door, past the moving men who were lying on the floor, grousing about their situation.

"You're going to jail for this," said one of them.

"Please be quiet," said Sugarman politely. For some reason, perhaps the politeness frightened them, the movers shut up.

"What are we going to do with her?" I asked Sugarman, as though he had created the problem.

"I do not know, Kemo Sabe. I am not the one who planned this very well-organized caper."

But an answer came to us. Not though creativity, but serendipity. An ambulance drove into the parking lot of the Longevity Institute. It pulled up in front. The driver got out. I recognized the ambulance company as being one that I had seen regularly in the desert, ferrying people to several medical centers. It did not belong to Forster or his crew.

Medical personnel got out. I didn't wait for them to enter the building, whatever their mission. I wheeled Cynthia outside.

"Is this the stroke victim?" asked the young, dark-haired medical technician who came toward me.

"We're not sure," I said. "She needs to be checked out. Take her to Eisenhower." Eisenhower was a medical center that I had passed several times during my days in the desert. At least that way I would know where she was.

It took a few minutes to provide enough information to satisfy them before they took her away. I lied about her health insurance. I put myself down as her brother, Wallace Billings. I told them I would be coming to the hospital within the hour.

"You'll be all right," I told her, feeling guilty that I could not stay with her. "We'll be there to check on you soon."

She didn't reply, just looked at me the way a puppy looks at you when you hand them to the vet. They closed the doors and sped away.

I went inside, where Sugarman was having a spirited conversation with the moving men.

"They want to know what we are doing here. They want to know what we are going to do with them."

"If you don't stop worrying about the small stuff," I told them, "we're going to shoot your kneecaps and ruin your career in moving." I hoped that I would never have to encounter these guys after the packing tape had been removed.

"What now, Kemo Sabe?" asked Sugarman.

"Back to the original mission," I said, and started back down the hallway.

We approached the elevator.

"Where to?"

"Top floor," I said. "That's Forster's office," and I pushed the "up" button.

But when the elevator door opened, we were facing an unexpected character. It was Dr. Walden.

As usual, the sonofabitch was wearing a Hawaiian-style shirt, slacks, and white shoes. His left hand held medical charts; his right was loaded up with syringes at the ready. His mouth grasped the stub of a cigarette, protruding from the right side of his lips, a half-inch of ash about to drop. Smoke curled up into his eyes. I was standing closest to him, so naturally he saw me first.

"You!" he said. He dropped the medical chart and lifted his right hand, filled with syringes. He hurtled himself toward me as fast as a fat man probably dying of lung cancer could.

"Hey, I could use help!" I yelled at Sugarman. But he was frozen long enough that Walden reached me and plunged the syringes at my face. I ducked sideways and grabbed at his arm, but that didn't prevent him from getting two of the syringes into my shoulder, right into the soft muscles of my neck.

Then I reacted. I brought all the anger fueled by being left for dead in a nursing home. I lambasted Walden with a fist to the side of the head. His cigarette went flying and he fell over like the torpid whale he was. He was silent on the floor. We stood there, looking at the syringes sticking out of my shoulder.

"Look at the bright side," said Sugarman. "Maybe now we can figure out what it was they were giving you."

I was about to punch Sugarman, figuring it would be my last chance before a period of unconsciousness. Instead, I said, "Pull these out."

Sugarman came to my side, put his right hand on my shoulder and pulled the syringes out with his left. There wasn't much blood, just the few drops you'd expect of an injection. My shirt soaked up the blood. It hurt deep down and stung on the surface. Still, I knew it wasn't serious and it was only pain. Pain was no stranger to me.

Walden was moaning now. He rolled over like an old man in a nursing home waking up in the morning.

As I was trying to figure out what to do with him, Sugarman produced a pair of handcuffs.

"You're more of a detective than I thought," I said, impressed that he had them.

"Detective, nothing," Sugarman replied, "these were left over from my marriage."

He pulled the doctor's hands around behind him and installed the handcuffs. He sat him up against the wall.

"You remember me?" I asked him.

"You're preventing me from giving medical attention," he said.

"Giving medical attention to who?"

"Forster."

I was curious about his statement, but I couldn't resist asking one question. "When I was in your care, what were the drugs you gave me? How did you cause my symptoms?"

"Just a little drug cocktail," he said. "Something Forster cooked up. A few psychoactive drugs, some barbiturate, antihistamines, a little cough syrup."

"Are you kidding?"

"Maybe."

"Where is Forster?"

"In his office."

I looked at Sugarman. "Do we believe him?"

"He's in handcuffs," Sugarman said. "I can go with him. Where were you going?" he asked the doctor.

"Just downstairs. Down to the convalescing ward where we have the medication I need. I'm waiting for an ambulance, too, but I don't know what the hell is keeping them."

I kept my secret that his ambulance wasn't going to show up. When I was finished with these bastards, they weren't going to need an ambulance. "Let's go," I said.

So we went down the hallway, holding Walden between us. We opened the medicine cabinet he directed us to and got the medicines and the syringes as he directed. Then we returned to Forster's floor.

As we neared the door to Forster's office, I said, "Who's in there?"

"Forster and the girl. I guess it's his niece."

"No bodyguard?"

"Oh, yeah, the bodyguard," said Walden. "He's like furniture. I never think about him; he's just there. Oh, and there's also the accountant. He came over to see Forster."

"The accountant?"

"Yeah. He works for the nursing home."

Sugarman now carried his gun in his hand. I drew both of mine.

"We'll put Walden through the door first," I said.

We opened the door and pushed Walden through. As we

came into the room, I saw that Forster was on a sofa by his desk. Xanthia was sitting in a chair pulled up beside the sofa. The big man, Doug, was hovering behind them.

He saw us and started to draw his gun.

"Don't!" I said.

But he did. He was the bodyguard after all. That's what bodyguards do. But before he could get his gun cleared, I had shot him three times in that arm. I fired the smaller gun almost involuntarily, with my internal personalities doing the aiming. Somehow I knew that I would hit him in the arm and nowhere else. However, I wasn't expecting that the bullets would go through his arm and blow out a few windows of the pyramid.

Douglas, the bodyguard, released his gun and sat on the floor near the sofa, no longer interested in firing a gun. His arm lay limp and bleeding at his side.

"You asshole!" screamed Xanthia. She rushed to his side, hugging him and covering him with kisses. She examined his arm to see how serious were the wounds. She turned to me. "You asshole! You asshole! I told you to go home! What have you done?"

"He'll be all right," I said, secretly glad that I had shot him. "Besides, he's only your bodyguard."

Tears streamed down her cheeks. She pushed against him as he stared daggers at me. "I love him," she said. "We're going to be married."

Oh, fine. That figures. Now I was really glad I'd shot him.

Walden began attending to Doug's wounds, while Xanthia gave me hateful glances.

I took the opportunity to look at Dr. Forster. He lay on his back on the sofa. He still wore his white doctor's jacket. He was not moving, but his eyes were open, wandering, confused. He had the look all of us in the nursing home had had at one time or another—that look of shock and recognition that something was going very wrong. The panic, the claustrophobia, were probably setting in. Someday I might feel pity for him, but right now I thought to myself, *good. Good, you sonofabitch. It's your turn.*

I walked over to Billings, who stood there wearing his accountant clothes, surveying the situation with what I thought was a certain satisfaction.

"What happened to Forster?" I asked.

"Stroke," he said, looking at me for my reaction. "Happened about an hour ago."

I looked at Forster. I looked back at Billings. He was still studying my face.

I laughed. Xanthia looked toward me, again with a look of hate. I stifled the laugh.

"Did you have anything to do with this?" I asked Billings.

"Your story of the other night gave me an idea. I had been about ready to turn Forster over to the prosecutors, but somehow it didn't seem the right punishment. Especially since he no doubt has a fleet of lawyers."

"You did this. You gave him something to induce a stroke."

"I didn't say that."

"It's quite a coincidence."

"Yes, it is that. It's quite a coincidence."

"What now?" I said.

"We're waiting for the cops. They don't know it since they still think I'm the accountant, but I called the cops. And within the day I expect investigators from the medical boards and the IRS. I haven't found Cynthia yet, but I had to act. I was afraid that if they had her, she would be dead before I could start a wholesale search for her whereabouts."

"You could have let us know," I said, peeved at him.

"I know. But I decided to act on Forster. And I didn't need any interference. We each have our vengeance to exact. I hope you'll forgive me for taking mine first." Billings reached into his shirt pocket and pulled out a pack of cigarettes. They were the first cigarettes I had seen him carry. He had always smoked mine. "Here, Scott," he said, "have a cigarette. This is good news."

"I have good news, too," I said.

"What?"

I told him about his daughter.

"Where is she?"

"Eisenhower Medical Center."

"I'll go there as soon as we have this situation in hand. How did she look?"

"Weak, but I think she's okay."

"I'm so glad she's all right," he said. "You know who I think was responsible for taking her captive?"

"Who?"

He pointed to the floor where Dr. Walden was bandaging the bodyguard's arm. "Your friend, Doug, there."

"I'm really glad I shot the sonofabitch."

"Me too," he said.

I called for two ambulances. Soon we were all out in the parking lot, as they prepared to load Forster into an ambulance for his ride to the hospital. And then to eternity in a nursing home.

Billings, Sugarman, and I stood together talking to detectives who had arrived shortly after we came out of the building. One man seemed to know Billings, which made it easier for Sugarman and me to stay out of serious trouble. They were a little unhappy with us for tying up a bunch of moving men, and my shooting Doug didn't please them either. But for the moment they were willing to wait for further explanations rather than put us under arrest, at least so long as our protector, Billings, vouched for us.

Forster had been loaded up and taken away and Doug, the bodyguard, was going into the second ambulance. As she passed by us with Doug, Xanthia spoke in quiet fury to me and Billings.

"I'll show you bastards! This place will be mine! I'll run it. My uncle's dream won't die. I won't let it. I'll show you sonofabitches by keeping it alive."

"You're going to keep the institute going then?" Billings asked her.

"Yes, you bastard, yes," she said.

Billings was touching the pistol that still bulged under his shirt.

I put my hand on his shoulder. I shook my head no.

"Sue them out of existence," I said.

Billings moved his hand away from the pistol as Xanthia followed Doug into the ambulance.

The authorities proceeded against the Longevity Institute and the Convalescent Home of the Desert, closing both institutions and moving patients elsewhere. The records were boxed and sent to a floor of a government building, where prosecutors were reviewing them for evidence of fraud, financial malfeasance, theft, tax evasion, and more. Medical investigators had brought action against Walden, Forster, and several others on the staff.

At first Dr. Walden was pretty cocky. He convinced the local authorities to charge me with assault for hitting him and putting him in handcuffs. However, as the facts of his past transgressions and current crimes came to light, he was quick to cut a deal and the relationship between the Longevity Institute and the Convalescent Home of the Desert began to come out. Dr. Forster's former life as an auto-body man was an embarrassment, not only to his family, but to the medical authorities who had not discovered his little secret sooner.

I spent a week answering questions before local authorities allowed Sugarman and me to leave—at which time they encouraged it. Billings escorted us to the airport.

"Well, you should be clear of this now," Billings said to me, as we waited for boarding of the plane. "Your police department has been provided with Cynthia's deposition that Jake Longfellow killed Welch."

I had read the statement. It suggested simple rage as the motive. Jake Longfellow might not have been much of a human being, but he'd loved Cynthia Billings and had hated Welch for hurting her so, for despoiling her beauty. When he'd finally encountered Welch at his house, he had exacted a fitting revenge, slashing Welch's face before finishing him off by cutting his throat. Then he had traveled to Colorado to kill Welch's business partners before pursuing Xanthia.

"What bothers me is that we still don't know who Welch was," I quibbled.

"I was saving this for you. I got a report on him last night. I know who he was now."

"Who? Where was he from?"

"Seattle boy—born and bred. Hubert Rosewood."

"There's a reason to change your name right there."

"A better reason was a long record of fraud—most of it a lot less profitable than Program Nine. He did all kinds of things— bank examiner impersonation, charity fraud, and, finally, he was in the health foods business. Then he disappears in the records—about 1960."

"Right when he moved to Mill City."

"Yes. I think that's when he started working with Dr. Forster. Probably on other medical frauds, then working into the Program Nine thing as they perfected the idea."

"How does a guy get into that kind of business? He seemed such an intelligent man."

"I don't know. But Welch, I mean Rosewood, started out as a social worker. Maybe the work turns you bad."

I smiled. I liked that idea. Social-worker sociopath.

"I know something about his sister, too," said Billings.

"What's that?"

"She's no relation. We managed to identify her. She doesn't have a brother."

"Does Xanthia know?"

"I'm not going to waste my time disillusioning her."

"You don't know who Xanthia's mother was?"

"Nope. We can't even find a record that Welch had a daughter."

I looked at Billings. I shook my head. The girl I loved had been a complete illusion. She had no known father. Her ersatz father had been a fraud. Where had she come from that I had loved her?

"You take care," Billings said.

As we boarded the plane, Billings gave a little salute and faded back into the airport crowd.

We took the flight to Seattle, and I gave Sugarman a ride to his apartment.

"Take a shower," I told him, as he gathered his stuff from his car.

"How droll," he said. "I'll always remember that sense of humor."

"Maybe you'll remember me for this, too," I said, as I held out twenty hundred-dollar bills.

"A bonus?"

"Something like that." He had earned it, but it was easier to pay since I had kept all the money Xanthia had left behind in Seattle. I had more than forty thousand dollars left. I wasn't going to sue the bastards for my grievances—I had made an out-of-court settlement on my own.

"You're a gentleman, if not a scholar," he said, tipping his hat. He wandered up the walkway to the apartment.

# Fourteen

I assumed that things were finally cleared up with the police in Mill City, so as I drove into town it was with a good deal of optimism, even exhilaration. I was going to see my daughter. I was going to see my ex-wife. I was going to begin clearing up my reputation.

The only thing wrong with that idea was that a warrant was out for me—flight to avoid prosecution—and Officer Blaine decided to act on it. He took me into custody just after I crossed the bridge into town.

"I know I look like a local shitkicker," said Chief Ryder, when he visited me in my cell, "but I don't like people fleeing my jurisdiction. So I'm going to lock you in solitary for a while."

So he put me into solitary confinement. But if he thought this was going to bother me much, he would have been disappointed. I had been to the center of the pyramid of my fears in Palm Springs. This place was comparatively cozy. I could wait this out—even calmly. Two days later, I was released. The officer who did the paperwork to release me was not Blaine, and I didn't see the chief anywhere.

"Did you guys get the information from the authorities in Palm Springs?" I asked.

"What information?"

"Why are you releasing me?"

"I don't know," he said. "The charges have been dropped."

"But why?"

"I don't know."

"Can I speak to the chief?" I asked.

"It will be difficult to see the chief."

"Why's that?"

"Because he's in jail over in Spokane."

"In jail?"

The officer looked at me with a certain impatience that said he was going to tell me something once and only once. "Okay, the chief got into a little trouble. Seems he and Officer Blaine picked up a fifteen-year-old hitchhiker the other night. Right now they're both charged with statutory rape. They are accused of letting her go in return for sex.

"Now sign this form."

I signed the form and I was out of jail.

"Andrea?" I said, as she answered the phone. I was calling from a pay phone near the jail. The receptionist at the *Sun* had transferred me to her desk.

"Scott? Is that you? Thank God! Are you out of jail?"

"Yes," I said. "A little older and a little wiser, but out of jail."

"I can't believe that bastard Ryder held you."

"That bastard Ryder is getting his just desserts," I said.

"That's what I hear. Look, Allison is at the day care. You can go see her."

"That's where I'm going now," I said.

"I couldn't stop them from selling your stuff," she said.

"My stuff?"

"Yes. You weren't paying any rent. They sold all your stuff."

"Oh." I laughed that familiar gallows laugh. "I guess I wasn't meant to keep anything permanently." All my stuff had been sold once before—when I went crazy and abandoned my apartment.

"I'm glad you're so philosophical."

"I'm nothing if not that."

"I'm about to move, Scott."

"Move? Where to?"

"Seattle. I got a job on a newspaper."

"I thought you were destined to become editor of the *Sun*."

"Well, Albert is gone, and Jan the Barracuda is the new editor. I think she's already worried about one of the new employees she hired—thinks he's going to take her job."

"She's probably right."

"So what will *you* do?"

"I'll move to Seattle."

"What will you do for work?"

"I'll find something." I thought about Sugarman. I didn't think I would work with him as a private detective—one incompetent was enough. But I might see if he could get me a job at his cab company.

"By the way, there's a car for you at my place."

"A car for me? What does that mean?"

"Just go by there. You'll see."

We said our good-byes and I drove to Andrea's place. I knew what she meant when I saw the old Buick in the driveway. Frosty Shields's old car. I had made my friend wait too long.

I got out of my car and opened the driver's door on the Buick. The keys were in the ignition. There was an envelope on the steering wheel. I opened it. It was a little note from Frosty. "You seemed to like this old car, so I wanted you to have it. Good luck, son. Frosty."

That was the beginning of a flood that was hard to stop. His death brought it all home to me—all the pain of thinking I was going to die in the nursing home, all the pain of missing Allison, the pain of losing Xanthia forever. I just sat in the old Buick for an hour, letting the tears go as the waves of sorrow and regret flowed over me.

Eventually I had to let go of my self-pity because I couldn't let it interfere with a real responsibility—seeing Allison.

I drove the old Buick to the day-care center. Amid a cacophony of children's shrieks, squeals, and crying, Allison and I hugged each other tightly and she cried a little—as she always did if we were separated too long.

Then we got into the Buick.

"You want to go for a drive?"

"Yes," she said. "Let's go see Mommy."

"She's working right now. We'll see her later. Let's go to that place across the lake and have ice cream."

"Okay."

So here we were. It was now September. The weather was cool and sunny. The leaves were beginning to change. We were cruising across the long bridge out of town. My daughter had a big smile on her face and all the windows were down.

"Are you going to go away again, Daddy?" she asked me out of the blue.

"I hope not."

"Come live with me and Mommy."

"I'll live nearby," I said.

"And I don't want you to die!" she said. It was a command, and a strange one.

"What makes you think I'm not going to live forever."

"Frosty didn't live forever."

"When did you meet Frosty?"

"We visited him in the hospital."

"Did you like him?"

"He was crabby."

I laughed. "Yeah, he was crabby."

"*Are* you going to live forever?" she asked, wanting to continue the subject. It was kind of a game. I think she was a little anxious, but she was being playful. She was too young to be concerned about something like this for long.

Was I going to live forever? It was a nice thought, but the closest I was likely to get to eternity was to be buried in the center of that pyramid that I had dreamed about as a child. I couldn't tell her that. This was my daughter, my five-year-old.

"Well, honey, I'm going to be around for a long, long time. I'm going to be around so long that you'll become a little old lady. You can't even imagine that, can you?" She shook her head no. "Well, it's a long time. It's such a long time it may as well be an eternity. So you can just figure on me being around forever."

"You won't be around forever if you keep smoking cigarettes," she said matter-of-factly, a sweet and innocent little oracle.

"Oh," I said. "I get it." I took my cigarettes out of my pocket. "Okay, kiddo, you win." We were going by the Quick-Mart at the far end of the bridge. I pulled into the parking lot and deposited the cigarette pack in a trash can. "I won't smoke anymore. Now I will live forever. I will be e-ternal."

She smiled a big smile. Even at five she knew it was a fable, but we both liked the idea; and we both loved each other, and those little instants of love is about all the eternity we're going to get.